ONCE A WITCH

Lalette's gaze focussed, and suddenly she felt tired and very old and not winestruck anymore . . . for without thinking she had traced the witch-patterns her mother taught her long ago, and now they were smoking gently on the table-cloth.

"Witchery!" croaked Count Cleudi, recovering his composure quickly. "Madame, my congratulations on your skill in deception, which should take you far.

"You and your precious mother made me believe you pure!"

". . . there is peril and derring-do aplenty, which suits well the ingenious treatment of magic."
—Poul Anderson

THE
Blue Star

Fletcher Pratt

BALLANTINE BOOKS • NEW YORK

Copyright 1952 by Twayne Publishers, Inc.

All rights reserved.

SBN 345-24537-7-150

First Printing: May, 1969
Second Printing: July, 1975

Cover art by Darrell Sweet

Printed in the United States of America

BALLANTINE BOOKS
A Division of Random House, Inc.
201 East 50th Street, New York, N.Y. 10022

Contents

THE
Blue Star

Prologue

Penfield twirled he stem of his port-glass between thumb and finger.

"I don't agree," he said. "It's nothing but egocentric vanity to consider our form of life as unique among those on the millions of worlds that must exist."

"How do you know they exist?" said Hodge.

"Observation," said McCall. "The astronomers have proved that other stars beside our sun have planets."

"You're playing into his hands," observed Penfield, the heavy eyebrows twitching as he cracked a nut. "The statistical approach is better. Why doesn't this glass of port suddenly boil and spout all over the ceiling? You've never seen a glass of port behave that way, but the molecules that compose it are in constant motion, and any physicist will tell you that there's no reason why they can't all decide to move in the same direction at once. There's only an overwhelming possibility that it won't happen. To believe that we, on this earth, one of the planets of a minor star, are the only form of intelligent life, is like expecting the port to boil any moment."

"There are a good many possibilities for intelligent life, though," said McCall. "Some Swede who wrote in German—I think his name was Lundmark—has looked into the list. He says, for instance, that a chlorine-silicon cycle would maintain life quite as well as the oxygen-carbon system this planet has, and there's no particular reason why nature should favor one form more than the other. Oxygen is a very active element to be floating around free in such quantities as we have it."

1

"All right," said Hodge, "can't it be that the cycle you mention is the normal one, and ours is the eccentricity?"

"Look here," said Penfield, "what in the world is the point you're making? Pass the port, and let's review the bidding." He leaned back in his chair and gazed toward the top of the room, where the carved coats of arms burned dully at the top of the dark panelling. "I don't mean that everything here is reproduced exactly somewhere else in the universe, with three men named Hodge, McCall and Penfield sitting down to discuss sophomore philosophy after a sound dinner. The fact that we are here and under these circumstances is the sum of all the past history of—"

Hodge laughed. "I find the picture of us three as the crown of human history an arresting one," he said.

"You're confusing two different things. I didn't say we were elegant creatures, or even desirable ones. But behind us there are certain circumstances, each one of which is as unlikely as the boiling port. For example, the occurrence of such persons as Beethoven, George Washington, and the man who invented the wheel. They are part of our background. On one of the other worlds that started approximately as ours did, they wouldn't exist, and the world would be altered by that much."

"It seems to me," said McCall, "that once you accept the idea of worlds starting from approximately the same point— that is, another planet having the same size and chemical makeup, and about the same distance from its sun—"

"That's what I find hard to accept," said Hodge.

"Grant us our folly for a moment," said McCall. "It leads to something more interesting than chasing our tails." He snapped his lighter. "What I was saying is that if you grant approximately the same start, you're going to arrive at approximately the same end, in spite of what Penfield thinks. We have evidence of that right on this earth. I mean what they call convergent evolution. When the reptiles were dominant, they produced vegetable-eaters and carnivores that fed on them. And among the early mammals there were animals that looked so much like cats and wolves that the only way to tell them apart is by the skeleton. Why couldn't that apply to human evolution, too?"

"You mean," said Penfield, "that Beethoven and George Washington would be inevitable?"

"Not that, exactly," said McCall. "But some kind of musical inventor, and some sort of high-principled military and political leader. There might be differences."

Hodge said: "Wait a minute. If we are the product of human history, so were Beethoven and Washington. All you've got is a determinism, with nothing really alterable, once the sun decided to cast off its planets."

"The doctrine of free will—" began McCall.

"I know that one," said Penfield. "But if you deny free will completely, you'll end up with a universe in which every world like ours is identical—which is as absurd as Hodge's picture of us is unique, and rather more repulsive."

"Well, then," said Hodge, "What kind of cosmology are you putting out? If you won't have either of our pictures, give us yours."

Penfield sipped port. "I can only suggest a sample," he said. "Let's suppose this world—or one very like it—with one of those improbable boiling-port accidents left out somewhere along the line. I mentioned the wheel a moment ago. What would life be like now if it hadn't been invented?"

"Ask McCall," said Hodge. "He's the technician."

"Not the wheel, no," said McCall. "I can't buy that. It's too logical a product of the environment. Happens as soon as a primitive man perceives that a section of tree-trunk will roll. No. If you're going to make a supposition, you'll have to keep it clean, and think in terms of something that really might not have happened. For example, music. There are lots of peoples, right here, who never found the full chromatic scale, including the classical civilizations. But I suppose that's not basic enough for you."

For a moment or two, the three sipped and smoked in the unspoken communication of friendship. A log collapsed in the fireplace, throwing out a spray of sparks. McCall said: "The steam engine is a rather unlikely invention, when you come to think of it. And most modern machines and their products are outgrowths of it in one way or another. But I can think of one more peculiar and more basic than that. Gunpowder."

"Oh, come," said Hodge, "that's a specialized—"

"No it isn't," said Penfield. "He's perfectly right. Gunpowder destroyed the feudal system, and produced the atmosphere in which your steam engine became possible. And remember that all the older civilizations, even in the East, were subject to periodic setbacks by barbarian invasions. Gunpowder provided civilized man with a technique no barbarian could imitate, and helped him over the difficult spots."

McCall said; "All the metal-working techniques and most of chemistry depend on the use of explosives—basically. Imagine digging out all the ores we need by hand."

"All right, then," said Hodge, "have your fun. Let's imagine a world like this one, in which gunpowder has never been invented. What are you going to have it look like?"

"I don't know," said McCall, "but I think Penfield's wrong about one point. About the feudal system, I mean. It was pretty shaky toward the end, and the cannon that battered down the castles only hurried up the process. There might be a lot more pieces of the feudal system hanging around without gunpowder, but the thing would be pretty well shot."

"Now, look here," said Hodge. "You've overlooked something else. If you're going to eliminate gunpowder and everything that came out of it, you'll have to replace it with something. After all, a large part of the time and attention of our so-called civilization have been spent in working out the results of the gunpowder and steam engine inventions. If you take those away, you'll have a vacuum, which I'm told, nature abhors. There would have to be a corresponding development in some other field, going 'way beyond where we are."

Penfield drank and nodded. "That's fair," he said. "A development along some line we've neglected because we have been too busy with mechanics. Why couldn't it be in the region of ESP, or psychology or psychiatry—science of the mind?"

"But the psychologists are just operating on the ordinary

principles of physical science," said McCall. "Observing, verifying from a number of examples, and then attempting to predict. I don't see how another race would have gone farther by being ignorant of these principles or overlooking them."

"You're being insular," said Penfield. "I don't mean that in another world they would have turned psychology into an exact science in our terms. It might be something altogether different. Your principles of science are developed along the lines of arithmetic. The reason they haven't worked very well in dealing with the human mind may be because they aren't applicable at all. There may be quite a different line of approach. Think it over for a moment. It might even be along the line of magic, witchcraft."

"I like that," said McCall. "You want to make a difference by substituting something phoney for something real."

"But it might not be phoney," insisted Penfield. "Magic and witchcraft are really pretty late in our world. They began to be talked about at the same time and on the same terms as alchemy, everything surrounded by superstition, lying and plain ignorance. In this world we're imagining, somebody might have found the key to something as basic in that field as gunpowder was to the physical sciences. Some people say we almost made the discovery here. You know the story about this house?"

McCall nodded, but Hodge said: "No. What is it? Another ghost story?"

"Not quite. The old part of the house, the one where the bedrooms are now, is supposed to have been built by one of the Salem witches. Not one of those they hanged on false charges, but a perfectly genuine witch, who got away before she was suspected—as a real witch probably would. The story is that she came here and set up business among the Indians, and as they weren't very expert at carpentry, she helped them build that part of the house with spells, so it would be eternal. The old beams haven't a bit of iron in them; they're all held together with pegs and haven't rotted a bit. There's also a story that if you make the proper preparations at night, something beyond the normal will happen. I've never done the right thing myself, apparently."

"You probably won't," said Hodge. "The essence of the whole witchcraft business is uncertainty. Haven't you noticed that in all the legends, the spells never quite come off when they're needed?"

"That's probably because there isn't any science of witchcraft, with predictable results," said McCall.

Penfield said: "It may be for another reason, too. Have you ever noticed that magic is the only form of human activity which is dominated by women? The really scary creatures are all witches; when a man becomes a magician, he's either possessed of a devil or is a glorified juggler. Our theoretical world would have to start by being a matriarchy."

"Or contain the relics of one," said Hodge. "Matriarchies are socially unstable."

"So is everything," said McCall. "Flow and change from one form to another is a characteristic of life—or maybe a definition of life. That goes for your witchcraft, too. It would change form, there'd be resistance to it, and an effort to find something to replace it."

"Or to remove the disabilities," said Hodge. "The difficulty with any power we don't really know about is not to define the power itself, but to discover its limitations. If witchcraft were really practical, there would be some fairly severe penalties going with it, not legally I mean, but personally, as a result of the practice. Or to put the thing in your terms, McCall, if there weren't any drawbacks, being a witch would have such high selection value that before long every female alive would be a practicing witch."

McCall carefully poured more port. "Hodge," he said, "you're wonderful, and I love you. But that's typical of the way you put things. You cover up a weak point by following it with one that attracts everyone's attention away from the feebleness of your real case. Penalties for everything? What's the penalty for having an electric icebox?"

"A pampered digestive system," said Hodge, readily. "I doubt whether you could survive the food Queen Elizabeth ate for very long, but she lived to be well over sixty. If there were witchcraft, or ESP or telepathy running around in the world, there couldn't but be defenses against it and troubles for the practitioners. Had it occurred to you that even a witch couldn't spend all her time stirring cauldrons, and might want to lead a normal life, with a husband and children?"

Penfield got up and stepped to the window, where he stood looking out and down at the midnight Atlantic, throwing its surges against the breast of the rocks. "I wonder if it really does exist," he said.

Hodge laughed; but that night all three men dreamed: and it was as though a filament ran through the ancient rooms; for each knew that he dreamed, and dreamed the same dream as the others; and from time to time tried to cry out to them, but could only see and hear.

1

Netznegon City: March Rain

I

It was raining steadily outside. The older woman's tears and words fell in time, drip, drip. Cold, for the tall window at the room's end would never quite shut close, bottom and top not nest into the frame simultaneously. Lalette in her soutane felt goose-pimples and tried to shut out the sound by thinking of a man with a green hat who would give her a handful of gold scudi and nothing asked, merely because it was spring and she put a small spell on him with a smile, but it was not quite spring, and the voice persisted:

". . . all my life—I have hoped—hoped and planned for you—even before you were born—even before you were born—daughter of my own—" (Yes, thought Lalette, I have heard that before, and it would move me more, but the night you drank the wine with Dame Carabobo, you told her how I

was the product of a chance union in a carriage between
Rushaca and Zenss) "—daughter—and after I saved and
worked so hard—you miss the only chance—the only
chance—don't know what I'm going to do—and Count Cleudi's not like most—"

"You told him what he offered was frightful. I heard you."

(Sob) "It was. Oh, it was. Oh, Lalette, it isn't right, you
should be married with a gold coach and six horses—but
what can we do?—oh, if your father had left us anything
before the war—all I sacrificed for him—but that is what all
of us must do, make sacrifices, we can't have anything real
without giving something away . . . Lalette!"

"Madame."

"You will be able to employ the Art and have everything
you want, you know most of the patterns already, he does
not go to the Service often . . . and after all, it's something
that happens to every woman one way or another, and with
the Art, even if he doesn't marry you, he'll find you a
husband you won't mind, it's only men like Cleudi who want
to be the first, a man who marries would really prefer a girl
to have a little experience, I know . . . Lalette!"

Lalette did not answer.

"All the young ones come to the ball after the opera,
Lalette. Count Cleudi will present you, and even if you don't
bring—"

(He would have not only a green hat, but southern-made
lace at wrist and throat and a funny-looking man who spoke
in a Mayern accent, thick as cream, and carried the purse
because it spoiled the fit—)

". . . as though he were just one of those . . . so considerate
. . ." (I suppose we cannot control how we come by our
parents) ". . . your father, like an angel out of heaven, and I
could have taught you so much more if he—" (Now she is
waist-deep in the past again. I'm going to hear it all over)
". . . really, for it is more like one step up than a leap down
from a high place, which is always what we think before the
first time . . . Lalette!"

"Yes, mother."

Someone knocked at the door.

Lalette's mother hastily daubed at her cheeks, heaved herself heavily from the chair, looked sidewise, saying; "We could sell the stone." But before the girl could reply, the tap again. The older woman waddled across to the door and opened it a crack; a long jaw and long nose under a wet turn-down hat poked in.

"I was just saying to my daughter—" began Dame Leonalda.

A pair of thin shoulders pushed past her as though not hearing, the man stood in the center of the room, sniffed and wiped his nose on his sleeve. "Listen," he said, "no more stories. I have heard too many."

Dame Leonalda gave him a doleful look and bustled back to her seat. "But I assure you, Ser Ruald—"

"No more stories," he said again. "I have charges to meet and taxes."

She put her hands to her face. (Lalette thought: her only device; I hope I shall not grow like that.) Ruald said; "But I do not wish to be hard, no, and I know you have no money just now. So I will be fair, and if you render me a small service, why then, it is not beyond me to forgive the whole four months' arrears."

Dame Leonalda took down her hands again and said; "What is the service?" (Her voice had something like a tinge of dread.)

Ruald sniffed again, darted a glance at Lalette, another at the door, and stepped close. "I have heard that you belong to one of the families of the Blue Star."

"Who told you that?"

"It does not matter. Is it true?"

The dame's lips worked. "And what if it is?"

"Why this, dame: it will not peril your soul to place a small witchery—"

"No, no, I couldn't do such a thing. You have no right to ask me."

The man's face sneered. "I have a right to ask you for my money, though."

"No, no, I tell you." Her hands waved the air. "That

Dame Sauglitz, they punished her with five years and stripes."

"They will punish nobody for this; utterly private between you and myself. Is not your skill enough so that no suspicion of witchery will fall on you? Come, I'll do better. I'll more than forgive the arrears, I'll give you quit-rent for four other months to come."

"Mother," said Lalette from the corner.

Dame Leonalda turned around. "This does not concern you," she said, and to Ruald; "But how am I to know that having done as you wish, you'll not denounce me before the episcopals?"

"Why as for that, might I not want your help another time?" She put up a protesting hand, but he; "Come, no more stories. I'll—"

There was another tap at the door. Ruald looked annoyance as Dame Leonalda crossed the room in another rustle of skirts. Her voice was almost gay. "Come in, Uncle Bontembi."

Rain shook shining from his cloak. "Ah, charming Dame Leonalda." The paunch hindered his bow. "The greetings of the evening to you, Ser Ruald. Why, this is a true evening gathering."

"I was just leaving," said Ruald, tugging at his jacket. "Well, then, Dame Leonalda, bear in mind what I have said. I'm sure we'll reach accommodation."

She did not get up as he went. When the door was closed she turned to Uncle Bontembi. "It is such a problem, dear Uncle," she said. "Of course the child is perfectly right in a way, and it would be different if her father had left her anything at all, but with such a man as Cleudi—"

"The Count is a splendid gentleman," said the priest. "I have seen him lose fifty gold scudi on a turn, but never his composure. And he is in high favor. Is there a problem relative to him? Not that his eye has fallen on our little Lalette? I would call that a matter for consent and rejoicing."

"Ah, Uncle, it is this, if men only behaved as nobly toward women as they do to each other! He has set his eye on this dear child indeed, but not his hand, and says he will pay all our debts and give her a hundred gold scudi besides, if she will only accompany him to the opera and ball of the spring festival."

Uncle Bontembi plucked at the button of his chin, and the smile left his face. "Hm, hm, it is certainly on the face of matters a proposal ... You are certain you have not been employing the Art, Dame Leonalda?"

"Oh, no, never, never. And my dear little girl, how could she?"

The priest glanced sly-eye at the girl. "Yes, yes, she has her first confession to make. Well, well, let us think this out together. I will say the Count Cleudi is highly held in other circles beside the political. There was some theological discussion at the Palace Bregatz lately, and the Episcopal was of the opinion that he had never heard sounder doctrine or better put than by Cleudi. Wherefore he cannot be very far from the laws of the good God and right moral, can he? And so his plan may be of greater benefit than first appears."

"I do not want such benefits," said Lalette, (but thought: then I should have the Art!)

"Oho! Our junior niece resists; this is not the true humility. Come, Demoiselle Lalette, let us look at it this way: we can only truly serve good and vanquish the eternal forces of evil through the happiness of others, for if it is our own happiness we seek, then others doing the same will make all unhappy, and so give victory to evil." He signed himself. "Thus to bring joy to others is the true service of religion and moral, no matter what the appearance may say. Now in this case there would be three people given happiness. Yes, yes, the doctrinal point is somewhat delicate, but I cannot find it in my mind to disapprove. There is a technical violation of moral law involved, and I am afraid the Church will have to assess a certain fine against you, but I will make it as light as possible. Enough to remind that a good action should be done for moral gain and not material."

"I do not love him," said Lalette.

"All the more unselfish, all the more." The priest turned to Dame Leonalda. "Have you not made it clear to our niece that the true love which puts down evil in the name of the major glory of God is something that rises out of and after union? Why, if she talks so, I will have to lay church-duty on her for approaching the doctrines of the Prophet."

"Oh, I have told her, I have told her." (The mother's voice began to cloud toward another rain of tears.) "But she is so romantical and sensitive, my little daughter, just like those poems by Terquid. When I was a girl—"

Lalette let her face smooth out (as she thought about the opera ball and what it would be like), but even that was not much use, their voices kept picking at her until she went behind the curtain to her bed in the corner, where it was even colder beneath the blanket at first, so that she curled up tight. (If I were really married, the Blue Star would belong to me and my husband, and . . .)

II

"But is it a genuine Blue Star?" asked Pyax. He turned toward Dr. Remigorius, who should know if anyone.

"Ah! Of that I cannot say. We have been deceived before. It is certain that the old woman has practised veritable witcheries; the Center of Veierelden found a record of a conviction against her in the church there. The only surety is in the test; and that is a test that only Friend Rodvard here can make. If it should be genuine, our game's won."

The lower lip of Pyax hung open among his pimples and Mme. Kaja's ravaged face changed line. "It would be wo-onderful to have it," she said, drawing out the long sound, and Rodvard felt the blood run warm beneath his skin as they all looked at him. "But I do not think her mother would permit a marriage," he said. "How will you have me do?"

"Do? Do?" said the doctor, the little white planes at the corners of his mouth shining against the black fantastic cut of his beard. "Shall we school hens to lay eggs or rats to suck them for you? Do what is most natural for a lad with a willing girl in his arms, and the Blue Star is ours. Will you have Mme. Kaja to teach you?"

The flush warmed Rodvard, and he said; "I—will you—"

Mathurin in the background opened his thin, tight lips. "Our friend is lapped in the obligation of the Church. Hey, Rodvard Yes-and-No, what moral do you follow? If it's to be that of the priests, you have no place with us. You are engaged as a soldier to the overthrow of all they stand for."

"O-o-oh, you are so wrong, friend Mathurin," said Mme. Kaja. "I understand. There is the heart—" she pressed a hand to a pendulous right breast "—but as my old friend, the Baroness Blenau used to say, hearts do not guide but to sorrow. Ah, friend Rodvard, believe me, if one is to have the great peace, one must deny the heart's message and seek the good of all beyond what gives pain at the moment." She slapped her breast again and turned to the others. "I know; he is in love with another."

Without reason, Mathurin said suddenly; "When I went to the court service with Cleudi last night, the old hog was drunk again. Fell on the floor at her royal prayers and had to be helped—"

Dr. Remigorius; "Will you still distract us, Mathurin? There is but one present question before this Center—the bidding of the High Center that friend Rodvard here obtain the Blue Star from Lalette Asterhax. Can we report to them that the task is undertaken?"

Pyax spoke, running his tongue across lips; "If he will not, I can offer through marriage and lawful lease. My father would be willing to give a dower—"

Rodvard burst into laughter with the rest, over the thought there could be enough money in the world to buy a Dossolan bedding for one of Pyax' Zigraner birth. (But the laugh ended bitterly for the young man at the thought that because they could see no better way he must give up his ideal of honor and true love. He tried to imagine how it would be to live with someone who did not love one again, but whom for honor's sake he must have married, and for a moment the intent candle-lit faces dissolved away; he felt a momentary strange sweet painful thrill before the picture in his mind changed to that of his father and mother quarreling about money, and she began to scream until his father, with contorted face, reached down the cane from the mantel . . . Oh, if one gives in love, it should be forever, ever, love and death—)

"—still place him," Dr. Remigorius was saying, "but that will be a matter for the High Center. No, there's only the one thing, and we'll have the answer now. Rodvard Bergelin, we summon you by your oath to the Sons of the New Day and your desire to overthrow the wicked rule of the Laughing Chancellor and the old Queen, to take your part."

Pyax smiled nastily. "Remember Peribert? We know how to deal with those who fall away."

"It is not good to be hard on those from whom you seek help," said Mme. Kaja.

"Be still," said Remigorius. "Young man, your word."

(One more effort.) "Is it so vital that we have this jewel?" said Rodvard.

"Yes," said Remigorius, simply; but Mathurin; "This is the only true Blue Star of which we have record, and even this one may not be true. But if you will not make the effort to win it, as ordered, there's still an escape. You are a clerk to the Office of Pedigree; find another Blue Star that we can have, and you're excused. But with matters so approaching a crisis at the court, we must have one; for we are the weaker party."

Rodvard saw Pyax touch his knife-hilt and once more wetly run out his tongue, so like a lizard's. Beaten; had he not himself in those long conversations until daybreak, maintained that among free men the more voices must make the decisions? With a sense that he was assuming an obligation to baseness, he said:

"I will do as you desire."

Dr. Remigorius' face cracked into a red-and-black smile. "Pfo, young man, you'll make a witch of her and she will gain her fortune."

Mme. Kaja came over to take both his hands as he left. "The heart will follow," she said.

2

April Night

I

Lalette looked up through branches to the purpling sky, then down from the little crest and across the long flat fertile fields, reaching out toward the Eastern Sea, where night was rising. "I must go," she said. "My mother will be back from the service." Her voice was flat.

"Not yet," said Rodvard, lifting his head from arms wrapped around his knees. "You said she would stay to talk with the fat priest. . . . In this light, your eyes are green."

"It is the sign of a bad temper, my mother tells me. She looked in the waters for me once, and says that when I am married, I will be a frightful shrew." (It was almost too much trouble to move, she was glad even to make a slender line of conversation that would hold her immobile in the calm twilight.)

"Then you must be fated to marry a bad man. I do not see—if you really loved someone, how could you be shrewish with them?"

"Oh, the girls of our heritage cannot marry for love. It is the tradition of the witch-families." She sat up suddenly. "Now I must absolutely go."

He placed his hand over hers, where it rested on the long green moss under the cedars. "Absolutely, I will not let you go. I will bind you with hard bonds, till you tell me more about your family. Do you really have a Blue Star?"

"My mother does. . . . I do not know. My father would never use it, that is why we are so poor. He said it was wrong and dangerous. My mother's father used it though, she says, before she got it from him. It was he who told her to choose my father. He was a Capellan in the army, you know, and was killed in the war at the siege of Sedad Mir. My mother's father could read through the Star that my father wanted my mother for herself and not for her heritage. It was a love-match, but now there is no one that can use the Star." (Lalette thought: I really must not tell stories like that that are not true, it only slipped out because I do not wish to go back and hear her talking about Count Cleudi again.)

"Could not you sell it?" asked Rodvard.

"Who would buy it? It would be a confession that someone wanted to practice witchery, and then the priests would come down and there'd be a church trial. It is a very strange thing and a burden to have witchery in one's blood." She shuddered a little (attracted and yet depressed, as always when it was a question of That). "I do not want to be a witch, ever—"

"Why, I would think—" began Rodvard, (really thinking that in spite of her beauty, this was the reason she more than a little repelled).

"—and have people hating me, and those who want to like me not sure whether they really do, or whether it is only another witchery. The only real friend my mother has is Uncle Bontembi, and that's because he's a priest, and I don't think he's a real friend either, but keeps watch of her so that when she makes a witchery he can collect another fine for the Church." Rodvard felt the small hand clench beneath his own. "I'll never marry, and stay a virgin, and will not be a witch!"

"What would happen to the Blue Star then? You have no sisters, have you?"

"Only a brother, and he went overseas to Mancherei when the Prophet began to preach there. Somebody said he went beyond to the Green Isles afterward, when the Prophet left. We do not hear from him any more. . . . But he couldn't use the Blue Star anyway, unless he were bound with a girl from one of the other families, who could witch it for him."

Overhead the sky was deepening, with one faint easterly star agleam, a long slow smoke rose in convolutions from the chimney of a cot down there, (and Rodvard thought desperately of the lovely light-haired girl who had come so many times to search witch-family records at his clerk's cabinet in the Office of Pedigree, but she was a baron's daughter by her badge, and even if he did obtain the Blue Star from this one, and used it to win the light-haired girl, then Lalette would be a witch and put a spell on him—oh tangle!). The hand within his stirred.

"I must go," said Lalette again. (He looks something like Cleudi, she was thinking, but not so old and hard and a little romantic, and he had eye enough to catch the wonderful tiny flash of green among the blue when the sun dipped under.)

"Ah, no. You shall not go, not yet. This is a magic evening and we will keep it forever till all's dark."

Her face softened a trifle in the fading light, but she pulled to withdraw her hand. "Truly."

He clung the tighter, feeling heart-beat, vein-beat in the momentary small struggle. "What if I will not let you go till lantern-glass and the gates are closed?"

"Then Uncle Bontembi will expect me to make a confession and if I do not, he will put a fine on me, and it will be bad for my mother because we are so poor."

"But if I kept you, it would be to run away with you, ah, far beyond the Shining Mountains, and live with you forever."

Her hand went passive again, she leaned toward him a trifle, as though to see more surely the expression on his face. "Do you mean that, Rodvard Bergelin?"

He caught breath. "Why—why should I say it else?"

"You do not. Let me go, let me go, or I'll make you." She half turned, trying to rise, bringing the other hand to help pull loose his fingers.

"Will you witch me, witch?" he cried, struggling, and his grasp slipped to her wrist.

"No—." She snatched at the held hand with the other, catching the thumb and crying fiercely; "I'll break my own finger, I swear it, if you do not let go."

"No. . . ." He flung her two hands apart. Lithe as a serpent, she wrung one and then the other from his grasp, but it was with an effort that carried her off balance and supine asprawl. He rolled on his hip to pin her down, hands on her elbows, breast to breast, and was kissing her half-opened mouth till she stopped trying, turning her face from his and whispering: "Let me go. It's wrong. It's wrong."

"I will not," and he released one hand to feel where the maddening sensation of her breast came against him and the laces began. (The thought was fleetingly seen in the *camera obscura* of his inner mind that he did not love her and would have to pay for this somehow.)

"Let me go!" she cried again in a strangled voice, and convulsing, struck him on the side of the head with her free hand. At that moment the laces gave, her hand came round his head instead of against it, drawing his face down in a long sobbing kiss, through which a murmur, softer than a whisper; "All right, oh, all right, go on." (There was one little flash of triumph across her mind, one trouble solved, Cleudi would never want her now.)

Afterward, he knelt to kiss her skirt-hem. Her lips were compressed at the center, a little raised at the corners. "Now I understand," said she; but he did not, and all the way home was eaten by the most dreadful cold fear that she would revenge herself on him with a witchery that would leave him stark idiot or smitten with dreadful disease. And the other, the other; his mind would not form her name, and there was a cry within him.

II

All three of them were waiting, with that man of Count Cleudi's—the olive-skinned one with such intense eyes—what was his name? Lalette curtsied: Uncle Bontembi smiled. Said Cleudi; "Mathurin, the baskets. I commenced to think we should miss the pleasure of your company tonight, charming Demoiselle Lalette, and my heart was desolated."

"Oh," she said, (thinking—what if they knew?). "But here is Uncle Bontembi who will tell you that to be desolate of heart is to serve evil and not true religion, since God wishes us to be happy; for since he has created us in his image, it must be an image of delight."

"You reason like an angel, Demoiselle Lalette; permit that

I salute you." She moved just enough to make his kiss fall on her cheek. Dame Leonalda simpered, but there was, flick and gone again, a frown across Cleudi's high-cheekboned face. "What a lovely color your daughter has!"

Mathurin laid out the table with napkins which he unfolded from the baskets. There were oysters packed in snow; bubbling wine; a pastry of truffles and pike-livers; small artichokes pickled entire, peaches that must have come from the south, since it was only peach-blossom time in Dossola; white bread; a ham enriched with spices; honeyed small sweetmeats of dwarf fruit. (If he were only more to me and less for himself, thought Lalette, he might be possible; for he does not stint.) They sat down with herself and her mother opposite each other and the two men at the sides of the table, so small that knees touched. Mathurin the servant stood beside her chair, but flitted round to give to the rest as occasion demanded. Cleudi discoursed—a thousand things, eating with his left hand and letting his right now and again drop to touch the fabric over Lalette's leg, which, laughing with talk and wine, she did not deny him. (An aura, like a perfume of virility and desire and pleasure, emanated from him; Lalette felt as though she were swaying slightly in her seat.)

"Lalette Asterhax; the name has fifteen letters," said Cleudi, "and the sum of one and five is six, which fails by one the mystical number of seven. Look also, how you may take it by another route, L being the twelfth letter of the alphabet, so that to it, there is added one for A, another twelve for the second L and so on, the sum of all being eighty-seven." (He has prepared this in advance, she thought.) Being itself summed up again this eighty-seven is fifteen, so it is evident that you will be incomplete and thus lacking in happiness, until united with a man who can supply the missing figures."

"I am not sure that the Church would approve your doctrine," said Uncle Bontembi. He had moved his chair around to place his arm over the back of Dame Leonalda's, and she had thrown her head back to rest on the arm.

"You are clearly wrong, my friend," said Cleudi. "The Church itself takes cognizance of the power of numbers, which are the sign-manual of enlistment under God against evil, rather than being the protection itself, as some ignorant persons would make them. Look, does not the Church in Dossola have seven Episcopals? Are there not seven varieties of angels, and is it not dulcet to make seven prayers within the period? Whereas it is the heretical followers of the Prophet who deny the value of numbers."

"Then," said Lalette, "I must never complete myself by union with you; for you have five letters and the seven of my first name being added to them, make twelve, which is three by your manner of computation, and an evil omen."

Cleudi laughed. "Ah, divine Lalette, your reasoning is unreason." He poured more wine. "For it is clear that man and woman are each incomplete by themselves, not to be completed until they are united; else we were not so formed. Now such union is manifestly to the pleasure of God, since he arranged it thus, so that if anything prevent true union, it must be contrary to the ordinance of God. Is this not exact, Uncle Bontembi?"

Through Dame Leonalda's giggle the priest smiled, his face curling in wrinkles around the fat. "Your lordship lacks only the oath and a drop of oil in the palm to be an Episcopal. I resign in your favor my chance of preferment."

"But I'll resign no chance of perferment." Cleudi reached to squeeze Lalette's hand, where it lay on the table. "A stroke of fortune. I happened to fall in with His Grace the Chancellor only this morning. He spoke of the difficulty in finance, which is such that—would you believe it?—there is even some question whether Her Majesty will be able to take her summer holiday in the mountains."

Dame Leonalda raised her head. "Oh, oh, the disgrace!" she sighed.

"I do not see the stroke of fortune," said Lalette simply.

"A disgrace, yes," said Cleudi, his mobile face for a moment morose. "But I was happily able to suggest to His Grace that the matter of taxes be placed in the hands of the lords of court, themselves to be taxed an amount equal to that due from their seignories, and they to collect it within their estates."

"Again—the stroke of fortune?" said Lalette, not much interested, as she dipped a finger in the wine and drew arabesques on the table-napkin in the damp.

"His Grace was so much charmed with my plan that he offered me a place in the service, with the directorate of the lottery, so that I now am happy enough to be no more a Tritulaccan, but Dossolan by service of adoption." He lifted his glass to Lalette. "I shall drink to your grey eyes, and you to my fortune."

The glasses touched. "I do wish you good fortune," she said.

"What better fortune could there be than to have you attend with me the first opera-ball of the season, and make the drawing of the lottery as its queen?"

Said Uncle Bontembi, in a voice as rich as though he were addressing a congregation; "Spring is the season most calculated to show forth the victory of God over evil and the beginning of new growth and happiness. Not only do we celebrate the return of the sun, but the rejection of darkness, as the former Prince and false Prophet." Lalette did not look at him.

"I will send a costumer to make you one of the new puffed bodices in—yes, I think it must be red for your coloring..." began Cleudi, and then stopped, his eyes seeming to jut from their sockets, as he stared at the wet design under Lalette's finger. Her own gaze focussed, and suddenly she felt tired and very old and not winestruck any more, for without thinking at all she had traced the witch-patterns her mother taught her long ago, and now they were smoking gently on the table-cloth.

"Witchery!" croaked the Count, but recovered faster than the shock itself, and slid in one motion to his feet, with an ironical bow. "Madame, my congratulations on your skill in deception, which should take you far. You and your precious mother made me believe you pure."

"Yes, witchery." She was up, too. "It would have been the same in all cases. I don't want your filthy costume and your filthy scudi. Now, go!" Before he could sign himself, she splashed him with a spray of the dazzling drops from her fingertips. "Go, in the name of Trustemus and Vaton, before I bid you go in such a manner you can never rest again."

Off to one side Lalette heard her mother sob; Cleudi's face took on a look of dogged blankness. Without another word he let his hands drop loose to his side, trotted to the door and through it. Cried Uncle Bontembi; "We'll see to her later. I must release him," and rushed after, his fingers fumbling in his robe for the holy oil, his flesh sagging in grey bags above his jowls.

Lalette sat down slowly, (her mind devoid of any thought save a kind of regretful calm now she had done it), as her mother raised a face where tears had streaked the powder. "Oh, Lalette, how could you—" (the girl felt a wild flutter of being trapped again), but both had forgotten the servant Mathurin, who stepped forward to grip urgently at Lalette's elbow. "Rodvard Bergelin?" he demanded, and she recoiled from the temper of his face, then remembered her new-won power, and touched his hand lightly as though to brush it away, saying:

"And what business of yours if it was?"

"He is the only one can save you. The Blue Star, quickly! Cleudi will never forgive you. He'll have you before the Court of Deacons; he'll—" He ran round the table to Dame Leonalda. "Madame, where is the Blue Star? It belongs to your daughter, and she must leave on the moment. You will not know her if she has the torturers to deal with."

The older woman only collapsed into a passion of alcoholic sobbing, head on arms across the table. "I suppose I must trust you," said Lalette. "I think I know where it is."

"Believe me, you must. He is as cruel as a crocodile; would strew your grave afterward with poems written by himself, but not till he had the fullest pains from you. . . . Is it in that?"

Lalette had pulled aside her mother's bed, beneath which lay the old leather portmanteau with the bar-lock. Mathurin tried it once, twice; it would not give. Before the girl could protest, he whipped a knife like a steel tongue from beneath his jacket and expertly splashed around the fastening. The portmanteau fell open on a collection of such small gauds and bits of clothing as women treasure, Mathurin shovelling them onto the floor with both hands until at the back he came on an old, old wooden box, maybe a handsquare across, with a crack in the wood and a thin slab of marble that might once have borne an inscription set in its cover.

"That must be it," said Lalette, "though I have seen it only outside the case. I cannot be certain now."

"Why?"

"A witchery is needed, and—"

"Get your cloak and what money you have. Rodvard lives in the Street of the Weavers, the third house on the left as you turn in, the one with the blue door. Do not wait; I must attend my master."

3

Escape

I

There was a moon to throw black shadows on passing cat and man; Lalette's little sharp heels clicked so loud on the pave that she almost changed to tiptoe. The Street of the Weavers was known to her; at its gate she had first met Rodvard, amid booths gay with bunting for the autumn festival. He slapped her with a bladder then, and challenged her to dance the volalelle among the reeling violins and sweet recorders . . .

"Fair lady," said a tentative voice. Not even looking round, she pulled the hood closer and hurried her steps until those behind her sounded irresolute and then died away.

One, two, three; moonlight showed a door that would be a worn blue by day, clearly a pensionnario. Lalette caught her breath at the loud flat rap of the knocker through the silent street, held it for a long minute and was just wondering whether she dared strike again, when there was a sound of fuzzy disturbance within, and a wicket window beside the door came open on an ill-tempered face, with a long, drooping, dirty moustache.

"What do you want?"

"I—I must speak with Rodvard Bergelin."

"This is a respectable house. Speak with him in the morning."

"It is—a matter of life and death—Oh, dear God!" as the wicket began to close. "Here." She reached in her purse and recklessly thrust at the face one of the three silver spadas that were all the money she had in the world (What will mother do tomorrow morning?). The face expressed a sour satisfaction; an inarticulate grumble came out of it, which she interpreted as a command to wait where she was. (The musicians' booth had been where the shadow of a turret split the corner in particular shapes.)

A sound of footsteps approached the door from within and it opened upon Rodvard yawning, hair awry, hose wrinkled at the knees, jacket flung around unlaced.

"Lalette! What is it? Come in."

The moustached face hung itself in the background. "She cannot come in this house at night."

"The parlor—"

"I say she cannot come in so late. This is a respectable house. Go down to Losleib Street."

Face closed the door; Rodvard, all anxious, came down the single step, pulling his jacket together (with the fine brown hair curling on his chest in the form of a many-pointed star). "What is it?"

"Can you help me? I do not want to be a burden, but there is trouble. Truly, not meaning to, I set a witchery on Count Cleudi, and they said he would have me arrested to the Court of Deacons."

He was all wideawake and grave at once. "Is there no legalist or priest you could—"

She stamped. "Would I come here, to your respectable house?"

"I did not mean—I only asked—forgive, this is to be thought on. ... Attention; I have heard of an inn by the north gate where provosts never find anyone who pays. I will go with you."

"I have hardly any money."

Even in that uncandid light, she saw his face frown and alter, almost as Cleudi's had, another resemblance. (That is what he imagines I am like, the quick thought crossed her mind, bitterer than the doorman's suspicion.) "Wait; I think I know where you'll be safe for tonight, with a friend of mine who is no friend of provosts or court lords, either. But I must get my cap and knife."

She was quick enough dodging his kiss to make it seem she was only missing the intention. He went round on his heel and up the stair, back in a minute with the feathered cap he had worn that afternoon, and properly belted with his knife. "This friend of mine is a Dr. Remigorius, have you heard of him? A great man to roar at you like a lion, but of good and generous heart. For the poor he has always a kind word, and often physics them or delivers their children without ever asking payment."

They passed into the night city. "How did it happen?" questioned he at a turning.

"In the beginning an accident—ah, do not ask me." She gestured impatient, then put the hand that did not hold his arm up to her face. "And now I am a witch, and I swore I never would be."

"It is my fault. I am sorry. Will you wed with me?" (The words were out; he felt a thrill of peril run up his spine.)

"Do you wish—no you do not, I know it. Beside, how would we find a priest who'd make a marriage without episcopal license—and for a witch?"

"But I do truly desire it. I swear—"

"Oh, spare me your false oaths. Since you ask forgiveness, I'll forgive anything but those." She gripped his arm suddenly so hard it hurt. At the corner of the next street was a watch of two, one with halberd and helmet, the other sword and lantern, but the sight of late-walking couples would be less than novel to them, they only gave a glance in passing.

Rodvard brought her round another corner and before one of those houses built with jutting overstoreys in the Zigraner fashion. Small-paned windows were beside a door, where a stiff stuffed lizard hung to show that someone within practiced the art medic. The bell tinkled crackedly; Rodvard's arm came nervous-tight around the girl. "It will turn to a happy issue," he said. "No harm can touch us, now we have—found each other." She did not try to draw from the warm sweet pressure, and it endured until a second ring brought the man out, with a fine beard ridiculously done up in a sleeping-bag to hold its shape, and a robe like a priest's hastily corded round him.

"This is the Demoiselle Asterhax," said Rodvard. "Can you help her? She has put a witchery on one of the court lords, Count Cleudi, and is searched for by the provosts."

Sleep fell from the older man's eyes. "A witchery? The Tritulaccan count? He has enough favor to be deadly if he will, and it would involve me in the overthrow.... But I am sworn by the practice of the healing art to refuse help to none who come in distress. Enter from the cold."

Lalette caught a darkling glimpse of shelves lined with jars in glass or stone as they passed through. Rodvard half stumbled against a stool and they were at an inner door, where Dr. Remigorius said; "Halt," struck flint and steel to a candle and stood in its light beside the untidy bed, pulling off his beard-bag. "Now you shall tell me a true tale of how this came about," he said, "for a physician must know the whole nature of the disease he is to cure, ha, ha. Will the demoiselle sit?" He swept the pile of his own garments from the only chair to the bed.

The wine in her limbs and the long double walk had left Lalette tired and safe and not caring very much now. She sat down slowly. "It was only that Count Cleudi came with some baskets of supper and was trying to persuade me to go to the opera-ball with him, and I was toying with my fingers in some spilled wine on the table. You know how one does—" she made a little gesture of appeal. "I accidentally drew witch patterns and when he saw what they were, he—he—he would have had me against my will, so I witched him. That's all."

Not a line changed in Remigorius' face. Said he; "I see—

all but one detail. What made you flee so fast by midnight to my friend Rodvard? What do you know about this Count Cleudi?"

"It was his servant, a man named Mathurin, said I must instantly take my mother's Blue Star and go. Because he would have had me killed."

She saw Rodvard flick up his eyebrows as he glanced at Remigorius. (The expression round his mouth might have been triumph, which was incomprehensible); her brow knit, but the doctor's voice was smooth as ice; "It is not your mother's Blue Star, but your man's, while he is your lover, and I think this must be the case, or you would not have witched this southern Count. You have Ser Rodvard's bauble safe, then?"

(A faint perfume of suspicion—was it to herself or to this Blue Star that he was offering kindness?) Lalette said; "I have it here," and took the box from under her cloak.

The doctor, gravely; "Then you will have the provosts much the hotter on your trail, since the lords temporal and spiritual are not desirous to have these things in hands they are not certain of. I think you must fly from the city as fast as you can, perhaps even beyond the Queen's writ, up to Kjermanash. Not Mayern, because of the Prince and his prophecies. But before that it would be well to provide this Blue Star with the needed witchery and let Ser Rodvard bear it. When you are not easily found, be sure they will set spies out for you, and with this tool you may be sure of people you meet."

Lalette frowned, but looked at Rodvard. "Is this your word also?"

"How could it be other? I think we may need the protection."

"Very well." She lifted one palm to her forehead. "This witching is, I think, something that leaves one without force or will, and I have performed one tonight. But I will do it. I would be private."

"There is the shop. Do you require materials, demoiselle?"

"Only a little water—though wine would be better."

Remigorius produced a bottle half-filled with wine from a

tall cabinet against the wall, lighted a candle-stub, and swung the shop-door with a bow. When it had closed behind her, Rodvard said; "I do not see how, if she is to be taken instantly from the city, I can use this Blue Star for our purpose."

The doctor glanced sidelong and whipped a finger to his lips. "Tish! Matter for the High Center. But who said you would go with her?" They were quiet; a small sound, like the mewing of a kitten, came from the shop, then it stopped, and Lalette came back in. The hood was on her shoulders, and her face was white to the hair-roots; the wooden case stood open in her hand, and in it, lying on a bed of white silk so old it had faded to yellow, the Blue Star, the witch-stone, smaller than might have been imagined, barely a finger-joint across, but seeming to have depth, so that even in the candlelight all the sapphirean fires of ocean and cold hell were in its heart.

Rodvard shivered slightly. Lalette said; "Open your jacket," and when he had done so, hung the jewel round his neck on its thin gold chain.

"Now I will tell you as I have been taught," she said, "that while you wear this jewel, you are of the witch-families, and can read the thoughts of those in whose eyes you look keenly. But only while you are my man and lover, for this power is yours through me. If you are unfaithful to me, it will become for you only a piece of glass; and if you do not give it up at once when I ask it back, there will lie upon you and it a deadly witchery, so that you can never rest again."

She came forward to take his face in both hands and kiss him on the lips. The stone lay like a piece of ice against his bare chest. Rodvard felt no different, unchanged, but as he looked deep into the girl's eyes before him, he knew without words but beyond any doubt that a black shadow had closed round her mind, she would never witch him, she had decided, but was hating all this and Remigorius and him too, for the moment. He turned his head, the thought flashed away, and the doctor said, with a twist at the corner of his lips:

"Now we will see if this star is a true marvel or only another of the bogey-tales made up by the lords of court to keep men in submission. Look in my eyes, Ser Rodvard, and tell me what I am thinking."

Rodvard looked. "Why, why," he said, "I do not altogether understand, but it is as though you were saying in words that you would try on a living person whether an infusion of squill in vinegar is useful in a stoppage of the passages." (It was not the complete thought, there was a formless shadow at the back of his mind, something about a treason.) Remigorius shook his head and turned from the gaze with pressed lips.

"God's splendor! You are become a dangerous man, Ser Bergelin," he said, "or a cleverer one than I think." Then; "I count the night more than half gone, and you will need rest, having far to travel in the morning. I leave you two my bed while I arrange for your journey." He picked up his clothes and bowed himself into the shop to dress. Rodvard and Lalette were left alone.

II

She remained in the chair, with her head drooping and slightly to one side, so he could see only the angle of cheek and chin. "The bed," he said. "I am so weary," said she, "that it's not needed. Do you take it and let me rest here. I'll turn my back if you wish to undress."

(The thought went tingling through his mind that after this afternoon—so long ago, now—they needed no more be modest with each other.) It almost reached his lips, but instead; "No, you shall have the bed; you need it," and held his hand to help her up, but she hardly touched it, on her feet with a sweep of skirts, to take one stumbling step to the towseled bed, where she flung herself down in her cloak, and as he could tell from her breathing, was asleep almost at once.

He, wakeful as an owl-bird with excitement and having slept earlier, sat in a chair with the ice-cold jewel unfamiliar around his neck—bodily contact had not warmed it at all—half daydreaming, half thinking. A high destiny? Not with a witch and through witchery. All he thought revolted against that, it was cheating, if witchery should rule, there was an end of free choice where choice meant most, all hopes were then fled. There's no new day if this rules, we may as well make our beds under the old Queen's rule, and that of Florestan, the Laughing Chancellor.

Remigorius. The doctor would say this was not what he thought, but what he had been taught; they had quarrelled on this issue before, and Remigorius would say how Rodvard's reasoning led straight as a line to the support of all the things that both desired to throw down; how it was precisely the rejection of witchcraft as devilish and unclean that Episcopals and Queen stood for. If there were a good God, as the Church said, He could not allow a free choice that might be turned against Himself and so deprive Him of godhead.

Mathurin would chime in at this point to say that no man under tyranny would by free choice choose freedom, the generality preferring rather to have a chance of rising to the tyrant's seat. They must be compelled to take the better way to their own betterment, so that even in the secular affair free choice was a dream—and then he, Rodvard, would be overborne by the whirl and rush of their arguments.

A high destiny? Let us, Sons of the New Day, compel them, then; ride the stormwind to greatness by setting men free. Oh, it would be noble to be acclaimed as one of those who had brought about the change. But no; no; that honor would go to those of the High Center, the leaders now hidden in shadow, whose forms would stand forth in granite with the dawning of the New Day—while the name of Rodvard Bergelin was never heard.

A high destiny? He thought of battle, the close combat where steel bows flung their sharp messengers against the double-locked shields and horsemen went past, while the trumpets shouted. The war-tune rang through his head— "Lift the star of old Dossola, brave men rise and tyrants stare . . ."

No. The star would never rise in this time. Dossola, defeated and dead to honor, bound down by treaties which Queen and Florestan upheld merely to keep their own place. Shame—no high destiny could come from serving such a cause. For so much, what could Rodvard Bergelin do in war, even if the cause were better? There had been Dagus of

Grödensteg, to be sure, the archer, the great hero who sprang from night and nowhere when Zigraners were a terror to the land—Rodvard thought of his statue in the Long Square, one arm aloft to hold the deadly bow, the star-badge in his cap. But that was in the far-off glorious times, when one could clap on a hat and run forth to adventure instead of a day's toil over yellow documents at the Office of Pedigree. What could one do in this modern war, where noble birth and twenty years of service were needed to make a commander? He'd lay some captain's bed, no doubt, and clean his tent; or enter for a ten-year man, learn the halberd, how to shoot the bow and form square—a dull depressing life, with a cold lone grave at the end of it; "stupid as a spearman" said the proverb, and all he had known were stupid enough. No; no destiny. "The destiny of all is to service, for only so can happiness be won." Who had said that? Some priest; member of what Mathurin called the conspiracy against poverty. Yet if it were not true, one must save one's services for oneself and be false as hell to all the world beside. Let conscience die . . . and dawn began to poke behind the gray window at the sound of the doctor's entry returning.

4

Daylight; Refuge

I

Lalette sat up sleepily and sipped a little wine; there was nothing to eat but the end of a loaf, most of which Rodvard devoured, surprised to find that he was hungry, (and a tingle running down his veins as he thought of the evening under the cedars). Remigorius did not even wait for the end of the meager breakfast before breaking out with; "Hark, the provosts are already forth. This must be hurried, and you two must leave. I have arranged matters to

the least peril. There's an inn on King Crotinianus' Square, at
the north end, called the Sign of the Limping Cat, where the
north-going coaches halt to pick up travellers from that side
of the city. Go there; you can wait on the bench outside and
had better, to avoid talking with someone who might be a
spy. I trust you, demoiselle, to keep your face as much
covered as possible; Rodvard, you shall use that devil-stone
to know the purpose of any who approach.

"There will be a blue-painted coach which goes to Bregatz
by way of Trandit and Liazabon. The driver's name is Morsens; inquire. Before Trandit you should make an argument
for the benefit of others in the coach, you being a young
couple just wed, so joyous in the bridal that the new dame's
trunk has been forgot. At Trandit, then, Ser Rodvard will
descend to return for it, while Demoiselle Asterhax rides on
to Bregatz in the care of Morsens the coachman and reaches
those of the Center there. Are you players enough to play
these parts? . . . It will thus not be strange when Morsens
protects her, which he will gladly do. But you must give him
a gold scuderius, for he is not one of ours, and his danger is
very great."

Lalette, who had begun to take down her hair with fingers
swift and sure in order to do it up into the bridal braids,
stopped with pursed mouth. "But I do not have a scuderius,"
she said. "I have hardly any money at all."

An expression of furious indignation held the doctor's face
as it turned toward Rodvard. "You?" But the young man,
flushing, reached in his jacket-pocket for a handful of coppers and one single silver spada. "Perhaps we can make it up
together," he said. "They are so deep in arrears of pay at the
office where I'm employed . . . or if we can find a Zigraner
with his shop open early, I might pledge my wage . . ."

"Or if we find a kind-hearted provost with scudi instead of
bilboes for those he pursues!" cried Remigorius. "Madam,
you will need all the witchcraft you can muster, for you are
surely the most improvident fool that ever tried an evasion
with what did not belong to her. I've no money, either." He
tugged at his beard, looking at her from anger-filled eyes, but
before Lalette could more than begin the sound of a hot

retort, changed expression, shrugged, and spread his hands:

"There's a night's work gone glimmering, then. But I'll not send you back to Cleudi and the Deacons' Court, even though you were other than friend Rodvard's mistress." He mused (and Rodvard, catching his eye as the head turned, saw in it a flash of deadly acquisitiveness for the Blue Star, no real interest in Lalette's fate whatever). The young man started as from a blow; Remigorius spoke again:

"You must hide in the city, then, till somehow transport's found. Would be welcome to this abode, but too many come here for physic; the matter would be bruited about. Nor your place, neither, Rodvard. The Queen's provosts will not be long in finding your connection with this demoiselle, no. Your mother know of it?"

Said Lalette; "If you mean of Rodvard, I—I do not think so. We met always while she was at the Service. He never came to the house and there was only my gossip, Avilda Brekoff, who was ever with us."

"Then we may have a few days before they come on the scent. Were you seen coming here last night?"

"Only by a watch of two from a distance, and by the doorman where I live," said Rodvard, but Lalette; "I had to give the man a silver spada to call Rodvard and there was some slight bargle over whether I might enter. I fear I was not only seen, but noted. I regret."

"You may well. Here's the few days lost again. If the matter's pressed, they will surely question the doorman of every pensionnario in the city." Remigorius swung knit brows to Rodvard; "You had best go to your working place today, for the absence might be noted. But I will let you return to your pensionnario for only the once, and then to bring away nothing but your most intimate needs. Stop for no meal, where there's talk—at least, till we can be sure of this doorman. What's his name?"

"Krept or something like it, I do not know for sure. We call him Udo the crab. I have one or two books I would not willingly lose."

"Would you rather lose your life?" The doctor scrabbled for a piece of paper and began to write. "This is more dreadful than you know of. Demoiselle, you can be secure for a little time with a friend of ours, a certain Mme. Kaja, who used to be a singer in the opera. She lives on the top floor of an old goat's nest in the Street Cossao and has young girls visiting her all the time for instruction in music, so there'll be no comment at your appearance." His pen scratched, he stood up, threw sand on the paper and let it slide to the floor. "This be your passport. Your lover—" (the word was accompanied by a lip-turn that made Lalette shiver) "—can join you there this twilight. But wait—you may be known in the street."

He bustled into the shop-room and returned with a pair of quills. "Up your nose, one on either side. So. I'd like it better if there were another cloak for you, but leave the hood of this one down; with your hair changed, and your face ..."

II

It would be the morning after his wedding breakfast on new wine and old bread with fear for a sauce, that *she* should come to the Office of Pedigree again—with her bands of light hair, fine chin line and cheekbones, and the pointed coronet badge in her hat that showed her a baron's daughter. All morning Rodvard had been dozing and drowsing; she greeted him gaily; "Have you found more of this matter with which the stem of Stojenrosek is to confound Count Cleudi, or has the weather been too fine for work indoors?"

"No, demoiselle." (There was a twist in his chest, he could barely get the words out.) He passed the chair where she showed a turn of ankle, to one of the tall dark wall-files, and took out a parchment. "One of the recorders lighted on this—see, it is from the reign of King Crotinianus the Second, the great king, and bears his seal of the boar's head, with that of his Chancellor. It is a series of decisions on inheritance and guardianship for the province of Zenss. At the eleventh year of the reign there is one here—" he handed the pages over carefully "—giving the son of Stojenrosek leave to wed with one Luedecia and pass the inheritance to their daughters, though she's but a bowman's daughter herself, there being no heiresses female to take the estate, which would thus have fallen to the crown."

She had stood up to look at the old crabbed chancery hand of the document where he spread it on the table and her shoulder brushed his. Said she; "Did they wed, then?"

"Alas, demoiselle, I cannot tell you." (Shoulder did not withdraw.) "So many of the records of that time were destroyed in the great fire at Zenss a quadrial of years ago. But I will search."

"Do so ... I cannot read it," she said. "What does this say?" Her fingers touched his in a small shock, where they were outspread to hold the parchment, and the contact rested as she bent to look, in the spring light filtering through the dusty panes. The inner door to the cabinet adjoining was closed; down the corridor outside, someone was whistling as he walked; she turned her head to face him slowly, he felt the witch-stone cold as ice over his heart, and to shut out what he feared was coming, Rodvard croaked chokingly;

"What is your name?"

"My name is Maritzl." (No use; it came over sharply—if he kiss me, I will not stay him, I will marry him, I will take him into my father's house, I will even be his mistress if he demands it ... this disappearing in the lightning-flash of Lalette saying, "If you are ever unfaithful—" and flash on flash what would happen if he lost the Blue Star for which he had sacrificed so much. Sold, sold.)

She caught her breath a little. He disengaged the parchment from her hand. "I will have it copied for you in a modern hand," he said.

III

Under Remigorius' order, Rodvard did not go home to the pensionnario at sun-turning as usual, but took his repast for a pair of coppers on small beer and cheese at a tavern near his labor. He had been there not often, but it seemed to him that the place bubbled with talk beyond custom, and he wondered if the cause were some tale of Count Cleudi's witching and

Lalette's escape, a speculation dispelled on his return, for there came to him young Asper Poltén from the next cabinet with:

"Did you know that girl you squired to the harvest festival turned out to be a witch? She has witched Count Cleudi, and stolen all his money; they say he's going to die. They have closed the city gates and set a price on her. Your fortune that you carried matters no further with one like that."

Rodvard shuffled papers. Some reply was necessary. "Why are they so urgent over a foreigner? People have been witched before without having all the paving stones in Netznegon City torn up about it."

"Do you forever live in dreams? He's the new favorite—named director of the lottery only yesterday. Perhaps that's the reason the witch rode him—for jealousy more than the scudi. She's not to be blamed if, as I hear, he's more than a proper man in the parts that matter most to women. They say Cleudi and the Florestan held an exhibition for Her Majesty and the Tritulaccan was longer. Speaking of which, Ser Rodvard, you are not far from fortune yourself. I saw the Demoiselle of Stojenrosek here again today. She'll have a shapelier body than Cleudi will ever press, and bring you a fortune in addition."

("Did you see her indeed, curse you? and what business is it of yours?" Rodvard wanted to cry; or "Mine's the high destiny of the witch.") But aloud he could only say; "There's nothing in that. She's only searching out some old family records. I must go to Ser Habbermal's cabinet; he has a project forward for me."

He stood up with a trifling stagger, leg tingling with the pain of the position in which he had cramped it. Asper Poltén made offended eyes. "Ah, plah, you are too nice for anything but priesthood!" He turned away, flung open the door to the next cabinet, and could be heard uttering to the three within; "Bergelin again; this time pretending he does not know what women carry between their legs or what it's used for—" with a whoop of merriment from the rest.

Rodvard himself, before they could all come in and begin their usual sport of baiting, walked to the outer door,

through it, and without so much as pausing at the garderobe
for his cap, straight down the corridor to the street and
away, the last steps running. If there were stares at seeing
him without headgear or mark of condition, he did not
return them, but hurried on to his own living-place. The
pensionnaria was at the foot of the stairs, the little black
hairs on her upper lip quivering as she administered some
rebuke to a maid who held a trayful of dirty dishes, but her
eye lighted as she turned to perceive a new victim.

"You are too late, Ser Bergelin. If we make a rule good
for one, it must stand for all, because it is only so that I can
keep up a place like this, as cheap as it is, and I simply can't
have you bringing girls here late at night, I have told
Udo. . . ." The end of it he did not hear, as he broke past her
up the stairs, bounding.

The extra set of hose must come, of course, but his best
jacket would not go on over the other, so he had to make a
bundle with underclothing and wrap it in the cloak that it was
too fine a day to wear. The festival-cap must stay behind,
even though it might bring some coppers from a dealer; also
the pair of tiny southern-made health-goblets for carrying at
the waist on feast days, of whose acquisition he had been so
proud. At the last moment he added the volume of Dostal's
ballads; of all the books, he could spare that one least. There
was a moment of fear when a glance through the glass-
windowed door showed callers closeted with Udo the Crab,
but side vision registered the fact that they were only a pair
of rough fellows in leather jackets, not blue-and-green provosts.

He had been to Mme. Kaja's only once before, and then at
night, for a meeting of the Sons of the New Day. Under this
more vivid light the Street Cossao showed as a dirty court-
yard with a running sore of gutter down the center, garbages
piled in the corners, yelling children underfoot and somewhere among the upper stories a hand that practiced the
violon monotonously, playing the harvest-song, but always
going sour on the same double-stop passage. Rodvard elected
the wrong house first, the doorman did not know of Kaja,
but the next one at the back angle of the court was it; he

went up a narrow dark winding stair smelling of yesterday's cabbage and knocked at the topmost door.

Mme. Kaja herself answered, clad in an old dressing-gown, pink silk, and dirty grey where it dragged along the floor, with her hair packed untidily atop her head. Past her a space of floor was visible, with light coming through a pair of dormer windows, a keyed musical instrument and chairs. "Ser Rodvard!" she squealed, her voice going into a high musical note. "You are sooo welcome. We did not expect you this early. The dear girl is waiting."

A door against the slant of the garret opened and Lalette came out, unaffectedly glad it was he, and this time not avoiding as he ran forward to kiss her on the lips. The older woman; "I leave you to your greetings, while I make myself beautiful." She passed through the door from which Lalette had come; the girl sat down. After the door had closed behind Kaja, "Rodvard," she said, very still and looking at the floor.

"Lalette."

"I have given you my Blue Star. Whether to marry you now I do not know. I think not—it seems to me that you are not altogether willing; I feel you are holding something back from me. But this I say, and you may look into my heart and find it true—" she raised her head in a blaze of grey eyes "—that I want to be a good partner to you, Rodvard, and will honestly do all in my power never to fail you."

From the inner room came the sound of Mme. Kaja, running scales in what was left of her voice (and what could he say? thought Rodvard, who had won this loyalty for Remigorius' reason and not his own desire. Let conscience die, but not with a tear at the heartstrings.) "I will do as much," said he, and as her lip quivered at his tone, "if we ever pass this peril with our lives."

She lifted a hand and let it fall beside her. "It is life without account of peril that I have offered," she said. "I do not—"

"How do you know? Lalette, look at me. Will you lie with me this night, in peril or whatever?"

But she would not meet the questioning eyes now (and he

thought, she thought, they both knew there had been somehow a lack of communication). Lalette said; "You have
come before time."

He shuddered slightly. "They picked at me till I must
leave. You will hardly believe how—how base—"

The inner door sprang open and Mme. Kaja emerged with
almost a dance-step, dressed to the eyes in withering finery.
"For a little while I must go forth," she said, "but you will
hardly miss me, he, he. I'll bring sup from the cook-shop, is
there a delicacy you desire or any other way I can lighten
captivity for my two caged birds?"

She beamed on them fondly. Rodvard thought of the cap
left at the office and prayed her for a new one, with the
badge of his condition, which took more of his slender store
of coppers. The door closed; and now they two had not much
to say to each other, having agreed that all that mattered
should be left unsaid.

The end of it was that Lalette in all her clothes lay down
on the bed in the corner to make up for some of the sleep
lost last night, while he undid his parcel and set out to lose
himself in Iren Dostal's harmonies and tales—but that did
not do very well either, the poems he had always loved
seemed suddenly pointless. He fell into a kind of doze or
waking dream, in which the thought came to his mind that if
he were really ready to let conscience die in exchange for
high destiny, he had only to give this witch back her Blue
Star, call for the provosts, and claiming the price set on her,
seek out Maritzl of Stojenrosek. A destiny not high by the
standards of the Sons of the New Day, no doubt. But love
and position, aye. Remigorius would approve; would call it
the act of a great spirit to seek an inner contentment, no
matter what others thought of how it was achieved, no
matter if others were hurt during the achievement. But
Remigorius thought the struggle more important than its
end—and it might be that the reason he, Rodvard, could see
no high destiny, was that he did not possess such a spirit,
immune to scruple, willing to serve any cause.

Now he fell on to wondering what was the tangle of ideas
and thoughts that made up himself, Rodvard Bergelin, where

they came from and how they were put together—could they be altered?—and so drifted deeper into his daydream till it began to grow dusk and Mme. Kaja came back with a covered dish of fish and red beans.

5

Night; Generosity; Treason

She was less cooing than before, having learned of the closing of the city gates and the price on Lalette. (For the first time she knows what it is to be a conspirator, Rodvard thought.) There was a self-sacrificing debate over where to sleep, for the singer had only the one bed and tried to insist that the pair use it, or at least share it with her. In the end Rodvard composed himself across a pile of old garments on the floor. They smelled, he felt ill-used, and went to sleep wondering rather desperately what to do about money.

That problem became no easier with the morning, when Mme. Kaja said her own funds were very low and she could not receive her pupils while the two were there. As she was going out Rodvard gave her his last silver spada, whose breakup would keep them nourished for a couple of days. Lalette added that she was much concerned over her mother; could the singer obtain news?

Hardly had the receding footsteps left the first flight when Rodvard, burning inwardly with anxiety, suspense and the thought of another do-nothing day, which combined to translate themselves into desire, swung the girl off her feet in his arms and bore her toward the bed without a word. She struggled a little and the Blue Star told him she was not very willing, but the contact of their bodies soon caught her, she only asked to be careful of her dress as she pulled it off—and Mme. Kaja's voice said; "Oh."

Rodvard rolled over, blood running hot through his cheeks. "I am so-o-o sorry," the older woman said. "I was going to the Service and found I had forgot my Book of Days. But you must not mind, really you must not, when I was in the opera, His Majesty used to make three of us attend him together and when the heart speaks . . ." rattling like a broken music-box in terms that Rodvard scarcely heard, as she crossed the room to take the Book of Days and left again without looking at them directly.

Lalette (feeling as though she had bathed in a sewer and never wanted to touch anything clean again) took her dress to put it on. When Rodvard touched her shoulder, she shook his hand away and said, simply; "No."

"It was my fault," he said, "and I regret—"

"No. I am the one most to blame. It does not matter now for any reason." Her mouth moved and she looked down, tieing laces. "Dear God, what your fine friends will think of me! I should have accepted Count Cleudi's offer; at least I would have been well paid for the name I'll have."

He felt himself flush again. "Well, if they call you any name you do not wish to have, it will be your own fault," he said. "I have offered you marriage—"

"Ah, yes, indeed, with me furnishing the priest's spada for the ceremony."

"—and I will hold to the offer. Demoiselle, you are not just."

She turned and sat down, (feeling suddenly weary, bitten with the edge of concern about her mother, so that it was not worth while to quarrel). He made one or two beginnings of speech, but could settle on nothing worth saying; moved about the room, clanking the coppers in his pocket, and looked out the window; picked at one or two keys of the music in a manner that showed he had no training with it; found a book of Mme. Kaja's and standing, skimmed a few pages, then set it down; resumed his pacing; abandoned it; walked to where he had placed his few belongings on a chair, took his own book and settled himself purposefully to read, in a position where his face was mostly in shadow from her."

(The angry shame had run off Lalette now, she could only see that he was truly unhappy.) After a little while she ran across the room, put her arms around his shoulder and kissed the side of his face. "Rodvard," she said, "I really meant it all. If you want me, you may have me any time you wish."

He swung her down to his lap, but (now afraid of interruption) would go no farther than kissing her and holding her close, so for a long time they remained thus lip to lip, speaking a little to exchange memories of things pleasant in their few meetings and not noticing they had missed a meal, until they heard Mme. Kaja's step outside the door, which this time she made firm enough to give them warning. The singer began to talk at once about the Service and how as the chanters intoned the celestial melody and the violet vestments fluttered among the flowers that fell from the galleries to crush fragrantly beneath the worshipers' knees, she could feel every power of evil roll from her mind—"though the second baritone was flat in the *musanna*. Oh, if only the court would have religion in its heart, as the poor people do, who sat with tears in their eyes." She smiled suddenly on Lalette:

"I spoke to my own priest, too, for you. I know you must have a confession to make by now——" she held up outspread fingers before her face and tittered through them "——so I made up a story for you, about a jealous husband, and he will hear you after dark, when all's safe, and you won't have to pay but a copper or two."

Lalette looked up. "But there's no confession to make. . . . Did you find out about my mother?"

Rodvard saw Mme. Kaja's eyes open wide, and felt the cold stone (she was not believing Lalette at all, and for some reason was desperately frightened that the girl should lie). "Oh, you pooooor child," she said. "It was so unthinking of me to forget to tell you. I did not find out much, but I know the provosts have not taken her, and Count Cleudi is not as ill as pretended, that is only a story."

She set down packages of food, a dish of lentils with bread and wine; began to make ready the table, keeping her eyes averted, so Rodvard could not read her thinking (it came to him that he would not be the first Star-bearer she had met) as she talked rapidly, about the Service once more. The priest had said that when anyone admitted evil to his heart, peril lay upon all persons approaching the lost one. "For these powers of evil increase like mice in a granary, running from one soul to another, and as farmers will often burn an old grain-bin to keep the vermin from spreading, so it is lawful and even necessary to destroy the body of one infected by the powers of evil. He was talking about this poor child here, it was easy to see."

Rodvard (to whom this was interesting, if somewhat questionable discourse) would have inquired more as she paused for breath, but Lalette (who found it more than tiresome) broke in to ask what of the city? what of the hunt for her?

"Oh, they have opened the gates again, though I did not go to see, and put guards everywhere. But it will be all right. Have I ever recounted to you, friend Rodvard, that I was in arrest once myself? It was because of that Oronari, who was so jealous because I could carry the high note in 'The Mayern Lovers' while she could not, and had me accused of stealing some of the jewels that were loaned for the spring festival performance. I felt very badly about it, because she was a friend of mine, but it's just as the priest said, the power of evil had gained control over her, and there was nothing I could do but complain to the Baron Coespel, who was my protector then, and he had her banished the . . ."

She stuffed food into her mouth, masticating noisily as she babbled. Rodvard caught a flash of Lalette's eye (and knew she was thinking how thin the veneer of half a lifetime around the court was over someone with a peasant's background). To change things he asked; "Madame, is there any word of the doctor?"

"He did not send the fruiterer from his street?" She sighed and turned to Lalette. "Then it is likely that he has no money as yet. He is so good and kind and works for so little that it is often so. Dear child, have you no funds at all?"

Said Lalette; "Only two spadas. But I took all the money in the house when I left, and my mother—"

"Dear child, of course we all love our parents and do all we can for them, but after all, they are only our relatives by accident and not the choice of the heart—" she smote her breast in the gesture Rodvard remembered "—and when the heart speaks, God dwells in us to drive out the powers of evil. Then we are grateful to those who speak to us through the heart, and if we have anything we give it to them. I denied the heart once—"

"Your pardon," said Lalette, and stood up to leave the table. Her face was a little white.

Mme. Kaja finished the last of the wine and wiped her mouth. "I know it is hard for you, being of the witch-families, dear child," she said. "But Uncle Tutul, who is the priest we are going to see tonight, says that even a witch may save herself if she gives up everything to those she loves, and oh, my dear, I really do not mind missing my pupils, but—"

Lalette's mouth strained. She stood up and plucked from her waist the tiny purse. "Here," she cried, "are the spadas," and flung them ringing silvernly against the plates. "Take them; I am going to the provosts myself. To be seduced, I will, it was my fault. But I will owe no obligation for it." She turned to the door so fast that Rodvard barely barred the way before her.

"No," said he, as she tried to push him from the way. "You shall not go like this." Their hands caught and she struggled for a moment. "Or if you'll say you do not love and never will, go; and I will join you before the Deacons' court. But it was another tale that you told lately."

Said Mme. Kaja; "Oh, dear child, you must not resist such love." She tittered (and the nerves of both the others jangled).

Lalette sat down. "I am at the mercy of you two," she said.

"Mercy? Mercy?" The singer's bracelets clanked. "Ah, no, we are at yours, and seek to help you at our own risk. Not so, friend Rodvard?" She swung to face him for an unguarded moment (and he was staggered till he must grip the table-edge at the blast of hate for Lalette behind her eyes. There was a strange mother-thought in it too, he could not make out the detail). Kaja's glance went restlessly on across the room. She stood up in her turn, saying; "I do not know the hour, my watch is being repaired, but I am sure by the dimness outside it must be late, and Uncle Tutul is waiting. Demoiselle Asterhax—no, I shall call you Lalette, it is so much more friendly—will you come?"

(Rodvard thought; if I let her go, everything will arrange itself to my utmost advantage.) "Maritzl," he said, "do not go out this evening. There's no—"

Mme. Kaja tittered once more. "Ah, friend Rodvard," she said, "if you have women kind to you, you must remember their names. Will you come, Demoiselle Lalette? Even if there's no confession, it will be a joy to hear Uncle Tutul's discourse."

Rodvard; "Lalette, I beg you, by all you have said this day and all we hope for in the future, do not go out now. I have a reason." He reached one hand and took hers, as she looked at him (wondering why he was so vehement in such a small matter); a child's look, with trust in it.

"Well, then," and she sat down again. A glassy smile appeared on Mme. Kaja's face, and she shook one finger at Lalette as she hurried to the door. "You naughty Rodvard; she will certainly have a confession to make before I return," and her steps were audible, going down.

Lalette's hands lay listless in her lap. For a minute there was silence, in which she rose, walking slowly to the window to gaze out and down, not turning around. "What is your reason and who is Maritzl?"

He had begun to make up his bundle with quick fingers, the volume of Iren Dostal inside. "We must leave here forthwith. The Blue Star—she will do you a terrible harm if she can."

"You have told me nothing I did not know without that bit of witchery. A pattern would be useless against her, though, she is too close to the Church. . . . Rodvard."

"What will you have?" He pulled the edge of the cloak tight.

"I am sorry I said what lately I did . . . about being seduced. Will you forgive? I do not wish to be a shrew, as my mother said, and I will say that I do not regret—what we did."

He dropped the knot half-made and ran over to her, but she shifted in his grasp, pointing. "Rodvard!"

Down the line of her finger he saw hurrying figures pass the lantern at the gate of the Street Cossao. Impossible to miss Mme. Kaja or the priest, or the provost with bare alerted sword. Said Rodvard; "I did not think her so quick in her grimness. Is there another stair?"

"Not that I know. I am sure not. No escape. Oh—"

"That cannot be true. Life is to those who struggle for it, says Dr. Remigorius." He threw the latch and pushed the window outward; not a foot down lay a broad rain-gutter, which being proved solid by foot-weight test, he went three rapid steps across the room to sling his bundle over one shoulder, stepped out cautiously, caught a grip at the edge of the dormer with his right hand (not daring to look down into the dizzy dark), and stretched the other to Lalette. "Come."

"Oh, I—"

"Come!"

He could feel her shiver dreadfully as she took the step, she almost tripped over her dress on the sill, but once out, it was she who stretched to the limit of his restraining hand to swing the window closed. By good fortune it was a suave spring night; Rodvard could see stars past the rim of the house as they edged rightward, free hands pressed against the slates of the mansard, until contact was made with the second dormer, the one in the dressing room. He gripped at that edge, sliding foot against foot, the bundle almost pulling him off balance where he came against the projection. "Hurry," whispered Lalette. "I can hear them."

Ahead and beyond the roof turned; one might work round that backslope but it would only lead to the opposite side of Mme. Kaja's garret. Rodvard halted his sliding progress and looked over his shoulder to see the loom of the house at the back of the court, fortunately of the same height. A glance down showed another gutter, with something more than a thigh-length of black space in separation. He turned again, face brushing slates, to make out that Lalette had seen it, too.

"Shall we try it?" he whispered, and then, incontinently, "I love you" (which was for that enchanted moment true). For answer she disengaged her hand from his and began to tuck up her skirt, leaning with cheek against the roofslope. He swung and tossed the bundle to the other gutter; set foot on the edge where they were, teetered, and with perspiring palms, pushed himself into the long step, almost going down when the lip of the opposite gutter proved higher. But it was wider as well, it held, he was able to reach a hand out and pull her across.

There were no windows on this side of the other house, they found it easy to slide along leftward to the corner, and by the especial grace of heaven, there was a drain at the angle, in which Rodvard's foot caught to keep them from tumbling where the gutter ended suddenly, with the back of the building going down sheer. They both stood breathless as a window in the building they had just left cracked open, a voice said; "No, not along the gutter there. Perhaps they jumped." Mme. Kaja's titter was raised. "We must get more men and search—"

Lalette pressed Rodvard's hand; the window closed, and they stood mute on the roof-edge, finger laced in finger, for it seemed a long time. From below in the court, voices floated up, clear as though they were only a few feet away, except that one could not make out words, only that Kaja's tone was among the rest. Lalette drew him to her and whispered; "We must go back through before she returns," and began to lead to where they had crossed the gap. She was clearly right, they had no future there, the roof where they were had no break, was only the side of the building, which went to its peak at the front as well as the back.

The return, with its repetition of peril already overcome, was worse than the passage. Rodvard had to stand on the very edge of the gutter to swing back. Lalette followed lightly. By the time he had reached the window of the dressing-room, worked it open with one hand, and had a leg across the sill, he dared look down—and saw what might have made them earlier hesitate about making a return, namely a blue provost standing watchfully under the lamp at the street entrance, while two or three figures more were

moving about. But like most searchers, they never looked
aloft.

"Where?" whispered Lalette as they stood in the room, and
he:

"We dare not leave the building now. Even if they were
not below, the doorman will be awake. Have you seen
anyone else here?"

"I have been a prisoner."

"Then we must try at random whether it is true, as the
priests say, that not all men are evil."

Crossing the outer room, hand in hand in the dark, Rodvard stumbled against a chair, swore softly, and they both
laughed under breath. A board creaked, so did the hinges of
the outer door, and they were going down, each in turn
tripping a little at the short end of the steps where the
stairway turned. By unspoken mutual agreement, they tiptoed
past the door of the outer apartment of the fifth and to that
at the rear of the house. Rodvard gathered his breath and
knocked.

6

Night and Day; The Place of Masks

I

No step sounded, but as they stood close to catch any
stir, a clear, childish treble came muffled through the wood:
    "What is it?"

Rodvard squeezed Lalette's hand. "I cannot tell you from
here," she said with her mouth close to the door, "but we
need help. Will you let us in?"

Pause, in which a chain rattled. "In the name and protection of the God of Love, enter," and the door melted before
them into a darkness different because it held shapes. "Stand

here till I make a light," said the young voice. "You must be careful not to break things."

There was a small sound of fumbling, flint and steel clicked and the candle came slowly into light on a scene that made Rodvard and Lalette both almost cry out, for the small room seemed crowded with people; princes and queens with coronets, richly and gaily dressed, beggars in rags of silk, yellow warriors with ram-horn helmets, Zigraners with want-chins and sliding eyes and all other fantasies of human shape, so life-like in the uncertain gleam that it was an eye-flick before they could be recognized as festival masquerades. In the midst of them a smooth-haired boy of it might be anywhere from twelve to sixteen stood bowing gravely in his tight-hose, candle held at arm's length.

"I am glad to see you," he said. "My name is Laduis Domijaiek."

It was a good name for them, from the northwestern provinces, where Queen and Florestan were least popular. Said Rodvard; "We are pursued by the city provosts because a court lord wishes harm to this lady. Will you help her get away?"

The boy looked at Lalette, cocking his head on one side, as though listening to a distant voice. "Yes," he said. "My heart says it is right and we must always listen to the heart. Besides, we don't like the provosts."

"Thank you," said Lalette. "Where are your parents?"

"Father is in another world, and mother's at the Marquis of Palm's palace to make the costumes for the spring festival. She's going to stay all night and she told me I must go to bed. But this is more fun." He looked at Lalette again, and his eyes widened suddenly. "Oh, are you the witch? Witch something for me."

In spite of her situation, Lalette smiled. "Aren't you afraid I would hurt you?"

"Oh, no. We are Amorosians, and so witches can't hurt anything but our outsides. I'm not supposed to tell anybody that, only the provosts are after you, too, so it's all right."

From outside came the sound of feet, tramp, tramp, on the stair, and distant voices. "They are going to search," said

Rodvard. "Laduis, the lady will come back and witch something for you another day, but just now we must get her away from the provosts. Is there any way out of this house except by the main stair?"

The boy was all seriousness. "Not from this floor, Ser. I used to go down the drain-pipe from Ser Tetteran's quarter, but that was when I was thirteen and it isn't dignified."

"Then we must hide her." Rodvard's eye darted round the small room, took in the door to that still smaller, where beds must be. "The masks; can you help us into some of these?"

Laduis Domijaiek clapped his hands, and they set to work—for Lalette a Kjermanash princess, whose billowing imitation furs would hide the trimness of her figure; a hunchback Zigraner moneylender for Rodvard, with a bag of brass-plated scudi. Her dress had to come off, but the boy took it to hang with his mother's and came back to help Rodvard adjust the face-mask as furniture was moved overhead. The thumping came to an end, there was the sound of feet on the stairs once more, Rodvard and Lalette squeezed past the ghostly figures at the front of the assembled masks, and the boy blew out the candle.

Bang! "The Queen's warrant!" said a voice outside. "Open!"

Rodvard could hear the boy's feet go pad, pad, on the floor from the bedroom, acting his part in all detail. "What is it?"

"Queen's warrant; we're looking for an assassin."

Chain rattled. Through the eye-peeps of the mask, Rodvard could see the priest in the light of the provost's lantern, and held his breath.

"My mother is not here."

"We don't need her. Stand aside." Rodvard stood rigid, cursing himself for a fool to have put on this Zigraner guise with its bag of false coins that might jingle. "By the Service, the whole assembly's here." The priest held high his amulet; this was the moment of test, but it passed so lightly there might have been no test at all. The provost raised his lantern; "Anybody call on you tonight, sprout?"

"I was asleep, ser provost."

The man grunted, light flickered as he went into the bedroom, there was a thud as though he might be kicking something, and he came back into the sweep of sight, a naked shortsword showing in his hand. "Not there," he said. "Ah, bah, she's a witch and has spirited herself to the Green Islands. But I'll have my revenge." He swung his sword at the neck of a yellow-armored Mayern fighting man, and Rodvard heard the head crack to the floor as the boy cried; "Oh, no." The provost; "Three scudi reward for a foeman down. Tell your mother I saved you from a villain. Hark, now; open your door this night to none more; an order in Her Majesty's name."

The door banged to leave it dark for those within and feet retreated beyond. Rodvard stirred cramped muscles. "Will they come back?" Lalette's voice whispered.

The candle lifted slowly into light. Laduis Domijaiek was on one knee beside the fallen head, whose nose was broken off. The eyes that looked up held tears.

"That man killed Baron Mondaifer," he said, fiercely, "and I would like to kill him, too."

Lalette slipped off her head-mask and ran a hand across her hair, looking very princess with her dark head against the white Kjermanash fur. "A true sorrow and it is our fault," she said. "Do you have names for them all?"

"Oh, yes. You are the Princess Sunimaa, and she's always getting into trouble because it's cold where she comes from, and her heart is all ice, and the others don't like her except for Bonsteg the beggar, who is really a prince in disguise, only she doesn't know it yet. But Baron Mondaifer was one of my favorites. He's from Mayern, you see, and he's always lived in the forest, even if he is in favor of Prince Pavinius, and thinks he's still a good prophet."

Said Rodvard, undoing laces to get out of his Zigraner dress; "Your mother will get someone to fix him and bring him back to life."

"No. His spirit's gone away to another body, like father's and now there isn't anything left but dust. If mother has a new head made, I shall have to give it a different name."

The boy looked at Rodvard solemnly, and though the Blue

Star was cold as cold upon his breast, he could not somehow draw quite clear the thought behind those young candid eyes—something about a place shrouded in clouds, an old house somewhere, with a diffused golden light. Weariness slit his jaws into a yawn. "There is a place where we can sleep?"

II

They had to take his mother's bed, not meant for more than one, so that for the first time they lay close wrapped in each other's arms with a night before them; and this, with the sharp memory of the peril shared on the rooftops hand in hand, was a little more than either could quite bear unmoved, even though the boy was in a corner of the room. They began kissing and holding each other very tight; presently deep breaths said Laduis was asleep. She did not resist (nor desire to). Afterward, Rodvard lay for a long time wakeful (thinking that this had been the sobbing, true union, not an arranged accident like that under the tree; they had pledged each other and were somehow one forever. Now he was committed, and there was a deep harsh sweetness in the thought of devotion and change, live and love, forgetting all ambition, high destiny and even the Sons of the New Day that had brought him to this.)

Of course lark and Laduis rose before them in the morn; the first the pair heard was a double rap at the outer door and the boy's voice saying; "Mother, we have guests."

Rodvard rolled out to make the best bow he could with half his laces still undone, and saw a small woman of careworn aspect and maybe thirty-five years, who had just set a heavy basket on the floor. "Madame Domijaiek, I am your humble servant, Rodvard Bergelin. Your son took my—sweetheart and myself in last night to save us from distress."

"Mother, I listened to the voice of the heart, as you said," piped the boy. "They are good. Besides a provost came and broke Baron Mondaifer."

"It is well done, son." She placed a hand protectingly on his shoulder. "Ser, I am glad that Laduis could help you. Have you breakfasted?"

"I left some of my bread and cheese for them, mother. The lady is a witch."

Rodvard saw the woman's face alter, and her eyes, which had held only a mild questioning, were taken away from him. She fumbled in her belt-purse. "Laduis," she said, "will you get another piotr-weight of millet from the shop at the market-square?"

Lalette came from the bedroom, looking only by the half as delightful as Rodvard's night memory painted her; curtsied and said straightly; "Madame, I am in your benevolence and honor, so now no concealments. I am Lalette Asterhax, the veritable witch on whom the provosts have set a price, and if my being here will trouble you, I'll leave on the instant. But I swear I have done nothing for which I might truly fear from a just God."

Doubt melted from Dame Domijaiek's face; she reached out both hands to take the two of the girl's, saying; "My dear, I could not let you go from here into danger, for that would not be love. But as for your witchery, we are also told that if one live in the true world, the outer appearance of evil on all of us, shall have no force. Each must find his own way to love. Now you shall tell me the whole story, while I set forth something to eat."

The girl gave it all fairly, hiding nothing, as they munched on bread and cheese and pickled onions. When she had finished on the note of Mme. Kaja's treachery, Dame Domijaiek said; "Ill done, but the poor woman's fault is partly your own."

Said Rodvard, surprised; "How can that be, Madame?"

"It takes more than one to make a murder. If you had been wholly ruled by the God of love, the good will you bore her could not but have been reflected back toward you. Was there not something, perhaps seeming of slight importance, on which you felt almost in fury with her?"

Rodvard flushed (recalling the moment when Mme. Kaja had burst in to find them on the bed), but Lalette said simply; "Yes, and on a question that most sharply brings angers; to wit, money. Speaking of which, have you the spadas, Rodvard?"

"Why, no. I reached for them where they were on the table as we went through the window, but they were not there, and I thought you had taken them."

Lalette's nostrils moved. "A victory for Mme. Kaja. She has left us penniless."

"Believe me, an evident result of the fact that you quarrelled with her on pennies," said Dame Domijaiek.

Rodvard; "I will not say I disbelieve you, madame; yet I cannot see how this is valuable in our present necessity. The thing's done. Now we have to ask how matters can be bettered, and how to carry word to my good friend, Dr. Remigorius, so that we can elude the body of this pursuit."

The widow looked at him steadily and though he was new to this Blue Star, he felt surprise that he could make out nothing at all behind her eyes, no thought whatever. "Ser Bergelin," she said, "you will one day learn that before you can escape the world's despairs, you must first escape the world's self. But now you have been sent to me for help, and helped you shall be. With what I know of mask-making, I can so alter your appearance that it will not be hard to pass a relaxed watch. But will your doctor provide security?"

"Assuredly," said Rodvard, (too quickly, Lalette thought), (and it was so, for he remembered the moment when he surprised the doctor's mind, his carelessness of what happened to Lalette.)

Dame Domijaiek gave a trifling sigh. "You will be safe here for the time. But there is a condition to my aid. I believe in a rule more certain than yours of witchcraft, demoiselle; and will ask that while you are under my roof, you will banish from your mind every thought of evil and horror and revenge, even toward those who have wronged you. It is a protection I ask for me and my son, though you will not believe it."

III

By this time it was clear to both Rodvard and Lalette that as the boy had said, they were certainly in the house of a follower of the Prophet of Mancherei. Though they did not speak of it, the thought gave them both an inner qualm, not over being found there, but at the thought of what might be done to their inner selves by one of these insidious probers in secret thoughts, who had so misused their own Prophet. But a mouse cannot choose the smell of the hole he hides in; they glanced at each other, and gave the widow their word, as she had asked. The boy Laduis returned. It was thought better that the pair be somewhat disguised again, in case of visitors. Lalette kept the Kjermanash furs; Rodvard at first donned the garb of an executioner, but the girl not liking him in that, took the gear of a hunter-guide from the Ragged Mountains instead.

It was a morning of nervous attent, through which they heard feet come and go in the apartment overhead. Between the promise to the widow and their own feelings, there was hardly anything that could be said of what they wished to say, so they spent the time listening to the lad, who told them tales of his imagined people behind the masks. It would be about the noon-glass when a man knocked, who said he was the butler of the Baroness Stampalia to look at a costume; coming so quickly to the door that Rodvard and Lalette were without time to don head-masks, and sought refuge in the bedroom. This was as well; the butler examined attentively everything in the outer room.

Not long later the widow returned, narrowing her eyes over the tale of the Stampalia butler. "She has her own dressmaker. Could he have been a spy?" Then to the couple; "You see, you obeyed my injunction as to thought, and were protected."

Rodvard would have made a point of this, but Dame Domijaiek gave him no time, turning to Lalette, with; "Touching your mother, my dear, I think you have not to be troubled. I have not seen her myself, but the gossip is that Count Cleudi has most generously sent her a present of money, which is an evidence of the working of the God of love, though the instrument may not be what we would desire."

Rodvard, whom this style of discourse filled with a discomfort he could not readily assay, asked about Remigorius. The dame had visited his shop; she produced a chit from the doctor which confirmed all Rodvard's discomforts on the matter of Lalette, for it commanded him in guarded words to come at once, and without her. Lalette did not understand when he showed her the paper, but she said he must clearly go. Dame Domijaiek added her voice to the same purport, saying that if Rodvard were needed to go elsewhere, Lalette would be the safer there for hiding alone.

From a cabinet she brought some of the false hair used on masks and skillfully affixed a fur of it to Rodvard's face, while Lalette, suddenly gay, changed the dress of his head and added a ribbon that make him quite a different person. He kissed her farewell; the widow simpered as though it were she who had been saluted, and said she would offer an answerable prayer to the God of love for the success of his going.

7

Sedad Vix: A New Life

I

The doorman did not glance from his cachet—a lazy doorman—and the provost on guard at the street entrance was equally indifferent as Rodvard went past, feeling a trifle unreal after so long close indoors. Remigorius was compounding a philter with mortar and pestle; he hailed Rodvard almost boisterously, laughing over the figure he made in his false facial hair. "What! Will you have a career as a ladies' lap-cat, now that you've turned seducer by profession? Well, I have summoned you here because things mount to a crisis. The court's finance is utterly broke, and the High Center holds that we must move fast, for though there are stirrings in the west, it seems they move in the direction of Pavinius."

Said Rodvard; "We are likely to be broke ourselves. Mme. Kaja's a traitor."

Pestle stopped in mortar; the doctor's face seemed to narrow over the midnight thicket of his beard and a soft pink tongue came out to run a circlet round his lips. "I'll mix that bitch a draft will burn her guts out. Give me the tale."

Rodvard told it all plainly, with the hiding on the rooftop and the household of the Amorosian woman, over which last Remigorius' eye held some anxiety. "The one who came here? You did not tell her of our fellowship? These people of the Prophet's rule lie as closely together as so many snow-flakes, and though they're as deep against the court as we, I would not trust them. But touching your affair of the old singer—" he placed one finger to his cheek and held his eyes averted, so that Rodvard could not see where his true thought lay "—you're too censorious. I see no real treason there; she's deep in double intrigues and must keep up an appearance, beside which, no doubt, there is something of an old woman's green-sickness for a younger man. It may all have been by order of the High Center, indeed; you'd certainly have been saved yourself by some tale, for you are now too valuable. Now for our affair; you are to take the stage at dawning for Sedad Vix, where you are to be writer for Count Cleudi at the conference of court."

Rodvard's eyes sprang open wide. "The court? Will I not be known?"

"Ah, nya, you're not involved now in this pursuit of the provosts. The only one that could establish your communion with the witch is cared for."

"What—who would that be?"

"Your pensionnario doorman. An accident happened to him last night but one; was found in the river this morning, thoroughly dead and green as a smelt." Remigorius waved a hand goodbye to Udo the Crab and whipped to his main theme, the conference of court. Florestan the Chancellor, the army restive for want of pay, the revenues hypothecated, the question of a great assembly, Cleudi intriguing, the time come for all terrible measures.

"But Mathurin can discover all this as clearly as I," said

Rodvard (a little quickfire of suspicion running through him).

"Better in the open, but we'd know the secret purposes, and whom to trust. Mathurin takes Cleudi to be a spy for the regent of Tritulacca, despite his ejection from the councils there. Is it true? You'll find the hiding place of his mind. Then there's Baron Brunivar, the people's friend, as they call him. A reputation too exalted for credit. He's from the West—is he not by chance in Prince Pavinius' service, seeking to place that worm-bitten saint on the throne, as prince and Prophet, both together? A thousand such questions; you'll play in high politics, young man, and earn yourself a name."

Rodvard (heart beating) said; "Well—"

"Well, what do you ask more?"

(His mind made up with a snap, and as though the words came from someone else;) "Two things. To write a letter to Demoiselle Asterhax, who will be expecting my return, and to know how I am to reach Sedad Vix without a spada."

Remigorius shot him a glance, hit and past (in which there was annoyance and something like a drop of ink about Lalette). "What, you grasshopper? Always without money. To Sedad Vix is a spada and two coppers." He drew from his pouch this exact amount. "As for the letter, write. Here's paper, I'll charge myself with the delivery."

Rodvard wrote his letter; discussed through a falling light what persons might be watched at the villa by the sea, and how to give the news to Mathurin; dined miserably with the doctor on a stew that had the sharp taste of meat kept beyond its time, and lay down exhausted on the floor, with a couple of cushions and his cloak.

Sleep withheld its hand; his mind kept running in a circle round the thought of being a controller of destinies, until he made up a kind of play-show in his head, of being accuser before a court of the people, with some man who bore a great name as the accused, and himself making a speech— "But you, your lordship, are a liar and a traitor. What of your secret adhesion to the Prophet? . . ." The scene he could fix clearly, with the accused's face, and the members of the court looking grim as the accusation was driven home, but somehow the people of his drama would not move around or change expression beyond this one point, and each time he reached it, the whole thing ended in a white flash, and he drifted for a while between sleeping and waking, wondering whether his Blue Star might not be driving him foolish, until the imagined play began again, without any will of his own. Toward day, he must have slept a little, for Remigorius was laying a cold hand on his face, and it was time to look toward the new day and new life.

II

From the city to Sedad Vix by the shore is a fair twelve leagues, through the most fertile fields in all Dossola, now jumping with new green orchards blooming in a row and pale yellow jonquils. Another time Rodvard had found the trip after they crossed the high bridge pure pleasure; but now he felt having missed his sleep, and the travel-mate in the opposite seat was a good-looking pregnant woman, who said she was going to join her husband, and babbled on about his position in the royal orchestra till one could not even doze. The Blue Star said coldly that she was a liar and talking to hide the true fact, namely that she hated her husband and pregnancy and the love of any man, and as soon as she was free of her condition, hoped to catch the eye of some wealthy lady and to be maintained for pleasures impermissible—so vile a thought that Rodvard closed his eyes. The man next to him was a merchant of some kind by the badge in his cap; he kept addressing heavy-handed compliments to the dame, saying that he would dance with her at the spring festival and the like. Rodvard, turning, could see he thought her licentious, and was determined to profit by it at some future time. At Masjon, where they stopped for lunch, the merchantman bought a whole roasted chicken and a bottle of that fine white Tritulaccan wine which is called The Honey of the Hills.

Rodvard himself was a little faint from lack of food when he reached the royal villa after a solid half-league of trudging beyond the stage-post, nor did the under-butler who received him offer food, but took him at once to a cabinet looking out over a terraced flower-garden, at the back of the rambling building. This guide said to wait for the arrival of Ser Tuolén, the butler-in-chief. The name had a Kjermanash sound; and sure enough, the tall man who came after perhaps half an hour's retard, had the high-bridged nose and curling hair of that northern land. Rodvard stood to greet him with extended hand, and as he looked into the eyes, received a shock that ran through him like poison-fire, with its indubitable message that he was facing another wearer of the Blue Star.

"You are Ser Bergelin?" The eyes looked at him fixedly though the lips did not cease smiling. "What is your function to be?"

"Writer to the Count Cleudi for the conference," Rodvard managed to say. (One almost seemed to drown in those eyes, liquid and northern blue, but he could not read a single thought behind them.)

The smile expanded. "You will find it easier to meet others who *know* when you have borne that stone for a time. I perceive it is a novelty to you. There are not many of us. Hmmm—I suppose it is little use asking you why Count Cleudi wishes a Blue Star with him. No matter; I have watched him before, and it is no secret that he wishes to be Chancellor; even Lord Florestan knows that. I trust you are not an Amorosian or one of that band of assassins who call themselves Sons of the New Day?"

"No," said Rodvard (and thought with the back of his mind that this was why all plans to deal directly with the court had broken, and others of the brotherhood been laid in the toils of the provosts, this Star-bearer here.) With the front of his thought he concentrated on looking at the detail in the painting of a milkmaid just beyond Tuolén's ear.

The butler-in-chief turned. "It is by Raubasco. He was not satisfied with the highlights in the middle distance, as I discovered by a means you will understand, so it was easy to persuade the painting away from him. Do you intend to bring your wife?"

"No," said Rodvard, (thinking quickly on Lalette and as quickly away).

"Oh, there is something wrong with the personal relation. Perhaps it is just as well if you do not; Her Majesty is not prudish, but she does not approve of witches at the court. Your room will be at the depth of the west wing, beyond the hall of conference. I will have one of the under-butlers show you." He stood up, then paused with one hand holding the bell-rope.

"One last word. A Bearer finds himself in a strange position here without his witch. I suppose your wife has given you the usual warning about infidelity, but you are clearly new to the jewel and young, and there are not a few ladies who might make the loss seem worth the gain—since you can read their desires. In particular I warn you to stand clear of the Countess Aiella of Arjen, in whom I have noted something of the kind. She is involved with the Duke of Aggermans, a man who'll protect his own dangerously. . . . Drop in tomorrow night after Cleudi releases you; it will be a pleasure to compare things seen with another Bearer. I have not met one for long."

In the room was a tray of food on the table, ample and well selected, with a bottle of wine; three to four books also, but they were all gesling-romances, and of a kind Rodvard found it difficult to bear even when well written, as these hardly were. He glanced at each in turn, then tossed them aside, and was only rescued from boredom by Mathurin's coming, who pressed his hands, and said he would come the next evening again, but for the now, he must hurry.

Rodvard replied that the high butler Tuolén was the bearer of a Star, and Mathurin must either avoid his eye or keep his own thought on innocuous subjects.

"And his witch? Wait, no, that explains much."

"I do not see," said Rodvard.

"Why, fool, the hold the court party has. No sooner a man turns up that's in opposition than your Tuolén knows his most secret purpose, and I do not doubt that his wife witches the man. This is something for the High Center of the New Day."

III

A pretty maid brought him breakfast in bed. She gave him a cheerful morning greeting but embarrassed him by hoping in her thought that he would not make love to her. Her mind held some memory of how the last man in this room had done so, but she shied from the thought of the outcome so much that instead of decently avoiding her look Rodvard was tempted to pry deeper, but there was hardly time.

She said it would be near to noon when Count Cleudi rose and that his apartment was in one of the pavilions set among tree and shrub and garden, west from the main villa. Rodvard dressed and went to stroll in that direction through curved avenues among intricate beds of spring flowers—tulip and narcissus, with pink azaleas just in the bud beside them and magnolia showing its heavy white wax. The pathways had been laid out so that each sweep brought somewhere into view through trees the pale blue bay, with the white houses of Sedad Vix climbing the slope beyond, their walls touched to gold by genial sunshine; bright yellow birds were singing overhead, or busily gathering morsels for their nests. Rodvard felt his heart expanding with a joyous certainty that all would yet be well, though in the same tick demanding of himself how men who dwelt in such surroundings could be given to evil and oppression. Ah, if all people could only walk in gardens daily! A question in philosophy to put to the doctor—but before he could frame it into words, a turn of the path brought him past a tall clump of rhododendrons to the front of a red-doored pavilion, where a gardener was letting into the ground plants of blooming hyacinth.

The air was rich with their fragrance. "Good morning to you," said Rodvard cheerfully, for joy of the world.

The man looked up with lips that turned down at the corners. "If you say it is a good morning, I suppose it must be one for you," he said, and turned back to his trowel.

"Why, I would call it the best of mornings. Does not the fine air of it please you?"

"Enough."

"Then what's amiss? Have you troubles?"

"Who has not?" The gardener slapped his trowel against the ground beside his latest plant. "Look at these flowers, now. Just smell that white one there, it's more fragrant than the blue. Aren't they beautiful things? Brought here at expense, and in this soil, see how black it is, they would grow more perfect than ever, year by year. But here's the end of them; as soon as the blossoms fade ever so little, poor things, they must be dug up and thrown away, because she—" he swung his head and rolled an eye in the direction of the red-doored pavilion "—can't bear to have any but blooming flowers at her door and will want new lillies."

"Who is she?" asked Rodvard, lowering his tone for fear that voices will sometimes carry through wood.

"The Countess Aiella. Her affair, you will be saying, whether flowers die or live; she has all that income from the Arjen estates, and doesn't have to provide for her brothers, who married those two heiresses up in Bregatz, but a man could still weep for the waste of the flowers. Ser, give a thought to it, how in the world we never have enough of beauty and those who destroy any part of it take something from all other people. Is it not true, now?"

He paused on his knees and looked up at Rodvard (who was growing interested indeed, but now felt the coldness of the Blue Star telling him that this earthy philosopher was not thinking of beauty at all, but only reciting a lesson and wondering whether his pretty speech might not draw him a gift from this poetical-looking young man.)

"I do not doubt it," he said, "but I have no money to give away," and turned to go, but he had not travelled a dozen paces when he met one who must be the Countess Aiella herself by the little double coronet in her drag-edge hat. Rodvard doffed to the coronet, noting in the fleeting second of his bow the passionate, bewildering beauty of the face surrounded by curves of light-brown hair.

She stopped. "Put it on," she said, and he looked up at her. The cloak did not conceal the fact that she was still dressed for evening; a leg showed through the slit in her dress. "I have not seen you before."

"No, your grace. I only arrived last night."

"Your badge says you are a clerk."

"I am a writer to the Count Cleudi for this conference." (He dared to look into the eyes a finger-joint length below his own; behind them there was boredom with a faint flicker of interest in himself and the thought of having spent a bad night; a weary thought.)

"Count Cleudi, oh. You might be him in disguise." She laughed a laugh that trilled up the scale, slipped past him with a motion as lithe as a gazelle's and up the path into the red-doored pavilion. Rodvard looked after her until he heard the gardener cackle, then, a little angry with himself, stamped on round the turn of the path, trying to recover the glory of the morning. Some of it came back, but not enough to prevent him thinking more on the comparison between this countess and Lalette than the difference between this day and any other day; and so he reached Cleudi's door, with its device of a fishing bird carved into the wood.

Mathurin greeted him properly in words to show he and Rodvard barely had met each other. The pavilion was all on one floor, the Count in a room at the side, with a man doing his hair while he sipped hot spiced wine, from which a delicious odor floated. Rodvard had heard of, but never seen this famous exile and intriguer; he looked into a narrow face with a broad brow above a sharp nose and lips that spoke of self-indulgence. Mathurin pronounced the name of the new writer; a pair of dark eyes looked at Rodvard broodingly (the thought behind them wondering what his weakness was and how he would cheat). Said Cleudi:

"I do not ask your earlier employment, since it is of no moment if you are faithful and intelligent. I cannot bear stupidity. Can you read Tritulaccan?"

"Yes, your Grace."

"You will gain nothing by attempting to flatter me with the form of address. On the side table are pens and papers, also a horoscope which has been cast in Tritulaccan and a poem in your own musical language. Make fair copies of both in

Dossolan. Have you breakfasted?" (His accent had the slight overemphasis on S which no Tritulaccan ever loses.)

"Yes, thank you."

The symbols on the astrological chart were new to Rodvard; he had to copy each by sheer drawing and then translate the terms as best he might. The poem was a sonnet in praise of a brown-haired lady; its meter limped at two points. Rodvard managed to correct one of them by a transposition of words and presently laid both papers before Cleudi, who knit his brows over them for a moment and smiled:

"You are a very daring writer to improve on what I have set down, but it is well done. Mathurin, give him a scuderius. Well then, you are to wait on me in the conference at nine glasses of the afternoon. Everything I say is to be set down, and also the remarks of the Chancellor Florestan, but most especially those of the Baron Brunivar, for these may be of future use. Of the others, whatever you yourself, consider worth while. You are dismissed."

Mathurin saw him to the door. "The scuderius?" asked Rodvard.

"Goes into the treasury of our Center," said the servitor.

"But I have no money, no money at all," protested Rodvard.

"Pish, you do not need it here. Would you starve our high purpose to feed your personal pleasure in little things? I will come to your room tonight."

8

High Politic

I

Although the day was bright outside, little light could seep through the leaded panes and what little light there was had been cut off by heavily looped curtains. There were candles down the long table and in brackets on the walls. In the marble fireplace at the high end of the room a small flame smouldered under the stone cupids; before it three men were standing, with goes of brandy in their hands. Baron Brunivar was recognizable by his description—tall, with a mane of white hair and a firm-set mouth that made one think of the word "nobility" without reference to civil condition. He was talking with a short, round man who looked as jolly as he could possibly be and a dark, grave-faced lord who held a kitten in his arm till the little thing struggled to be set down, whereupon it played round his feet, catching for the shoe-laces. In spite of his solemnity, this would be Florestan, the Laughing Chancellor; he was known to favor cats.

In a moment he looked around and signed to Tuolén the head butler, who rapped a little silver bell on the table. All the men from various corners of the room gathered. Three of them were episcopals in their violet robes with flowers of office. Florestan quietly waited till all were at rest, his visage in calm lines (but Rodvard could see just enough of his eyes to catch an intimation that this might be a grim business). He tapped the bell once more.

"My lords, if you were ignorant of this convocation's purpose, you had not been summoned; therefore, let us leave all preliminaries and turn straight to the matter of Her Majesty's finance."

Pause. The apple-faced man said; "What's there to say of it?"

"That it is a very dangerous thing to have the court in poverty when we are threatened with this question of the succession."

The faces along the table watched him attentively, all set in varying degrees of stubbornness, and as the kitten scratched at the leg of his chair, he reached down to pet it. "My lords, this has now grown so grave that we can dissolve our troubles only by measures never taken before; all the old means eaten up. Yet we still want money to pay Her Majesty's army, which is not only a disgraceful thing but also a perilous. Those who should protect us may become our persecutors."

The little round man's smile was jolly as before, his voice not; "Your Grace, a bug close to the eye may look as big as a lion. Is there proof of true disaffection?"

A man with silver-streaked hair and the breast-star of a general on his silk nodded gloomily. "I bear such proof. This brawl among the Red Archers of Veierelden has been given a light appearance; but my men have looked into it, and it runs deeper than you think. Namely, they were shouting for the restoration of Pavinius to the succession. We hanged one of his emissaries, a Mayern man."

"Pah," said the round man. "Since he was exiled every ruction has been a shout for his return. They do not mean it."

"Dossola will never bear a king who is himself the leader of a sect opposed to true religion," observed one of the episcopals. "Even his one-time followers of the Amorosian faith have rejected him."

Florestan held up his hand. "My lords, you wander. I summoned you here on this matter of finance to say that it is within the powers granted to me as minister by the Queen's Majesty to establish by decree the new form of tax-payment proposed by our good friend, the Count Cleudi. Yet as some of you have been good enough to let me know this plan will never succeed, I now ask what other you propose."

"It is a plan to steal from the nobles of the land, and it will surely not be borne," said a long-faced man with great force.

Said one of the episcopals; "The estates of the Church must of course be exempt from this plan; for it would be an affront to the most high God to make his spiritual ministers into tax-gatherers for the lesser, or civil estate."

Chancellor Florestan threw back his head with a burst of laughter so heartily sustained that it was not hard to see how he had won his calling-name. "The same spiritual ministers," he said, "have little trouble with their consciences when it is a question of collecting taxes to their own benefit. No, I do not contemplate that the lords episcopal shall be exempt, however ill that sits, and I tell you plainly that I will enforce this plan with every strength there is. Come, my lords, you waste my time, which belongs to the Queen; and so dissipate her resources. I ask again; who has a sharper scheme than Cleudi's?"

Now they burst in on him with a flood of words like so many dogs barking, which he hardly seemed to hear as he leaned down to pet the kitten. Rodvard, watching the calm indifferent face, could not catch a clear vision of the eyes in the candlelight and flow of movement. He saw Tuolén advance to pick up one of the glasses, with his eyes fixed on the horsefaced lord who had been so vehement (and it came to him that Florestan must know there was another Blue Star in the room, and be concealing his thought from reading). The Chancellor reached over to tap his bell once more.

"We will hear the Baron Brunivar," he said.

The lord he mentioned turned a stately head, (but though he was squarely in face, Rodvard could only make out a thought troubled and urgent; nothing definite.) "Your Grace," he said, "when I first learned of this plan, I thought it was put forward merely to provoke a better. Now I see that it is not, and though I have no plan for raising more money, only for spending less, I ask you to think what will happen if you persist in it. More taxes cannot be borne by the commonalty; they'll rise, and you'll have Prince Pavinius over the border with a Mayern army at his back."

The Laughing Chancellor turned his head and said to his own writer at the side table; "Be it noted that Baron Brunivar spoke of treason and wars in the west, where his seignory lies."

White eyebrows flashed up and down over Brunivar's orbits. "You shall not make me a traitor so, Your Grace. I have stood in the battlefield against this Pavinius when he was Prophet of Mancherei, with all Tritulacca to aid him; and there were some who fled." He looked along the table. "It is not exterior war I fear, but Dossolans at each other's throats, and an unpaid army against us."

Florestan's voice tolled; "Write it down that the Baron Brunivar doubts the army's loyalty to Her Majesty."

Brunivar's face became a grimace, but he plunged on. "Let

me beg Your Grace; could not enough be saved on the
household budget for the spring festival to keep the army
happy for long?"

"Write it down that the Baron Brunivar declares Her
Majesty to be extravagant."

"I'll say no more. You have my completest word."

Said Cleudi lightly; "I thank you, my lord Brunivar, for
having shown that no plan but mine will do."

Brunivar's mouth flew open and shut again. Said one of the
episcopals; "Let us think if there be not another plan. I have
heard that in some of the estates of Kjermanash, when
extraordinary measures are needed, they have a tax on flour
which is levied at the mill; most collectible, since no one can
avoid it if he wishes to eat bread. Could not a similar be laid
here?"

Florestan's lips twitched. Brunivar struck the table. "I said
I'd done, but this outdoes all. My lord, in the west it is
exactly that our people have not coppers enough both to buy
bread and pay their present taxes that has roused our troubles. Will you starve them?"

The little fat man said; "Yet the present revenues are not
enough."

A general murmur. Brunivar stood up in his place at the
table. "My lords," he said, "I am forced to this issue. The burden lies not on the court alone, but on all of you. The
popular can pay no more; whatever comes, must come from
our estates. It has been so since the Tritulaccan war and the
loss of the Mancherei revenues that kept us all in luxury. We
in the western seignories have made some sacrifice toward
the happiness of our people, out of free will and the love of
humankind. We have been without the troubles that such
seignories as yours, Your Grace of Aggermans—" he looked
at the round man "—and without witchings. And this, I
think, is because we show some love for those we rule."

Cleudi lifted his hand for speech and the Chancellor signed
to him. He said; "I speak here under permission, being a
foreigner, and not familiar with these new religions that have
vexed and divided the ancient realm of Dossola and its
former dominion overseas. I would ask whether the Baron

Brunivar's talk of love for humankind places him more
definitely with the Amorosians who follow the first doctrine
of the Prince-Prophet, or with those who now accept his
word?"

Head bent to set down these words, Rodvard did not catch
a glimpse of Brunivar's face at this accusation, but he heard
the quick gasp of breath that was covered by Florestan's
laughter. The Chancellor said; "My lords, and fellow-
scoundrels of Baron Brunivar's accusation, I think this most
happily clears the air. You see where the true resistance to
Count Cleudi's plan for taxes lies, and on what ground. Will
you make yourselves one with that purpose, which is clearly
nothing but the establishment over us of Pavinius and his
form of witchcraft?"

His eyes swept the table, and the noble lords and episcopals stirred in their seats, but nobody said a word. "Now I'll
add more. You are jealous of your privilege, my lords, as to
this new plan, and fear the government will be the only
gainer. By no means; it is only a device of finance which will
in the end work favorably for all. You are charged with the
taxes due from your seigniories, yes. But when this happens
there is created a class of financial paper which, having
value, can be bought and sold; I mean the warrants drawn by
the court on you for the tax-monies. Good; Her Majesty's
government will sell these warrants at discount to Zigraners
and others who love to speculate. There's a fine speculation;
for instance, will the tax on the province of Aggermans yield
twice what it did last year—or the half? Thus the paper will
change hands; but at every change of ownership in the paper,
the government takes a small tax on the transaction, small
enough not to discourage the purchase and sale. Thus we are
provided instantly with the full treasury we must have, ob-
taining it from the sale of the warrants; and at the same time
we have a steady source of income, while you, my lords, lose
nothing."

The small fat man who had identified himself as the Duke
of Aggermans spoke up; "It all sounds very well, but why
must the nobles of the realm be converted into money-
grubbing tax-gatherers as though we had Zigraner blood?

What! Can you not cheat the speculators as well by selling them paper on taxes collected direct, in the name of the Queen?"

The Laughing Chancellor flung out a hand. "Why, touching your first question, my lord, you'll be no more a tax-gatherer than you are today; only the agents who now speak in Her Majesty's name will be by degrees transferred to your service. From this you'll benefit; for some of these taxes will be paid in early and you will have the handling of the monies until the government's paper against you falls due. As to the second, why if we are to enlist the speculators to our work, it must surely be through having papers of different values, which go up and down from one seignory to another, instead of all being equal, as the government's own obligation is."

The general said; "The monies must come soon, if we're to have peace with the army."

Florestan stood. "The session may be considered closed."

II

Outside the hall it was a shock to come into bright flowers and green. The sun was just plunging down behind the low green hills westward, the birds singing sleep-songs and everything in perfect peace, not a leaf in movement. Tuolén the butler tapped Rodvard on the shoulder and when they were together in his cabinet, brought forth a bottle of Kjermanash ceriso, held it up to contemplate the ruby glow against the falling light and poured into goblets of crystal.

"You found it diverting, Ser Bergelin? His Grace is very astute."

Rodvard, sipping, perceived that a reply was asked. "Did he convince them, then?"

"Where were your eyes? Ah, over your papers. But surely you saw enough to know that conviction was beyond His Grace's purpose? The lords episcopal will never be convinced; the lords militant are convinced already. Did you watch Brunivar when Cleudi, accused him of being a follower of Pavinius, whether as Prince or Prophet?"

"No, I was writing."

"It would have been worth your trouble. There was that something like a golden flash which always comes when a man discovers that what he has said in innocency may be taken as the product of a guilty mind."

"Guilty?" Rodvard's surprise broke through the guard he had set on his thought. "I am new to this Blue Star, but saw no guilt, only an honest man who would help others."

The butler's permanent smile came up out of his crystal. "Honest? Honest? I imagine Brunivar may answer to that. A trademan's quality at best; I look for it in dealers who furnish the court with pork. But in high policy, that type will hardly gain one more than a length of cold ground—which it will now do for Brunivar."

Rodvard looked down. "Then—then His Grace was playing a game with Brunivar, to—"

"To make this public confession that he is either an Amorosian or a follower of the Prince. As you clearly discovered. The episcopals can never let that fall. They can no more have a man of such opinions as regent-apparent than they could have Pavinius for king. So now there will be an accusation and a trial and Brunivar walking the walk to meet the throat-cutter on the scaffold, for I doubt they can afford banishment. Not while Her Majesty insists on carrying through the old King's will that makes Brunivar regent-apparent for his honesty if the throne falls vacant. But mark the astuteness of His Grace, who at the same time destroys the popular party by taking off its best leader. But I do not think more will be until after the spring festival, since to condemn Brunivar now would give him the cancellation of punishments which the festival entails."

He gave a grunting laugh, drained his ceriso, refilled his own goblet and brought Rodvard's up to the brim, while the latter's thoughts whirled wildly, to cover which he asked; "The short man, always smiling, though he spoke so sourly, was the Duke of Aggermans?"

"Yes. One to watch. I have caught him thinking of schemes

by which he may one day reach the Chancellor's seat. That is why he opposes Cleudi. . . . Ser, why are you so deep in turmoil of mind?"

"I—I suppose it must have something to do with Baron Brunivar," said Rodvard (not daring to try to conceal). "I have always heard him well spoke of as a man who thinks of the benefit of others than himself."

The steady smile became a chuckle. "So he does. These are the most dangerous kind in politic. The next step beyond thinking on the good of others is deciding what that good will be. A privilege reserved to God. But is not His Grace astute?"

"Yet it seems to me shocking that a man who has done no wrong—"

"Ah, I see where you lead. Ser Bergelin, wrong is not in acts alone, or else every soldier would be a criminal, but in the thoughts with which they are done." He tapped the jacket just over his heart, where the Blue Star would hang, and for the first time the smile left his face. "When you have borne one of these baubles as long as I, you will learn something— namely, that few of us are different from the rest. I saw a man in a dungeon once, a murderer, whose thoughts were better than those of the deacon who gave him consolation. To my mind, that is. You or another might take those same thoughts for hideous. Take now your Baron Brunivar, who seems so lofty to you because on one range of topic his desires chime with your own. Yet you are not his identical; watch him, I say, and you will find his gold more than half brass in another light. Wrong? Right? I do not know what value they have to one who wears the Blue Star."

III

Let conscience die. The hours wheeled timeless past as they so often do when there is a change in outer circumstance so sharp that landmarks vanish. Let conscience die; was it true? Rodvard thought of the high ideals of service with which he had joined the Sons of the New Day—was any purpose as good as another? Lalette; his mind shot off on a

sudden tangent of tenderness toward her, who fairly desired
to be a good partner, it might be for her own interest, but
still making two instead of one against a world; and Mathurin came in.

When he was told that Baron Brunivar was likely to be
condemned only for being the best man in the state and its
appointed future regent, his eyes burned like coal-fires; he
said; "It is the thing we need; the people will not bear to hear
it; they will rise. First gain for your Blue Star, friend." He ran
out with his nose sharpened for excitement, his eyes glowing
like those of a rat.

9

Spring Festival: Intrigue of Count Cleudi

I

"Now the mask, Mathurin," said Count Cleudi. One corner
of his lip twitched (the black eyes glinting with malice). He
seemed as light and strong as one of those bronze statues of
the winged man, knuckles resting on the table. His own
costume was a rich purple, as he glanced from the mirror to
Rodvard's face, masked down to the lower cheeks, but with
the lips bare.

"The chin is much alike. Turn around, Bergelin, slowly,
pivoting on the ball of the right foot. So." He lifted his own
right arm, slightly bent, dropped his left hand to dagger-hilt,
and illustrated. Rodvard tried to follow him.

"Not quite right with the dagger; you are jerky. But you
will hardly be dancing a corabando. Have the goodness to
walk across the room. Stand. Mathurin, where does he lack
the resemblance?"

The servant's fingers came up to his lip. "The voice is
almost perfect, my lord, but there is something in the movement of the hands not quite . . ."

"It is only birth that does it," said Cleudi. "The wrist laces; he is not very used to handling them. But for the rest, Bergelin, you were born a most accomplished mimic and swindler. Remind me to dismiss you before your natural talent is turned in my direction. Now the instruction; repeat."

"I am to be at the ball when the opera is over, at least a glass before midnight. The fourth box on the left-hand side is yours. I am to look at the doorbase of the second box, where a handkerchief will be caught. If it is white, edged with lace, perfumed with honeymusk, I am to go below and make myself seen at the gaming tables. But if the handkerchief is blue and rose-perfumed, I am to take it away and leave in its place another; then without being seen on the dancing floor or at the games, go at once to my lord's box, but leave the panels up and the curtains closed. Someone will presently tap twice, a lady. I am to greet her with my lord's sonnet, eat with her; declare my passion for her . . . My lord?"

"Yes?"

"What if—that is—I would—"

Cleudi shot him a gleam (containing amusement mingled with a little dark shade of cruelty and the thought of shaming him with the full statement of his quaver). "You want money, apprentice swindler? You should—"

"No, my lord, it is not that, but—." The Count's toe tapped, his expression became a rictus, and Rodvard rushed on with heat at the back of his neck. "What if the intrigue does not succeed, that is if you do not appear in time—"

The rictus became a bark. "Ha—why, then you must suffer the horrid fate of being alone in a secluded apartment with the shapeliest and most willing woman in Dossola. Are you impotent?"

Rodvard half opened his mouth to protest in stumbling words that he was a promised man, who thought it less than honest to violate his given word, but Mathurin tittered and (the stream of hate and fury that flowed from those black eyes!) he only made a small sound. Cleudi barked again:

"Ha! Will you be a theologian, then? It is she who should make confession, not you—by the wise decision of the

Church, as I was discussing but lately with the Episcopal of Zenss. The minor priests will say otherwise; but it is a reflection from the old days, before the present congress of episcopals. Listen, peasant; is it not manifestly to the glory of God that men should seek women for their first and highest pleasure, as it is that daughters should have all monetary inheritance? Is it not also manifest that all would be under the rule of women, who have the Art as well as their arts, unless some disability lay upon them. . . . Ah, chutte! Why do I talk like a deacon to a be-damned clerk? Enough that I have given you an order. Greater things than you think hang on this intrigue, and you'll execute it well, or by the Service, I'll reduce you to a state where no woman will tempt you again. Now take off that finery; be prompt here at two glasses before midnight for Mathurin to dress you."

II

"But where does this intrigue lead?" asked Rodvard.

"Could not your Blue Star give you a clue?" asked Mathurin. They sat on a green bank behind the hall of conference, many-colored tulips waving in the light breeze about them, and Rodvard carefully tore one of the long leaves to ribbons as he answered:

"No. There may have been something about Aggermans in it, but he was not thinking of his central purpose at all, only about how it would be a nasty joke and a revenge. What—" (it was behind his lips to ask what he should do lest he lose the power of the Blue Star, but in midflight he changed) "—what have you done toward saving Baron Brunivar? Will there be a rising?"

(There was a quick note of suspicion and surprise in the eyes that lifted to meet his.) "Nothing for now, but to let Remigorius, and through him the High Center, know what's in prospect. There's no accusation as matters stand; it will gain us nothing merely to put out the story that the court plots against him. . . . Yet I do not understand why he has failed to fly when it's as clear as summer light that Florestan means the worse toward him."

"What I do not understand," said Rodvard, "is why the High Center has failed to make more preparation. It will be too late when Brunivar's been placed in a dungeon, under guard and accusation with a shar of soldiers around him."

"It would never pass . . ." Mathurin's voice trailed off; he contemplated the lawns, brow deep, and Rodvard could not see his thought. "I can understand the High Center."

"What would never pass? You are more mysterious than the Count, friend Mathurin, with your hints here and there."

The servitor turned on him eyes of angry candor. "Rodvard Yes-and-No, my friend, Cleudi is right in calling you more of a moralist than a churchman is. By what right do you question me so? Do you think I am of the High Center? Yet I will show you some of the considerations. It will never pass that the Chancellor should execute Brunivar and then have it proved that this fate came on him for some private reason. And now that you whip me to it, I will say as well that it will never pass that Brunivar should not be executed while we cry shame. We need a general rising, not a rescue that will drive many of us abroad. People will not leave their lives to fight until there is something in those lives that may not be sustained."

(Conscience again.) Rodvard set his mouth. "If you wish the reign of justice for others, it seems to me that you must give it yourself, Mathurin, and I see no justice in watching a good man condemned to death when he might be saved. I heard the Baron speak out in conference, and he may yet win something there. But even fled to Tritulacca, or to Mayern and Prince Pavinius, he would still be worth more than with his throat cut."

The serving man stood up. "I'll not chop logic against you; only say, beware. For you are a member under orders; your own will or moral has nothing to do with the acts of the High Center. Brunivar is nothing to us; down with him, he is a part of the dead past which is all rotten at the heart, and of which we must rid ourselves for the living future. I will see you later, friend Bergelin."

III

A tray had been left in his room as usual, but Rodvard hardly ate from it before flinging himself down to lie supine, watching the pattern of light through the shutters as it slowly ticked across the wall, trying to resolve the problem that beset him. Brunivar with his noble aspect and surely, his noble mind. "Free will and the love of humankind," the Baron had said, and they called it the doctrine of the apostate Prophet. Yet for what else had he himself joined the Sons of the New Day? What else had the Baron put into practice out there in his province of the west?

Yet here is Mathurin saying that no happiness could be bought by love of humankind, since certainly no love of humankind would let a high man go to shameful death when it might be prevented. No, perhaps that was not true, either; even barbarians had sacrifices by which one gave his life that many might live, though their method in this was all superstition and clearly wrong. . . . But only the consent of the one, Rodvard answered himself; only when there was no way but sacrifice.

Brunivar had made no consent; was being pushed to a sacrifice by malignance on one side, with the other accepting the unwilling gift he gave. Yet in that acceptance was there not something base and selfish? He remembered the curious unformed thought of treachery he had surprised in Remigorius' mind, Mme. Kaja's active betrayal, Mathurin's violence, and was glad they were joined with him, in one of the minor Centers of the Sons of the New Day. When that Day rose— but then, too late for Brunivar. Ah, if there were some deliverance, some warning one could give that would be heeded.

A clock somewhere boomed four times. Rodvard twisted on the bed, thinking bitterly how little he could do even to save himself, willing in that moment to be the sacrificed one. With witchery one might—Lalette . . . Little cold drops of perspiration gathered down his front from neck to navel at the perilousness of the intrigue in which he was now em-

barked for the night, perilous and yet sweet, delight and
danger, so that with half his mind he wished to rise and run
from this accursed place, come what might. With the other
half it was to stay and hope that Cleudi would not interrupt
the rendezvous in the box, as he had said, so that the
heart-striking loveliness he had now and again seen from far
in the last seven days (for he did not doubt that the mask to
meet him in the box would cover the Countess Aiella) might
lie in his arms, come what might to the felon of Lalette's
witcheries. Was he himself one of those whose purposes were
hideous, as Tuolén the butler had put it, with an inner desire
toward treachery toward her who had received his word of
love? Wait—the word had been wrung from him, given
under a compulsion, was the product of a deed done under
another compulsion. This, too. Before a high court I will
plead (thought Rodvard) that I myself, the inner me who
cherishes ideals still, in spite of Mathurin or Tuolén, had no
part in betrayals ... and recognized as he thought thus, that
the union in the place of masks was of that very inner me,
given forever ... or forever minus a day.

Flee, then. Where? A marked man and a penniless, trying
to escape across the seignories, with only a clerk's skill, which
demands fixities, to gain bread. Brunivar might perhaps be
held from flying to safety by compulsions as tight as these—
at which the wheel of thought had turned full circle; and the
realization of this shattering the continuance of the motion,
Rodvard drifted off into an uneasy doze, twitching in his
place.

He came fully awake with a final jerk, swinging feet to the
floor in the twilight; stood up, made a light, and not daring to
go on with his self-questionings, pecked a little at the gelid
remains of his noon viands, while speculating on Cleudi's
intrigue. But the Count had so buried the line of his plan that
nothing could be made from this, either; Rodvard went to seek
Tuolén, in the hope that he might have some light. Vain
hope; the butler's cabinet was dark and everyone else en-
countered in the corridors was hurrying, hurrying, with bur-
dens here and there, in preparation for the grand ball. There
was an atmosphere of anticipatory excitement that built up

along Rodvard's nerve-chains until he stepped forth into the spring eve to escape it.

Out there, the evening had turned chill, with a damp breeze off the Eastern Sea that spoke of rain before sun. All the flowers seemed to have folded their wings around themselves to meet it, and Rodvard felt as though nature had turned her back. He longed for a voice, and as a girl's form came shadowy around a turn of the path, he gave her good-evening and asked if he might bear her burden.

"Ah, no, it is not needed," said she, drawing back; but a shaft of light from a window caught them both and there was mutual recognition, she being the breakfast chambermaid whose name was Damaris.

"Oh ,your pardon, Ser," she said. "It is most good of you," and let him take her package, which was, in truth, heavy.

"Why, this must be gold or lead or beef, not flowers as it should be on festival eve," he said, and she trilled a small laugh before answering that festival it might be for those badged with coronets or quills, but for her class it was a night of labor—"and it is not gold, or I would run away with it, but one of those double bottles of Arjen fired-wine for the box of the Count Cleudi, whom you serve."

She turned her head, and in the light which threw across the path from another window, he caught a glint of her eyes. (She was very friendly after a week of bringing him breakfasts, in which he had treated her as courteously as though she were high born.) "Will you have no festival at all, then?" he asked.

"Oh, yes, tomorrow afternoon, when all the court's asleep. In the evening when they wake, it will be duty again." They had reached the door of the great hall; within workmen were attaching flowers to the bowered dais where the musicians would play, there was a sound of hammering from somewhere along the balcony behind the boxes, and Tuolén the high butler was revolving in the midst of the dancing floor, pointing where a flower-chain should be draped or a chair placed. His movement was that almost-prance which Cleudi had demonstrated. The girl's face turned toward Rodvard (her eyes suddenly said she wished him to ask her something, he could not quite make out what, they were so quickly withdrawn, but it was connected with the festival).

"I'll have no festival myself unless someone takes pity on me," he said.

(That was it.) "Would you—come and dance with me? It is only a servants' ball . . ." (She was a little frightened at her own boldness in asking someone so far above her in station, yet trembling-hopeful he would accept.)

"Why—have you no partner?"

"My friend has been called away to serve in the army. I have my ticket already and it will only be three spadas for yourself."

(Somehow he would get them; it would be an afternoon of real relaxation from complexities.) "You honor me, Demoiselle Damaris. Where shall I meet you?"

"Oh, I will wake you with breakfast as usual, and wait for you. Here is the door."

The box was larger than one might think from the outside, and already heavy with the perfume of flowers.

10

Prelude to the Servants' Ball

I

Under the colored lanterns swinging from trees, there were already a score of more carriages lining the side drives. Coachmasters talked in groups. The doors of the hall stood open, a wide bar of light silhouetting those who came on foot from the opera-hall, and turning to a more vivid green the tender grass. Violins sounded piercingly; as Rodvard joined the throng at the entrance, striving to walk with Cleudi's slight strut, he saw how all the floor beyond was covered with jewels and flashing feet, while nearby the mingled voices were so high that only the rhythm of the music was audible, with women's laughter riding on all like a foam. Right behind him a bearded Prophet of Mancherei showed the slim legs of a girl through an artfully torn silken robe, and tossed at him a rouge-ball which marked his white jacket; he must weave his way to the foot of the stairs around a group gaily trying with tinsel swords to attack an armored capellan, pausing to bow before one of twenty queens.

Halfway up the stairs in the dim of the balustrade, an archer of the guard, with his star-badge picked out in emeralds, was kissing a sea-witch in flowing blue. They disembraced at his footfalls; the sea-girl leaped up and threw her arms around Rodvard's neck, crying; "Snowlord from Kjermanash, I will melt you. Did I not tell you, ser archer, that witches are all fickle?"

"But are tamed by those who battle for them," said the archer, as Rodvard gave her the kiss she sought. (Behind her eyes was nothing but reckless pleasure.) "My lord of Kjermanash, I challenge you; will you duel or die for her?"

"Oh, fie!" cried the sea-girl. "No one shall ever tame me," and giving them each a box on the ear in a single motion, ran lightfoot and laughing down the steps to throw herself on the capellan, shouting that he was her prisoner.

"Lost! Lost!" cried the archer in mock agony. "Come, my lord, let us make an alliance for the conquest of witches less fickle than the marine. I will provide the arm and you the purse, from that secret gold-mine which all Kjermanash keep."

"Ah, ser archer, it is magic gold, and at the touch of a witch, would vanish." Rodvard bowed and turned up the stairs.

For most, it was still too early to retire to the boxes, the corridor behind them was empty of all but one small group of masks, laughing together. Rodvard waited a moment with beating heart, turning to toss one of his snowballs of perfumed fabric at random into the crowd below. He thought someone down there in the group might have cried, "Cleudi!" as the people at the end of the corridor entered their box and he was alone. The handkerchief was in place; it was more than a little dim for him to be sure of the color, but as he took it from its place with a little tear, there could be no doubt that the perfume was rose.

Eight paces counted in automatic nervousness carried him to the door of Cleudi's box. Music and voices were muted from within, it was an island of alone, the feeling deepened by everything in view. Other servants than Damaris had been busy; the reek of flowers was heavier than ever, even the chairs were garlanded and the odor enhanced by a tall candle which stood on the sideboard, left of the entrance, sending a tiny curl of perfumed smoke into the still air. Around the candle were viands; beyond the sideboard against the wall, a divan with rolling edges; round chairs facing the panels where the box would look out over the dancing floor if the panels were let down and the curtains drawn back. There were two chairs facing the table and it was laid, but in the center, only the bottle of fired-wine, its cork already drawn. Rodvard poured himself a dram and drank it rapidly, savoring the warm shock as it coursed down his throat.

He wondered if he dared take a second draft and decided against, he would need clear wits to play his part. A slice from the ham made him realize hunger, but again he forebore to go further, it would be ungentle to disarrange the meal before the arrival of his guest. He walked slowly across and seated himself in one of the chairs, looking outward toward the blank paneling, twisting his back into the comfort of the seat, but without finding rest. From below the high note of a violin in crescendo pierced the hangings; one might be one of those gods of antique legend, who sit on the Shining Mountains, with heads above the clouds, and control mortal destinies to whom all below would be what he heard now, a babble with an occasional note of agony. Ah, but to be the controller instead of the controlled—

The door was tapped.

So rapidly that the chair was overset, Rodvard leaped to his feet, picked it up, cursing his clumsiness, strode swiftly to the door and threw it open. On the threshold stood the Prophet of Mancherei, who had teased him with the rouge-ball. He bowed over her hand, drawing her in, and as the door closed, declaimed:

> "Now that winter's gone, the earth has lost
>   Her snow-white robes, and now no more the frost
> Candles the grass or casts an icy cream
> Upon the silver lake or crystal stream;
> Now do the choir of chirping minstrels bring
> In triumph to the world the youthful spring:
> The valleys, woods and hills in rich array
> Welcome the coming of the longed-for May.
> Now all things smile, only my love doth lower
> Nor hath the scaling moon-day sun the power
> To melt that marble ice, which still doth hold
> Her heart congealed and makes her pity cold.
> How shall we call it spring when she doth carry
> June in her eyes, in her heart January?"

—in a half-whisper, yet joyously, with laughing lips, as Cleudi might have done it, passing one hand around her shoulders, with the other holding tight to her hand.

"A northern lord to complain of the cold? And to instruct the Prophet of Love in love?" she said, in Countess Aiella's thrilling voice. (If it were only this one.) "I will not grant your right to sue until you have proved love your prophet."

"Ah, that would be epicene," said Rodvard (the fired-wine working in him; but it was too dim to wring truth from her eyes). "You must convert yourself to a woman before you can convert me to your sacred love."

"Oh, love does not remain true love when its longings are satisfied; therefore the sacred, which can never be satisfied, is above the profane," she said, stepping to one of the chairs at the table with a graceful play of ankle. Her hands went up to slip off the head-mask, and she sat back, hair falling round her shoulders. "I am a little weary, my lord of Kjermanash; give me something to drink that will warm your wintry wit."

Her fingers toyed with a goblet, but he took one of the festival-cups from his belt, poured it full, then as she drank, disengaged it from her fingers and finished it himself, lips carefully at the place where hers had touched the edge.

"Not worthy of you, my lord. Is this the promised originality? Go catch servant-girls with such tricks."

"Alas," he said, using the same half-whisper (the voice was the danger-point). "True love and longing has no tricks, only the expression by every means of its desire. Let us contest your heresy that satisfied longing is the end of love; for in love, the momentary assuagement only leads to further longings."

He poured her more from the bottle, and this time took the other cup himself. The glint of her eye, momentarily caught, held some slight anticipation of pleasure, but there was more in it of weariness with the world.)

"Ah, if it only would," she said, and turned her lovely head aside. "I am hungry, my lord."

He leaped up at once and began to serve her from the sideboard, while the joyous tumult from below and along the corridor became louder, and someone in the next box was making high festival, with squeals of women laughing and the rumble of men. They ate, talking a little more of the nature of love and whether it lives by satisfaction or by the lack of it. She drank more than he. There were springcakes; he set one before her, but she only tasted it and pushed it away, whereupon he left his own untouched and ran around the table to gather her in his arms. "You are the only sweet I need," he whispered, feeling at once strong and weak, but she avoided her head from his kiss, and when he essayed to hold her, shook herself free, with: "No. Ah, let us not spoil it."

"Lovely Aiella, do not say that, I implore," he cried, slipping down with one arm around her waist, his face close to the sweet hair of her turned head (and now with the fired-wine and nearness it was not of Maritzl of Stojenrosek he thought of, Maritzl lost, or of Lalette, or of the interruption that would come, but only of desire), and he slipped farther to one knee, not saying anything any more, only drawing her hands to him and kissing them again and again.

She took them from him and lifted his face gently to look him straight in the eyes, for one long breath in which the sound of the twittering recorders came from the floor beneath; then the Countess Aiella rose a trifle unsteadily to her feet, and as Rodvard rose also, holding her in the circle of his arms, said; "Shall we kiss?"

Her face was in shadow as the full lips met his, but as he swung her from her feet toward the divan, her eyes came open (and he saw in those deep pools that she would resist no longer, only hope that it would be better than the others). He half fell across her, with fingers and lips they devoured each other—

The creak of the opening door shivered through every muscle. "Be careful, my lord," said Cleudi's voice, strongly. "By the Service! What's here?"

Rodvard rolled himself afoot (the thought of that other union unconsummated in Mme. Kaja's garret shouting a trumpet through his mind and making him now glad, glad of this failure) and around to see Cleudi, all in his purple costume, with the pudgy Duke of Aggermans, and between the two a masque dressed as a bear. The man was very drunk; as the lolling white head came upright in its swing, Rodvard found himself looking into the eyes of the people's friend, Baron Brunivar, and even in the dim light, was appalled by what he saw there, for the man was not only drunk, he had a witchery upon him.

The mouth opened. "Sh' my always darling," said Brunivar thickly, and disengaging his arm from Cleudi's, swung it in a round gesture. "Glad you foun' her for me." Aggermans released the other arm; the Baron took three stumbling steps toward Aiella, and as she slipped his clutch, stumbled onto the divan, pushed himself around, focussed his eyes with difficulty, and cried; "Now I foun' her. Festival night. You go leave us, and I do anything you want tomorrow, my lor'."

Aggermans' round face had gone cherry-red. "That I can credit, my lord," he said, looking steadily not at Brunivar but at the Countess Aiella. "The more since I once would have done the same. But it is too high a price for the temporary favors of a bona roba."

The Countess laughed. "The pleasure of your Grace's company has been so small that you must not blame me if I seek elsewhere." She turned to Cleudi with a certain dignity. "As for you, my lord, I know whom I have to thank for this shame, and believe me, I will not forget it."

He bowed. "If the memory lasts until the next time when you laugh over having given a rendezvous you never meant to keep, I shall feel myself repaid for my troubles," he said.

"Ah, she has been deceiving you, too?" said Aggermans, and turned toward Rodvard as Brunivar made one more pawing effort to grasp the girl. "And who is this? I think I should like to remember him." (Concentrated venom streamed from his eyes.)

"Why, since this is another costume of mine, I think this will be my writer," said Cleudi. "Take off your mask, Bergelin."

Rodvard drew it off slowly, not knowing what to say, but the Countess Aiella spared him the trouble. "I see," she said. "It was all planned, not a part only. At least he has a heart, and so the advantage over any of you." She stepped over to take the young man's arm. "Ser, will you escort me as far as my pavilion?"

Cleudi stepped aside to let them pass through the door and down the stairs. "What, unmasked already, my lady?" cried someone in the gay crowd round the door, but she did not turn her head until they were out in the shadow, when she released his arm with; "Now, go."

From within the hall came the moan of violins.

II

He woke with scaly tongue, head spinning in the fumes of the fired-wine and body burning with unfulfilled desires, to the clink of silver on porcelain, as the maid Damaris bore in his breakfast tray. She was already in costume, a milkmaid and not badly done; her eyes and feet were dancing. "Oh, where did you get the lovely Kjermanash mask?" she asked as he propped himself up among the pillows, and giving him the tray, went to run her fingers lovingly over the white silk where it hung across the chair. "It's just the most beautiful thing ever. I'll be so happy to be with you in it."

"Count Cleudi lent it to me . . . Damaris."

"What is it?"

"Sit down a minute. On the chair, no matter."

"I'll ruffle your beautiful costume. Was it made in Kjermanash?" She sat facing him on the bed as he moved over to make room. The neck of her milkmaid's dress was cut low enough to show the upper round of her breasts with a little in between (and the Blue Star told him that she noticed, and wanted him to notice; that it was festival day, when all's forgotten in the new spring).

"Damaris—about this ball . . . I'm afraid I won't be able to go with you after all."

Rather than angry, her face was woebegone to the edge of tears. (A world was crushing in her thoughts.) "You don't want to be with servant-class people?"

He reached out and patted her hand conciliatingly. "Of course I do, with you. But Damaris . . . you said it cost three spadas and I haven't hardly any coppers, even."

"Oh." She perched her head on one side and looked at him birdlike under prettily arched brows. "I can let you have that much." Then, seeing the expression on his face; "You can give it back to me when you get it from your master."

(He did not really want to go at all, headache and the thought of his position with Cleudi and the Duke of Aggermans gnawed at him, he could not think clearly.) "I—I—"

"I don't mind, really."

"But I don't want to take your money. I may—may not get any."

She considered, looking at him sharply, with eyes narrowing. Then; "I know. You don't want to go with me because I'm not your friend." She tipped suddenly forward, one arm round his neck, and kissed him hard, then drew her head back, and with a long breath, said; "Will you go with me now?"

"I—"

She kissed him again, tonguewise, and as her lips clung, shifted her body, and with her free hand, guided his to the V

of her dress. Her eyes said she did not want him to stop, and
he did not. Near the end it came to him that the Blue Star
was dead, he could not fathom a single thought in her mind.

11

Kazmerga; Two Against a World

I

Mathurin entered on his almost soundless feet and let the
door close behind him in the dark before saying, "Rodvard,"
softly. Rodvard, who had been letting his mind drift along
endless alleys rather than thinking, swung himself up. "I will
make a light."

"Do not. There is danger enough, and its point would so
be sharpened. Do not even speak aloud."

"What is it?"

"The Duke of Aggermans. His bravoes are let loose. No
time. I only just now learned it from the Count." Outside
there was the soft sighing of rain.

"I am to go?"

"At once. Make your way south, to the Center of Sedad
Mir. The contact is a wool-dealer named Stündert, in the
second dock street. Can you remember? Change clothes with
me quickly. Do not even take the door, which is watched,
but go by the window, across the road, and south into the
country."

The serving-man began to undress in the dark; Rodvard
recognized the sound. "Is there any money?" he asked.

The rustling stopped. "You to need money, who have the
Blue Star?"

Even under the dark, Rodvard felt himself flush (did he
dare tell what had happened? No.). "Still, I will need some
small amount. I have nothing."

Even under his breath Rodvard could catch the fury in the

other's tone; "Ah, you deserve to have your bones broken."

"I know; but is there any money?" Rodvard fumbled for the unfamiliar lace-points.

The man snarled, but pressed a few coins into his grasp. "You are to regard this as a loan. Cleudi sends it."

"Oh. You did not tell me he was aiding this escape."

"He wants you to go south to Tritulacca, and gave me a letter for you to carry—which I will transmit to the High Center."

It might be a girl's light tap at the door. "Go," whispered Mathurin, fiercely.

The window swung wide; Rodvard felt rain on his face, and the mud of the flower-bed squished round Mathurin's soft shoes as he took the leap down. A light flamed up in the room behind him; he began to run, stumbling up the terraces with branches snatching at his body, zigzagging to avoid the pennon of light. A voice shouted across the rain after him (and he thought Mathurin was a mighty bold fellow to face the Duke of Aggermans' assassins back there). He came against a hedge; there was another shout and the sound of crashing footsteps from the left, in which direction the hedge ran, no way to turn, and he stumbled over a root, prone, to roll beneath the lip of the shrubbery, thinking concealment might be a better resource than speed.

So it was; shout echoed shout with an accent of lost, footsteps went past, but apparently no one had a light and before one could be brought, Rodvard rolled out, and began to work cautiously toward the end of the hedge, bending double. The bushes turned back to enclose a square of garden, but there was a locked gate, low enough to be climbed. Over; the gravel path beyond, for a wonder, did not run circular like most, from which he deduced that it must be the one leading down from the main road. It offered the only real clue to direction, for the lights had winked out back there, the villa's mass and the trees cut off the night-shine from the bay, and the slope was no help at all with everything so gardened. Rodvard pushed forward cautiously; presently the feel of ruts under his feet told him his reasoning was sound, and he paused to consider whether along the road or across it. The second alternative won; if Aggermans were so in earnest, his people would not give up easily, and they would likely spread along the road.

There was no hedge at the opposite side, but a narrow ditch, in which Rodvard got one leg well wetted to the knee and almost fell. Beyond a slope pitched upward into what, as nearly as he could make out by feeling, would be a sapling grove with low underbrush. Having no cloak, he was by this time so wet that it did not matter when he stumbled against small trunks and the leaves just bursting above deluged him with big drops, but the sensation was so unpleasant that it tipped him into a despairing mood, where his fatigues of the night and day rolled in (and he began to ask himself whether all pleasures must end in an escape of some kind). So he followed the pent of the hill blindly, not thinking at all of where he was going (but only of how he was trapped by unfairnesses somewhere; and that it could not be altogether a matter of man's justice, which was the plainder of the Sons of the New Day, since no justice of man's would hold men from fiery passion).

Beyond an easy crest there was a dip, and Rodvard hurt his knee against a wall of piled stone. In the field beyond, he could sense under his feet the stumps of last year's corn, he was sick with weariness and fear and had begun to sneeze; there was no light or life in the world. What direction? With no reason for any, he followed the line of the stone wall for a little time, and it brought him ultimately to a sodden straw-stack, whose hard surface yielded just enough to the persistence of his fingers so that he could get the upper half of his body in and slide down into unhappy sleep.

II

He woke with a headache at the top of his spine, which ran around inside his head to the place over his eyes; nose feeling as though driven with a wooden plug. Mathurin's decent black clothes were horribly stained and scratched. Down the way he had come—not at all far from where he had crossed the wall, now that one could see by the light of morning—the fooprints lay, a fingerlength deep into the soft ground. At once he was oppressed by the thought that only too easily could his path from the villa be traced, there was Tuolén's witch behind as well, and fear mounting over the illness, he climbed to the wall itself and tried to walk along its top to hide his marks. After the rain, sky and air had become clear, and there were violets visible on the grove-side of the wall, not that they did him any joy in his misery. The stones quickly tore a hole in shoes made for indoor walking, so he had to jump down again and consider.

Right across his direction, at a little distance, there jutted out from the stone wall a hedge which lack of care had let grow into a screen of low, sprawling trees. It slanted down leftward to where a gap would mark a field entrance; beyond, a slow trickle of smoke ran up the blue to signal breakfast. Rodvard, deciding what he would do if he were hunter instead of hunted, found more than good the argument against harborage so near the villa. He climbed over the wall again to wipe his streaming nose with a burdock leaf, whose bitter juice stung his lips, and perceiving that he left less marked traces in the ground on that side, stayed. The overgrown hedge proved to line a deep-cut track that in one direction wound down toward the main road past the villa. Beyond that track was true forest of old trunks and heavy underbrush. It was surely a good place to seek concealment, but Rodvard was ignorant of how far it might run or what it led to, and with illness galloping through his veins, felt he must have shelter early, so murmuring half aloud to himself that he might as well die in hot blood as in cold rheum, he turned up the track toward the cottage-smoke.

The building was more prosperous than most in the country, with a barn outside, and two complete windows under the thatch-edge. No one answered his knock; as he pushed open the door, a child's squall was sounding with irritable monotony from a trundle-bed on the right, and a woman who had been doing something at a table before the fireplace on the left turned to face him. She was bent and dirty; her face was older than her figure. "What do you want?" she demanded.

"A place to rest, if I can," said Rodvard, "and perhaps something to eat." He crossed the room and came down weak-kneed on a stool by the fireplace corner.

The lined face held no sympathy as her eyes swept down the detail of his torn, mudstained clothes and lingered for a tick at the servant's badge on his breast. "This is not an inn," she said sourly.

"Madame, I am unwell. I can pay." He fumbled at the waist-pouch.

"This is not an inn," she repeated, then spun on her heel, took rapid steps to where the child in its bed still bawled, and administered it a severe clout on the side of the head. "Will you be quiet?" The cries sank to whimpers. She came to stand looking down at Rodvard.

"I know about your kind," she said. "You're too lazy to work, so you run away from a good master down there at the villa and probably rob him, too, on festival day when he's drunk, and then expect honest country-people like us, who have to labor for everything we get, to hide you from the provosts. My husband and me, we have to get up at dawn and work all day as hard as we can, and we're never through till the sun goes down, winter or summer, while you servant-people are drinking and stealing behind your master's back." All this was delivered in a torrent as though it were a single sentence, ending as she uplifted one arm to brandish an imaginary weapon. "Now you leave here."

Too weary and ill for a reply, a trickle he did not try to disguise running from his nostril, Rodvard did so, out into the bright spring day and along the track. Where it turned round a boss of hill that thrust in from the westward, a sense of being watched made him look back. The farm-wife had come out to the end of the house to look after him, and the sound of the child's petulant wail was on the air. (Rodvard felt a surge of bitter anger; there was an unfairness in life, every pennyweight of pleasure is paid with double its measure in pain, and only those who grubbed at the ground were entitled to call themselves honest. Why, if this be so, then joy must be wrong, and God himself must be evil, in spite of what the priests say.) But his head was too muzzy to follow any rabbit of reasoning to its hole, so he trudged along for a while without thinking anything at all, until he heard the creak of a cart, and here was a mule coming out from the Sedad Vix direction. The driver somewhat surlily gave him the time of the day.

Rodvard asked to go with him, and when the man said he was bound for Kazmerga, declared that was his destination, though he had never heard of the place and possessed not the least idea in what direction it lay. The fellow grunted and let him climb in; sat silent for a while as Rodvard sneezed and drizzled, then was moved to remark that this was a heavy case of the phlegm, but it could be cured by an infusion of dandelion root with certain drugs, such as his old woman made, and so well that they often accused her of being a witch. "—But the drugs are costly now." He evidently wanted conversation in payment for his favor, and when this beginning failed on Rodvard's merely remarking that he would pay for any quantity of drugs to get rid of this rheum, fell silent for a couple of minutes; then leaned over, touched the servant's badge, and struck out again with:

"Running away, ey? What happened, ey? Lying with wrong woman on festival night, perhaps? Ah, there's many and many a high family has daughters born nine months from festival night that shouldn't rightly inherit, but lord, young man, don't you run away because of that. I say to you that ladies can forgive and be forgive for everything they do that night, when all's free, and I say to you, you ought to go back to your master."

He chuckled and waved his mule-goad. "I do recall, I do, when I was a sprout no older than yourself how one night I went all the way to Masjon for spring festival and at the dancing in the square there, I found a little cat as hot as ever could be, so we slipped away for some conversation, ey? And when I got back to where I was staying with a friend, what do you think I found? Why, in my bed there was his sister—Phidera, that was her name—and she was saying she had thought the bed her own, and no more clothes on her than a fish. So there were two of them in one night, all I could do, he, he, he, and that's the way it always is at spring festival, and maybe it would be with you."

He looked at Rodvard, and the latter was glad for once that the Blue Star had gone dumb over his heart, for there was a drop of moisture on the lip above the ill-shaven chin, which the gaffer did not bother to suck in or to wipe away.

"It was nothing like that," said he (and to keep from being drawn deeper into the morass of the old fellow's thinking); "Have you heard that Baron Brunivar is like to be decreed in accusation?"

"Ey, ey. Those westerners, half Mayerns they are. It will be a sad day when the snow melts from Her Majesty's head, with only the regents between that crazy Pavinius and the throne, and no female heirs. Ey, ey. Here we are in the Marquis of Deschera's seignory. For you servant-class it is no matter; you lay out the plates on the table and you have a scuderius in your hand, but for us farm-people with all the taxes ..."

("I am not a servant," Rodvard wanted to cry, "but a clerk who makes his gain as hard as you; and it is you we most wish to help." But he forebore), saying only; "Is there an inn at Kazmerga? I need something to eat, being without breakfast, and a place to lie down for the cure of my fluxions."

"No tavern—" the man stopped, and the expression above the uncut whisker became crafty (so that now Rodvard longed for the Blue Star); "Would you pay an innkeeper?"

"Why, yes. I have a little money."

"You be letting me take you to my home. The old woman will arrange your fluxions in less than a minute with her specific if you pay for it, and give all else you need for less than half what an innkeeper would ask, and no questions if the provosts come nosing, ey. Go, Mironelle." He leaned forward and rammed the goad into the mule's rump, which shook its ears, danced a little with the hind feet, and began to trot, so that Rodvard's aching head jounced agonizingly. There was a turn, the track was broadening, fields showed, pigs rooted contentedly in a ditch, and the trees gave back to show a church with its half-moon symbol at the peak, and around it, like the spoke of a wheel, houses.

"Kazmerga," said the mule-man. "I live on the other side."

III

She was fat and one eye looked off at the wrong angle, but Rodvard was in a state not to care if she had worn on her brow the mark of evil. He flopped on the straw-bed. There was only one window, at the other end; the couple whispered under it, after which the housewife set a pot on the fire. Rodvard saw a big striped cat that marched back and forth, back and forth, beside the straw-bed, and it gave him a sense of nameless unease. The woman paid no attention, only stirring the pot as she cast in an herb or two, and muttering to herself.

Curtains came down his eyes, though not that precisely, neither; he lay in a kind of suspension of life, while the steam of the pot seemed to spread toward filling the room. Time hung; then the potion must be ready, for through half-closed lids Rodvard could see her lurch toward him in a manner somewhat odd. Yet it was not till she reached the very side of the bed and lifted his head in the crook of one arm, while pressing toward his lips the small earthen bowl, that a tired mind realized he should not from his position have been able to see her at all. A mystery; the pendulous face opened on gapped teeth; "Take it now my prettyboy, take it."

The liquid was hot and very bitter on the lips, but as the first drops touched Rodvard's tongue, the cat in the background emitted a scream that cut like a rusty saw. The woman jerked violently, spilling the stuff so it scalded him all down chin and chest as she let go. She swung round, squawking something that sounded like "Pozekshus!" at the animal. Rodvard struggled desperately as in a nightmare, unable to move a muscle no more than if he had been carved out of stone, realizing horribly that he had been bewitched. He wanted to vomit and could not; the cottage-wife turned back toward him with an expression little beautiful.

Her grubby hands were shaking a little. She grumbled

under her breath as he felt her detach the belt-pouch with all
his money and then slip off his shoes. The jacket came next;
but as she undid the laces at the top, grunting and puffing,
her hand touched the chain that held the Blue Star, and she
jerked out the jewel. In all his immobility Rodvard's every
perception had become as painfully sharp as an edge of
broken ice. He thought she was going to have a fit, her
features seemed to twist and melt into each other, her hand
came away from the stone as though it had been a red coal.
"Oh, nonononono," she squealed, backing away. "No. No.
No. Ah, you were right, Tigrette; you were right to stop
me."

The cat arched against her. As though the small act had
released some spring in herself, the woman bustled to the
invisible end of the room, where Rodvard could hear wood
click on earthenware, then some kind of a dumb low-toned
chant she raised, then became aware of a different and
aromatic odor. He was wide awake now and hardly sick at
all any more; could see how the mist in the room was
clearing a little, then heard the door creak open and the
mule-driver's voice, saying:

"Did you get it done, ey?"

"Not I, you old fool, you rat-pudding, you dog-bait."

"Old fool yourself." Rodvard heard the sound of a slap.
"Call me old fool. You weren't so dainty with the last one.
Taken with the pretty lad, are you? Now go do it, or I'll slice
his throat myself and never mind mess. What's one runaway
servant more or less, ey? This is real money, hard money,
more nor you ever seen."

Now she was whimpering. "I tell you you're a fool. He has
a Blue Star, a Blue Star, and his witch will know what's put
on him and recoil it back to us, double, triple. Worms that
never die crawling under your skin till you perish of it. All
the hard money there is is not worth it."

A sound of steps. The scratchy face looked down at
Rodvard, he felt the man palm the jewel. "Blue Star, ey? Ah,
fritzess, this is some piece of glass." But the tone was little
sure.

"It is a Blue Star and nothing else, the second one I see. They are wedded with the great wedding."

The man turned, and though his own head did not, Rodvard could see how the expression of craftiness had come on back to him. "Blue Star? Now you witch it for him, wife, witch it for him, so it will be no longer good. You can witch anything. Then I'll take him away from here."

The whimper became a sniffle. "I'll witch, ah, I'll witch, mumble, mumble, mumble." Rodvard heard her tottering shuffle go and come, the fat face was over his again, all filled now with oily kinks that held little beads of sweat. She looked at him closely and then flung over her shoulder; "Go out, old man, and leave us. There's something not healthy for you to see," and began plucking at her garments to undo them, at the last moment pausing to throw an edge of stinking blanket over Rodvard's face. His heightened senses caught the stiff rustle of clothes sinking to the floor; the aromatic smell declared itself over all others, her fingers sought his burned chin beneath the blanket and applied relieving unguent.

"Mumble, mumble," came her voice, and he understanding not a word. "Meowrrr-row!" shouted the cat, as it raced through the narrow cot from end to end. He could have melted with relief as the fingers soothed his chest, but then his mind went off on a picture of Lalette become old in the manner of this one and he would have shuddered if he could have stirred. The crooning mumble ended, the witch-wife's ministrations at the same time. There was a silence set with small sounds, over which the continued mewling of the cat. He heard the woman at the door summon her husband, then the two of them speaking in voiceless sibilants, a contention going on, which terminated with the man's strong arms around Rodvard, heaving him up like a sack of meal.

Exterior air came through the edge of the blanket; step, step, he was borne, and with a grunt, dumped in what must be the mule-cart. A pause; the blanket was twitched from his face and he was looking up into the disparate eyes of the woman.

"Nice boy, nice boy," said her voice. "You tell your witch

now how I do good. You tell her I respect the great wedding. Not him; he keeps your hard money."

She patted his still unmoving cheek, a touch that made his senses creep; and the Blue Star was suddenly, shockingly cold over his heart, (he could see beyond any question that there was in the woman's mind a great fear, but also the great longing kindness of two joined against an armèd world).

From where he was leading the mule to hitching, the man's voice came; "Wife, get that badge we took from the last one, the mechanician. I say to you, you hurry now."

12

Netznegon City; A Zigraner Festival

I

After he had gone, Lalette cried a little, but the widow pretended not to notice, busying herself with sewing on one of the festival masks, a task at which the girl was presently helping, so far as she could, for she was no great artist with the needle, nor wished to be. When they began talking again it was about the robe they were working on, grey silk velvet which had been artfully torn here and there to a pretense of raggedness, through which the slashes were being backed with flame-color. Lalette passed her hands across the lovely fabric (longing to be gay and courted in such a gown, though it left so much of the leg bare that she would have felt a little shame to wear it). Who was it made for?

"The Countess Aiella of Arjen, for the festival ball at Sedad Vix. The younger Countess, that is, the unmarried one. I designed it especially for her. The mask is there." She nodded.

It hung on one of the standards, empty of eye and mouth, but no one could mistake the provenance of the high-bridged nose and the cheekbones from which the full rumpled beard flowed down. "Why," said Lalette, "it is Prince Pavinius when he was Prophet of Mancherei; I thought you were—" and stopped.

"Amorosians?" The widow Domijaiek smiled. "I am a follower of that doctrine, though not yet perfected in it. But in spite of what you have been told, it is not one of gloomy reverence. It does not prohibit joy, nor even keep us away from the world, only declares that the joys of the world are false beside those that come to us when we learn how we have been deceived by the flesh. You, who are newly married, have the other kind of love now, and will not know what I mean, but in the end you will come to see that kind of love as sin."

"I am not married," said Lalette, letting her needle fall (but doubting that her feeling toward Rodvard were indeed the love the poets carolled, and of which Dame Domijaiek spoke), "except in what we who have the Art call the great marriage."

"I would as soon not speak as to that," said the widow, "but in our church we are taught that to love a person is to love the world, which is a deception due to the God of evil."

II

Rodvard did not come back that evening, nor the next, and no word from him of any kind. Lalette felt unhappy and listless after so long indoors; above her she could hear from time to time Mme. Kaja's footsteps come and go, and when the door was opened, often one of her pupils in song, flatted usually and more frequently than not, off key. The boy Laduis soon held little more for her, and in any case with the spring festival now rushing on so fast, had to be taken from his academy to run errands for his mother, who now worked late every night. The widow said the court had gone down to Sedad Vix, the doubled guards at the city gates were withdrawn, and the provost somewhat relaxing in vigilance as to their search for the girl.

It might be safe to leave her refuge, if she had any place

to go. Surely, not to her mother's, who would still be watched by Uncle Bontembi the priest if by no other, and it seemed to Lalette there was no friend of her own age near enough to be trusted, now that all the world knew her for a witch. It was a box. For the present, one was able to pay in some sort for food and shelter by labor on the festival costumes, but that would soon be done. Ah, Rodvard, are you detained or faithless—which? She wished him there before her for an explanation that would also be the clue to her new life; and asked herself why a partnership of half an hour and not altogether of her own will, should bind her for life. Hold him she thought she could, and though hating the dependency into which she was thrown, hating the bond that made dependency her only resort, there was nothing to do but go see Dr. Remigorius, knowing that man hated her, and through him, try to find her lover. Oh, if I could ever be my own, not my mother's nor any his, she wished desperately, and though not a word of this was put into voice, the widow seemed to know her whole mind when Lalette said she thought it might be worth going forth on festival eve to seek tidings.

"Of course. You will want the mask of the Kjermanash princess, the one that Laduis calls Sunimaa. I will let you take it."

Nothing more was said at this time, nor until the afternoon of the festival eve itself, with horns and whistles already blowing in the street, though the sun had not yet touched the arm of spring, when the widow helped her into the fur-tipped robe, surveyed her all round, and bade farewell with a smile (which Lalette thought a trifle sad). "If all does not go as you would wish, return here. You may at all times come in the name of the God of love."

It was just falling twilight when Lalette felt stones under her feet again and breathed deep the fine air of spring. Someone had hung a pair of colored lanterns at the gate of the Street Cossao, one of them with a broken pane in its side, through which the candle within shed its beam on a group of three or four premature revelers gathered round a bottle. They hallooed to Lalette and began to follow her along the boulevard on uneasy legs, but gave it up when she saw a hired carriage come past empty and hailed it as if to mount. When she did not after all enter his vehicle, the carriage-master swore at her, but want of money to pay left her without choice.

At the market-place tables had been set out and musicians on a stand surrounded with flowers and green branches were already intoning the volalelle, but only three or four couples were dancing. There were some murmurs of appreciation for her costume from those sitting; none called nor gave her any sign. It was a poor district; she knew she must look by the half too lordly, and that was as well.

Some way farther along, a group all masked was holding a procession from a side-street behind a hand-drum, and laughingly begged her to join, but she pulled loose. The sound of bells began to hand over the gay din that rose from the city, and Lalette hurried, feeling more than ever out of protection and alone. The street where Remigorius had his shop was wider than her memory of it. Someone had affixed an absurd green paper ribbon to the neck of the stuffed lizard over the door, but all seemed dark within.

There was no answer when Lalette pulled at the bell. Her heart plunged down into dreadful syncope—Oh, what will I do without money if he is not there nor anyone? Not go back to that woman of strange gods, no. She rang again, twice, to make her insistence clear, and as someone down the street greeted guests with a glad shout of welcome, the door cracked open and a voice said that the doctor was abroad, not even in Netznegon City, but there was another medic around the corner and two stories aloft.

"Oh," said Lalette, "it is not for the curative that I wished him. I desire to find a friend of his and mine—Rodvard Bergelin."

Door came fully open. In the rapidly fading light the girl found herself looking at a young man whose chin and slanting eyes betrayed Zigraner origin. As always with that race, the smile was an effort to ingratiate, but there was something unpleasant about it. "Are you—?"

"Lalette Asterhax. Yes."

"Demoiselle, will you come in? The doctor has left me to keep his place for all that concerns the Sons of the New Day, since matters have reached such a crisis with what has been discovered at the conference of court."

Lalette followed him (with dreadful certainty clutching at her heart that this was the key, then, of so much she had failed to understand; Rodvard was an intimate of that gang of murderous conspirators and so must these others be.) The Zigraner indicated a stool in the shop and struck a light. "You permit that I introduce myself? I am Gaidu Pyax. Of Rodvard you should not be concerned. He is doing good work, and the High Center has forwarded to ours its praise of him."

(I am planets and centuries away from the man who has chosen me, she thought. How can I say it? What shall I ask?) "There was no word."

The Zigraner frowned. "The sub-leader of your center doubtless told you of the plot against Baron Brunivar, the regent prospective? It was Rodvard who uncovered it."

"Oh." (The conversation was going to stop.) She cried desperately; "I thought he would be back with me for the festival."

"And you have so lovely a costume, demoiselle. Duty bears hard on us." His smile changed to a little bark of a laugh. "But be tranquil for him; he will sport high with the court at Sedad Vix." The tongue of Gaidu Pyax came out and made a circle round his lips; he glanced where the clock ticked against the wall and darted his eye around quickly. "I will see you home, or if you will—it is only—that is—would you care to see how we Zigraners keep festival?"

Outside the dark was almost full; the bells were all chiming in chorus and Rodvard at Sedad Vix. (I have no home, she thought, and he has sent no word.) "It would be pleasant." (For one must do something.)

Pyax leaped to his feet, his mouth all twisted with joy. "Come, let us go at once. I do not wish to be late for the light." He ran into the rear room with blundering, skipping steps, tripping at the doorsill. Lalette heard him stumble and then, in a break of the street-noises, how a voice in that rear room growled at him heavily. (Remigorius is there after all, she thought, and maybe Rodvard; they are lying to me.) Pyax' high-pitched voice said; "I don't care if she is a witch. She's going to—" and was cut off by the long bellow of a horn blown nearby, and he was back, his face somewhat abashed.

He did not lock the door. In the street the festival was now full-met, with lights tossing along and the horns blown from every window under the steady bells. Gaidu Pyax wore only a simple eye-mask and his voice had a lilt of excitement. Lalette (knew it was because how all his family would boast of having a true Dossolan girl to keep festival with, but she) said;

"I thought you told me that Doctor Remigorius was abroad."

In the flickering light, his eyes were sidelong. "He is; he truly is, demoiselle."

"Was that not his voice I heard in the rear room?"

"Oh, no, that was one of our people for whom the provosts are searching, and it is your fault in a way, because he had to eliminate the doorman at Rodvard's house, who recognized you—" How much further he would have carried the useless lie she did not know or care, for at that moment, a girl in a passing group threw a scent-ball that struck him in the face.

III

There was a high hall of entry with upholstered chairs, whose members were tortured spirals of wood; and a pair of gigantic silver candlesticks from the floor, rhinanthus plants in form. A respectful doorman came to take her furs, but they were only festival imitations without weight, and she kept them. Pyax said; "At our festival we do not wear masks indoors," so she removed her headdress, and drew a glance of admiration when he saw the dark hair flowing across the white. The inner door opened and a middle-aged man with a grave, kindly face, came out, somewhat ridiculously caparisoned in the red under-jacket of a general. Pyax bowed low before him.

"Father, this is the Demoiselle Asterhax, who has come to keep spring festival with us."

A little uncertain where the line of politeness lay in a Zigraner house, she would have curtsied, but he, without showing whether he recognized her name, took her by the hand, with; "The friend of my son is welcome," and led her in. Beyond the inner door was a narrow hall hung with glyptics, in which he turned rightward through a second door, and releasing her, clapped both his hands together. "This is the Demoiselle Asterhax."

A dozen or more people, who had been sitting in a room so dim they were visible only as forms, stood up and chorused, "You are welcome!" then sat down again with a rustling of silks. The senior Pyax took Lalette's hand again and led her round through the gloom to a chair, where he bowed and placed a finger on his lips. Gaidu Pyax took the next seat to her own; no one spoke. The whole place had the strange, almost musty odor that forever hangs round Zigraners; the sound of the rejoicing city could not penetrate.

Lalette felt that the arm-pieces of her chair were carved into animals' heads and now turned her attention toward the center of the room, where a single very weak taper burned on a table of almost eye-level height before a bronze armillary sphere formed in interlaced tracery. A clockwork turned the sphere; its parts flashed dully. In that breathing silence the voice of the elder Pyax spoke out, deep and almost ominous:

"Father, in our darkness, we who have waited long, and long hoped, pray you not to turn your face from the children of your creation and the hope of your glory, but to give us light, light, that we may surround your throne with our praises."

Someone sobbed in the dim; Lalette's side-glance caught a glimpse of Gaidu's face buried in his hands. To her, as the older man went on with his prayer, the scene that might have been moving became painful and ridiculous—grown people playing make-believe like silly children, weeping before a

machine that must unfailingly come to the end expected of
it—while there were true matters of life and death and love
lying unsolved. So watching the dull repeated gleam from the
sphere, she swept into reverie till sphere and taper reached
the term of their movement in a sharp intake of breath from
those around. A tiny runnel of flame slipped across the base
beneath the device, its heart seemed to split apart, discharging a bright ball of purest fire, which threw the whole room
into color.

At once the people leaped to their feet, and shouting
"Light! Light! God sees us!" began embracing and congratu-
lating each other, while servants hurried in to light tall candles. Lalette found herself in the grip of a woman with a
haired mole on her chin, whose over-ample contours were
laced into a costume from one of the knightly legends. The
woman capered up and down as she talked.

"Isn't it wonderful?" she cried in a high voice. "We are so
glad to have you come! Ser Pyax never spends less than a
hundred scudi on his festival! You are the one who witched
Count Cleudi, aren't you? The other two Pyax boys couldn't
come for the ceremony, but they have no sisters, you know.
God never fails as the world turns. You must try some of our
Zigraner wine."

A servant was at Lalette's side, with the beverage in a
huge silver flagon on a huge silver tray, and Gaidu Pyax was
offering her one of his paired festival-cups, curiously carved,
and so heavy it must be pure gold. "My aunt Zanzanna," he
said. "A dog bit her when she was a baby and never since has
she been able to control her tongue."

"I will bite you and drive you madder than I am," replied
the woman with the mole. Lalette looked around over the
top of her cup from wine strongly flavored with resin. Everybody was talking at once and in all directions, disjointedly.
The room was a little smaller than it had seemed in the dark,
but still large, with heavy hangings worked to tapestry at all
the windows and pictures occupying every fingerspace of wall
between. The chair where the senior Pyax had sat was
jewelled around its top. At one end of the room musicians
were setting their instruments in order. Most of the people

were approaching middle age and were of a strongly Zigraner cast of countenance, but there was one girl of surprising loveliness, blonde enough to be a Kjermanash. The man with her did not look like one of these people either.

Now the musicians struck up and everybody began dancing, even quite an old woman in a corner who had no partner, but stepped alone through the figures. The groups did not form patterns, but each pair toed it by themselves until they reached the end of the measure, when all formed a circle, partners pledging each other in their festival-cups and crying; "Light! Light!" Gaidu Pyax danced well, swinging Lalette strongly when the step called for it. Food was presently brought in, and from time to time a servant would summon the elder Pyax, whereupon he would go to the door and return with a new guest on his arm, clapping hands to make everyone stop what they were doing, whereupon all shouted "You are welcome!" as before, and there would be more drinking of pledges.

Lalette began to feel quite giddy and happy, no longer minding that all these people seemed to be talking about how terribly expensive everything was, or staring at her across their shoulders, as though she were an actress. She did not think anyone here would betray her to the provosts; the women all seemed to be trying to be kind. The thought of what Dame Leonalda would say if she knew her daughter were in such a place struck Lalette as funny, and she sat down, laughing softly to herself over it, to find Aunt Zanzanna bending over her.

"Would you like to lie down for a while in your room? We have such a nice one for you."

It was easier to walk with the older woman's arm around her. The room was up two flights, heavily bowered with hangings, and Lalette thought she noted a scent of musk as she lay down on the rich bed in all her clothes. The mask made her feel sick; when she returned from the cabinet she felt so weak she had to lie down again, but the melody of the volalelle they were dancing down there would not let her alone, it kept going round and round inside her head as she slipped down through drowsing wakefulness to full dream and an uneasy sleep. It must have been nearly day when she woke again, and she felt stiff. The scrape of violins still came from below; for a few minutes she considered returning to the festival, then slipped off her clothes and got into bed.

IV

She woke again to see complete spotted sunlight bright across the wall, wondering for the first sleepy seconds where she was. It was a footstep that had roused her; she turned her head and saw Gaidu Pyax looking down, with spots on his costume.

"The greeting of the morning," he said. "It is spring."

"Oh," was all Lalette could say, pulling the covers close around her neck, and then; "Well, I greet you."

The smile she had once thought rather pleasant became fixed. "I have come to keep the spring with you." He laid his hand on the edge of the covers. "You are my partner."

"No. Not this time. No."

"It is festival morning. You must."

"No. What would Rodvard say?"

His laugh had an edge of nastiness. "His head will be on another pillow now. I know him. Why should you not do it as well as he?"

He reached down and began to paw at the bedclothes against her resistance, the scream she tried to give was only a squeak in that heavy-hung and distant room, and then he flung himself on her, catching her wrist to twist it around, crying; "Witch, witch, I will tame you or break all your bones." She bit at the hand that touched her face, and with her own arm swung a sweeping blow that took him where head and neck join. He was suddenly standing beside the bed again, and she was saying low and furious, through tears:

"If you force me, I will kill myself and you, too. I swear it by the Service."

Gaidu Pyax' lips pouted out like a little boy's, he sank slowly to one knee beside the bed, reaching a hand out gropingly. "Ah, I knew it couldn't be true," he said, and lifted toward her a face of wordless misery.

For a long minute she looked at him, all her fierceness and resolution melting in the face of that unhappy desire. (She felt no spark for this boy, only thought: and what if I do, they do not want me, it was all a deceit put upon me, and I can at least heal this one's hurt); and was just reaching from under the covers to draw him to her and comfort him—

When a flash of lightning wrote in letters of fire across the inside of her mind the words *Will you go with me now?* and though there was no meaning in what they said, she understood that it told the unfaithfulness of her lover.

The hand that had extended to take that of Pyax patted it instead. "I am sorry," she said. "Perhaps it was my fault. I should have told you. . . . When others do it, I never could. But I thank you for the good festival."

13

Farewell and Greeting

I

Back again to the place of masks through streets littered with the sour debris of festival, among which languid sweepers toiled. After what had happened, Lalette did not ask to say farewell to the elder Pyax or Aunt Zanzanna. There was a twitch at the corner of the doorman's mouth as he let them out; she would not let Gaidu accompany her farther than the market square (for morning had brought back all the anxiety of the price still on her apprehension). He remarked somewhat spitefully that he could understand how she would not wish to have her people see a Zigraner bringing her home.

Laduis answered her knock; he seemed truly happy to see her. The widow was at the cookshop; Lalette changed the mask of Sunimaa for her worn clothes, finishing just as the woman returned. They ate, talking but little, and that much in light terms. Dame Domijaiek sent the boy out, and as his footsteps went down the stair:

"Did you find him?" she asked.

"He is at Sedad Vix." Her mouth worked a little, and with the calm eyes fixed upon her, she could keep it back no more. "He has been unfaithful to me."

"I do not understand."

"In the witch-families we cannot help—"

"Ah. Then it is a knowledge gained through falsity and witchcraft, not through the God of love, and so will lead to no good end."

"I am unhappy," was all Lalette could whisper, (not understanding what the woman was trying to say).

"It is because you look on this man as personal to you. Love must share with all."

(There was something passionately wrong with this, Lalette felt, but rue and the after-lash of last night's wine and this morning's experience had left her too low to seek out the flaws.) She began to weep softly.

After a few minutes, the widow said: "Let us reason. If you owe him not less than all love, so he owes as much to you; and by destroying your joy, he has failed his obligation. Do you still love him, not as we must love all, but to yourself, as of the material world?"

(It seemed to Lalette as though there were something big and dark and heavy in her breast where her heart ought to be, and she had no clear thoughts at all any more.) "I did not—ah, I do not know, he is all I have."

"You have a mother, child."

"A mother who tried to sell me! And still would, if she could find me."

"Because she wishes to save you from distresses she herself has felt. That also is done in love, I think."

"Then I'll have no love!" cried Lalette, looking up furiously, tear-drops sparkling on her lashes. "I'll hate and hate and hate."

A tiny red spot appeared on each of Dame Domijaiek's cheeks. "I do not think you had better say that again in this house," she said. "I have an arrangement to make, and will return before evening. Tell Laduis."

She went out, leaving a Lalette who could hardly bear herself, nor find anything to do, in her mind going over and over the dreadful ground of Rodvard's treachery and the fact that he was one of the Sons of the New Day. Even if he came to her now, she would not have him, that book was closed by his own hand; and the boy Laduis coming in, she allowed him to draw her out of her megrims, so that when the widow returned, they were almost gay together. But it was almost dawn before sleep touched her.

II

She came awake with a start, and the sense that something dreadful had happened. It must be late morning; the widow was gone from the other side of the bed and Laduis' cot was empty and neatly made up. There was—

All at once the whirl at the back of her mind resolved itself into a pattern. There were two things in it, a picture of a strange room where men talked before a fire while a sea beat on a rocky shore, and running through it as though the picture were transparent, an appeal so naked and desperate that it brought her to her feet at once—mind speaking to mind without words to say that the holder of her Blue Star was lying bewitched and near death.

There was no wine; it was horribly hard to trace out the pattern of the counter-witchery in water, even with the help of some dust from the corner, and the effort of the projection left her so weak and shaken that when it was done she collapsed across the bed in the shift that had served her as a night-dress and did not even hear Dame Domijaiek come in.

"So you have done it," said her voice (and Lalette thought that she had never in her life heard anything so cold).

Lalette raised her head. The older woman was looking at the patterns which still moved faintly, not at her at all. "I ask your pardon," she said. "It was an emergency; I learned—"

"Nothing you can say will change the fact that you have brought witchery into my house."

Lalette struggled to her feet. "Well, I will go."

"Yes," said the mask-maker, "I think you must go. You have brought on me and my son even worse dangers than you dream of. You must go. When you spoke of hating yesterday, I thought it might come to that, but I foolishly let sympathy overrule my judgment."

In the room above them, Mme. Kaja struck a chord on her music, and after one false beginning, launched into the bride's aria from "The Disinherited." Lalette looked at the floor and there were tears in her eyes. The widow spoke again:

"Yet you were sent to me for help, and help you I will, if you will take it. I think there is only one chance in the world for you, and that is to go to Mancherei and place yourself under the dominion of the Prophet."

"But I have no money to get there, no money at all, and what could I do there?" said Lalette (now angry with herself for having jeopardized herself and the widow too, in some manner, for the sake of false Rodvard; and willing in her contrition to follow this leading, but not seeing how it could be done).

"Love forever finds a way to draw to itself those who need it. There is a fund for the transportation of those who would go thither; and under the ordinance of the Prophet, there have been established the houses called couvertines of the Myonessae, where there is shelter and gainful employ for such girls as yourself, who need them."

"I—I do not believe in this religion, and—I am a witch."

"Few believe in the beginning, but only turn to our doctrine for relief from some condition of the world. It is this witchcraft you must escape."

Lalette heaved a sigh. (Her head ached now, and what was the use of this struggle to be free and one's own? The strings tightened, one was drawn back to puppethood.)

"Very well. If you will tell me what to do."

III

The conventicle was held at the back of a warehouse; people sat on bales of wool, or leaned against them. Guards against the provosts had been set at the door. One, who was addressed as "Initiate" pronounced a discourse of which Lalette hardly understood a word, it was so abstract. She could hardly keep her eyes open; the descent into doze and the jerk back were agonizing. A desiccated woman who breathed through her nose was seated on the next bale. At the end of the discourse, she took Lalette's hands in both her own, with a gesture astonishing until one observed that all the people in the gathering were similarly greeting neighbors. To Lalette's surprise most of them seemed to be well-to-do people with an expression of almost dogged cheerfulness, but there seemed about them something lacking, as though they had bought this good cheer with the sacrifice of some quality.

The thin woman was still talking when a man with an engraved smile touched Lalette's arm and said that the Initiate would like to see her. The man's face was calm as though carved in stone; he asked her whether she was married? Had read the First Book of the Prophet? Drank fortified alcohols? Practiced the Art? He looked at her as though his glance would bore straight through when she answered the last honestly that she had done so, but would practice it no more. Then he pronounced a discourse as incomprehensible as that he had given to the company, ending by saying she must be reborn into purest love.

At the close of this he told her that he had looked into her heart and believed her honest, but that she must carefully study the Prophet's First Book. He gave her a letter for the cargo-overseer of a vessel even then at the wharf; the book, he said, would be furnished to her aboard by the third mate of the vessel. Dame Domijaiek had been her guarantee; love would be her protector. She was kissed on the forehead and they all went out into a spring twilight with drizzles of rain.

At the wharf someone was trying to lead a protesting horse into the ship, among stampings and confused shouts.

Lalette huddled in the shadow, as close as she could get to the widow Domijaiek and regarded the masts running up into the grey, with their climbing triangles of rope tracery. A wide plank led through a gap in the bulwarks before them, but now the horse was disposed of, the ship's people were engaged in some bargle at one end of the vessel; no one paid any attention to the two women who tripped to the deck and stood uncertain. At last a man detached himself from the group with a cheerful farewell and came along the deck toward them, cap on head and munching a piece of bread. He would have passed with a brief stare in the assembling gloom, but the widow halted him with outstretched hand and asked where was the overseer of cargo?

He halted with mouth open and cheek puffed out with food. "By the lazarette," and before either could put another question, disappeared round a wooden structure that rose from the planking. A few spurts of rain fell. Lalette shivered more snugly into her cloak (wondering whether "witch" might not be written on her forehead to make all shun her save those whom others shunned, as Amorosians and Zigraners). Now the chatter broke up and three or four men together came toward the head of the plank, porters mainly with their iron hooks in their belts. The exception had broad but stooped shoulders, a close grey mat of beard and an unlighted lantern in his hand. To him Dame Domijaiek addressed herself, inquiring where the lazarette might be.

He waved a hand. "Aft of the tri-mast, leftward"; then glanced at Lalette, stepped close and peered at her so directly that she shrank away. "For Ser Brog, mother?" he said, and turned to the older woman. "Looky here, mother, I ha'n't seen you before along Netznegon dock, eh? You come to see me when you finish with Ser Brog, and maybe we do business, eh? At Casaldo's." The porters laughed and one of them bubbled a derisive sound through his lips (Lalette was already repenting her undertaking).

A voice behind a door told them to enter. It belonged to a tall man with white hair, whose black fuzzy eyebrows leaped up a long face when he saw that his visitors were women. He did not rise, but cast a half-regretful glance at the sheet of computations on a leaf let down from the wall before him. The letter he at first held far away as though it were an affiction of proclamation; when he grasped its purport and had seen the signature, he rose, all courtesy. "Aye, hands must wash face," he said. "I trust you left Ser Nimred well? Will you be having a little wine?"

Dame Domijaiek excused herself, since she must return to her child, but as she embraced Lalette farewell, the girl felt thrust into her hand a little cloth pouch with coins in it, and was suddenly at the edge of weeping. When she turned, Ser Brog had set out a pair of pewter cups and was drawing the cork from a bottle of wine. He bowed her to the single chair, himself taking the edge of the built-in bed, which was so hedged about by cabinets that he must bend.

He said; "So you are seeking a sea-voyage, Demoiselle Issensteg?" (This was the name the letter had given her.) "Are you one of the inland Issenstegs from Veierelden? I hear there have been troubles in that region."

(Was he trying to draw her into indiscretion, and how much did he really know of her origin and purpose?) She said that she was not of the Veierelden branch and waited. He asked her politely whether she had had a joyous festival and were a good sailor. When she said that she had not been at sea before, his face took on some concern, and he regretted that the captain's wife, who usually sailed with them, would not do so this voyage. There were no other women aboard. He would provide her with a bell for summoning someone when needed— "Not that you will be molested, demoiselle, but I will say the third mate is as strange—as a dog with two heads."

With this, Ser Brog finished his wine and rose to light her to a duplicate of his own tiny cabin. She decided she had been mistaken about the question, he was only expressing interest in the friend of a friend. It was nice not to have to be afraid. An hour or so later, as she sat curled up on the bed, but not yet disrobed, came a demonstration of how well the Amorosians cared for their own. A knock on the door turned into a porter with a neatly-strapped small trunk,

painted with her assumed name. It held an assortment of
body-linens, shoes and a dress in her size, new and of good
quality.

IV

She was roused by feet beating in rhythm and the sound of
distant shouts; a big round spot of light swung slowly from
side to side across the door. Last night had shown her a jug
and a basin beneath the let-down leaf that formed a writing
table, but the water was so cold it gave her goose-pimples.
The new dress would need taking in at the shoulders, so after
trying it, she returned to the old before stepping toward the
deck along a passage that held three more doors like her
own. Two men in yokes were pushing and relaxing on opposite sides of a pivoted bar (to steer the ship, she supposed),
under the orders of an officer in a green cap. One of the
workers was the curl-bearded man who had occosted Dame
Domijaiek the evening before. He relaxed one hand to touch
his forelock and had the grace to look sheepish. The officer
hardly looked at her; he was watching the masts that rose on
every side and the small boats about, for they were well out
into the Bredafloss, moving steadily downstream, though the
sails hung so flat, it seemed they could contain no air at all.

Lalette stepped past the steersmen to watch the slow
pageant of river moving by, and heard a step. Ser Brog; he
touched his cap and invited her to breakfast, down a flight of
steep stairs and along another passage to an apartment at the
rear of the ship. A skylight threw dappled gleams across a
table laid for five, with food already on it. Another man was
standing by; Ser Brog presented the second mate, and as he
did so, a big officer with a firm chin and bags under his eyes
came in with an air of great hurry and sat down without
waiting for the rest. This was the captain, Ser Mülvedo; he
bounced half an inch from his seat when his name was
mentioned, and fell to eating while the rest were taking their
places.

Lalette thought his courtesy somewhat strange to one who
wore a badge of good condition, and it was stranger still

when a youngish officer entered, to be greeted by the Captain with; "You are tardy. You know the rule of the ship. Take your meal with the crew."

The young officer went out sourly, but not before Lalette recognized him as the one who had directed her toward the lazarette. The meal went on in silence; when the Captain rose, so did the others, and Ser Brog touched Lalette's arm to take her to the deck again. The spring air was fine, the stream-bank all tricked out in tender green. Lalette looked (and felt with a thrill of delight that all was really now spring for her, she was free from the old life and everything to win), but Ser Brog was speaking.

"I am sorry to dream," she said.

"Why, dreams do be what we grow by. I would be saying that you had brought luck and fair weather on our leave-taking—for all but Tegval."

"The one sent from his breakfast?"

"He." The cargo-overseer laughed. "Our third mate is an admirable young man, with only one flaw—that he has discovered how admirable he is and does not stint his own admiration."

(The third mate would give her the book.) Said Lalette, watching a tall unpainted barn without a window that walked slowly past along the shore; "Yet your captain seemed very harsh with him for so light a fault."

"Oh, that is only the rule of the sea. On a ship one learns early that in this world there is no such thing as following one's own desire; it is all a pyramid of orders."

"You are grim."

"No, I only see things as they are." Now he began to make remarks which she must have answered, for he smiled and continued (but now her mind had leaped far away, and she was wondering whether she would see Rodvard again ever, or recover her Blue Star? Bound out to sea and away; it was his fault, who had given her unfaithfulness and desertion in exchange for the offered kindness and the abandonment of her mother. And now she wondered why she had embarked on the counter-witchery without even questioning whether she should; she felt a tear behind her eye, and hoped he had

come to know what resources of fidelity and good will he had
lost in her. No, not again, I'll never let another have the
making of my joy.)

A whistle was blown; men moved along the deck of the
ship, and Tegval came toward them with his cap insouciantly
on one side to be presented. He had the same look of inner
peace as the Amorosians of the conventicle, but mingled with
it an air of dash and recklessness.

14

The Eastern Sea; The Captain's Story

I

A frond of white had spread across the sky as they talked.
Lalette went to her room in the round covered-house that
rose from the deck, and applied herself to the needle.
Making the new dress right was a problem, since she had
done little but broidery before, and she became so taken with
fitting and clipping as not to note the tick of time; then felt
drowsy, and lay down to be roused by a knock at the door.

It was Tegval, third mate. "Man I lead you to supper?"
The ship had no motion when they reached air; here they
were in the middle of a brown-blue tide, with flat shores
stretching to green-blue on either flank. Tegval helped her
graciously down the stair, and was this time prompt enough
so that all of them were waiting when Captain Mülvedo
came in. This officer was now at ease, cracking his face into
a smile for Lalette and trying to converse with her about
people a demoiselle of condition might be expected to know.
Some of them she did know, but was forced to avoid the
issue lest he learn the falsity of her name.

Tegval offered her his arm after the meal, and showed her
around the deck as far forward as the tri-mast, his discourse
being of the parts of the ship and the beauty of the sea. He

would answer little when she asked him about Brog, the Captain and other personalities, and as evening was now beginning to grow shadowy, with a hint of chill, she announced an early return to her cabin. He leaned close as he handed her in the door and said in a low voice that he would knock at the fourth glass of night with a book, then tipped a finger to his lips to prevent questions (and she realized that even on a ship trading to Mancherei, it was not too well to be an Amorosian).

With no desire for sleep, she stretched out on the bed and tried to solve her riddles—how it was that her mind should turn to the seldom-felt nearness of Rodvard. There had been about him the faintest trace of some odor like that of old leather, masculine and comforting. She was a little irritated at herself for feeling the lack of it, and her mind drifted off through other angers till she lay there in the dark, simmering with wordless fury over many things; the ship began to move. The change in circumstance made her conscient of what she was doing; she began to weep for her own troubles, the tears trickling into the hard pillow where her face was buried, thinking that after all Rodvard had perhaps been right to slip away from a witch with so vile a temper.

There was a lamp hanging from a kind of pivoted chandelier. She swung out of the bed to light it, but had to strike more than once to obtain a good spark. By this time there was the queerest feeling in her stomach as though it were turning; she lay down again, not sure whether this was the over-robust supper she had eaten or the veritable malady of the sea. Orderly stampings and the sound of shouts drifted through the cabin's small window as her illness declared itself more firmly; she was miserable, her mind going round like a rat in a slat trap until a whistle was blown four times and someone knocked at the door.

Tegval, of course, with an overjacket on that swung as he stood balancing to the motion of the ship on widespread feet. "We sail on a fair and rising wind," said he, in a lilt. "Good fortune. Are you troubled by the sea, demoiselle?"

"I am—ill." (Hating to confess it.)

"No matter. Give me your hand."

It was taken in both his in a manner curiously impersonal, the eyes were closed and his lips moved. They opened pale blue. "You will be well," said he and sat down on the chair which, for the first time, she noted as bolted to the floor. She did not believe him and the swing of the lamp made her dizzy (and now she could feel his personality reaching out toward her with an effort almost physical, and was enough ashamed of her former angers to put into her tone some of the kindness now felt toward the race of man):

"You are most good. I was told you would have a book for me."

He undid his lacings and produced from beneath the jacket a volume, large, flat and all bound in blue leather with the royal coat of arms of Dossola on it to indicate who was the author. "You should not let it be seen," he said. "Our cargo-overseer takes the law's letter so seriously that he would denounce his best friend—which I am not."

"You may count on me." Their fingers touched as he handed it to her, no longer impersonal, and she let the contact linger for a brief second, before leafing over the pages. They were printed in heavy-letter with red initials. "What a beautiful book!" she said.

"It is the word of love," he said. "A true word, a good word—" chopping off suddenly as though there were more it would be imprudent to tell.

"I will read it." She did not want him to go quite yet and sought for words. "God knows, I need some help in the tangle of my life."

Said he: "We make a distinction between the god of evil and the God of love, in whose arms we may lie secure from the savagery that infests the world. Ah, inhumanity! Today a plover lit in the rigging, and what must they do but net that bird to be eaten by the captain. I could barely consume my supper for thinking of it."

Lalette stirred. "I do not understand this feature of your doctrine. One must often go hungry by thinking so, it seems to me. Do we not all live by the death of other beings, and even a plant suffer when it is devoured?"

Tegval stood up. "In true love, as you will learn, all are

parts of one body, and must give whatever another needs for sustenance. Read the book and sleep well, demoiselle."

He was gone, and to Lalette's surprise, so was her illness.

II

It was a strange book, cast in the form of a marvellous tale about a young man whose troubles were manifold, and only because he sought at each step to control his actions by reason, as he had been taught; it seemed that reason forever deceived him, because something would arise that was not comprehended in his philosophy, but was born from the natural constitution of an imperfect world. Thus reason always led him into doing evil, from which he would only be rescued by rejecting reason for affection to his fellow-men. Lest the reader should miss any part of the thought, he who had set this down abandoned his romance from time to time to draw a moral, as: "None can turn from vileness to virtue but those unbound by the teaching of the academies that consistency is a virtue."

Lalette found such interjections an annoyance, but forgave many of them for the beauty of the words, which were like a music; and the great glory of the descriptions of clouds, trees, brilliant night, and all the things that one person may share with all others, but were polluted (said the author) when the one would hold them to himself. Yet the type of the volume made it hard reading, the swing of the lamp made it flicker, so after a time she turned out the light and drifted to sleep.

By morning the ship was leaning through long surges under a grey sky with all her sails booming. It was hard to keep food on the table; at breakfast Captain Mülvedo rallied Lalette hilariously, saying she was so good a sailor he must send her to the masthead to run ropes. Brog smiled at her paternally; the first mate, whose ears moved at the end of a long jaw as he chewed, laughed aloud at the Captain's light jest, and offered to teach her to direct the steering-yoke. On the deck she felt like a princess (that this adventure would succeed after all, glad that she had done with tortured

Rodvard), with her hair blowing round her face and salt spray sweet on her lips. The waters set forth an entrancing portrait of sameness and change; she turned from the rail to see Tegval all jaunty, with his eye fixed bow-ward, balancing lightly.

Said Lalette; "I would be glad to know what witchcraft it was you used to cure me so quickly."

"No witchcraft, demoiselle," said he, not turning his head, "but the specific power of love, which wipes out misery in joy. And now no more of this."

The ship heaved; she would have lost her balance but that he put out a hand to sustain her, and the Captain's voice bellowed: "Tegval! I will thank you to remember that an officer's duty is to watch his ship and not the pretty ladies. You will do better in the forward head."

He had come unobserved upon them; now as the third mate made a croak of assent, he touched his cap to the girl. "No disrespect to you, demoiselle. You know the legend old seamen have, ha, ha, of sea-witches with green hair that speak to the spirit of a ship and witch her to a doom that is yet ecstasy for her crew? Be careful how you handle the people of my ship; for at sea I have the rights of justice and can diet you on bread and water." He shook a finger and ruffled like a cock, laughing till all the loose muscles of his face pulled in loops.

"But my hair is not green," said she, falling into the spirit of his words for very joy of the morning (but thinking with the back of her mind—what if he knew I am a witch? and—this one can do nothing for me; why am I here?).

"There was a mate with me once," he said, "in the old *Quinada* at the time of the Tritulaccan war, which you are too young to remember, demoiselle." He ducked his head in a kind of bow to emphasize the compliment. "Yeh, what a time of it we had in those days, always dodging from one port to another, and afraid we'd be caught by a rebel cruiser or one of those Tritulaccans and finish our years pulling an oar under the lash in the galleys of an inshore squadron. A dangerous time and a heavy time; you cannot imagine the laziness of some of these sailors, demoiselle, who will see

heir own lives sacrificed rather than keep a sharp watch. I
lo remember now how we were making into the Green
slands in broad daylight, when I found one of them sound
sleep, cradled in the capon-beam forward, where he had
peen set as a lookout—and in the Green Islands, mind you,
vhere armed vessels would lie in among the branches to
pounce on you.

"Yet you shall not think it was an exciting life, demoiselle,
or the thing no one will ever believe is that in war you go and
go, attending death with breakfast and nothing ever happen-
ng, so that it is almost a relief to fight for life. This mate
now—what was his name? He was always called Rusty for
no reason I could ever plumb, since his head was not rusty at
all, but dark as yours—well, Rusty, the mate, you could
hardly call him handsome, but he was gay and lively and had
a good tongue. Always telling stories he was, of things that
happened, and the good half of them happened to other
people, though he took the name of it. But bless you, nobody
minded, he would carry off the tale so well. I call to mind
now one night when we were both together at the home of
Ser Lipon, that was our factor, Rusty started right in with
the story of a polar-bear hunt in the ice beyond Kjermanash
that I had no more than finished telling him about the day
before, just as though he had been in the center of it.

"I sat with my mouth open, but never saying a word,
because it had not happened to me, neither, and beside, the
Lipons had a daughter, a pretty little thing named Belella,
who seemed as much doting on Rusty as he on her, and it
was no part of my game to spoil him, since I was spoken for
already, y' see? So he told the story of the polar-bear hunt
and soon enough the two of them were off in an angle of the
parlor, and within a week they were married."

Brog approached, touching his cap. "Your pardon, Captain," he said. "There is a trouble among those bales of wool.
I can find but six marked for your account, whereas by the
papers it should be thrice that number."

Mülvedo frowned. "Ah, pest, I am engaged." He took
Lalette's arm tight under his own. "See me later, Brog."

They moved a few steps away, the captain steadying her

against the shuddering heave of the sea. "That was his name
now, Piansky, though why he should have been called Rusty I
never could see. They were married, as I said, after one of
those lightning courtships we sailors have to make because
we have no time for any others, and they went to live in a
big house in Candovaria Square, which the old man had
built, and some said it was a cruel waste of money for just
the two of them. But I could never follow that, since she was
the only daughter, so she would have come into the whole
inheritance in time, and she was only getting what would be
hers.

"One voyage Rusty missed while they were building their
nest, but after that he came back to us, happy as a rabbit,
and well he might be with a fine wife, a good home and his
fortune made. It was about that time my own wife died;
Rusty took me home to be with him while the ship lay over
for a new cargo. Dame Belella always had a great deal of
wine and a house full of people, different ones always, to
whom Rusty must forever be telling some tale of his adventures. She would laugh at the ridiculous parts and look proud
over him. They were very gay; at least up to the time of the
Tritulaccan war, which I was speaking of.

"I remember going to Rusty's house after the second or
third voyage in that war, and a dangerous running passage it
was, too, out with wool to the south and back with goods for
the army, but our captain had judged where the Tritulaccans
would be, and we never saw a sail of them. That was the passage where we slipped through the Green Islands, as I have
said. We reached Rusty's house late in the evening; the parlor
was already full with people sitting drinking round the fire,
and Dame Belella stumbled as she got up to embrace him,
which shows how much cargo she had taken aboard already,
ha, ha. She let him take her place while she sat down on his
lap, saying we must be quiet because here was Ensign Glaverth of the Red Shar, who had been on a raid right through
the Ragged Mountains, and was just telling about it. I did not
think a thing at the time, since this Glaverth was sitting on
the floor with his back to a red leather hassock, and besides
he was one of those Glaverths from Ainsedel, the family they

call the mountain Glaverths, to distinguish them from the
ducal branch.

"He was telling how he had requisitioned a bed in a
Tritulaccan farmhouse where there was a daughter, and
made love to her, so that she told him of an ambush that had
been set for the Shar. As I said, I had no hint that Rusty
would take it ill till he suddenly interrupted the tale by
throwing his cup into the fire and crying that he would have
no more of this southern red, which he called hog's water and
traitors' wine, but wanted the honest fiery beverage of the
north.

"Two or three of them laughed and Dame Belella put her
finger over his lips, and after that she had called the servitor
for fired-wine, she begged this Glaverth to go on with his
tale. When he had done and they were all murmuring to ask
him questions, Rusty pushed his wife off his lap as though she
had been a sack of meal and stood up next to the fireplace,
with his own cup in his hand.

"'You sows of soldiers,' he said (begging your grace,
demoiselle, but he said it so); 'You sows of soldiers talk of
your perils, but they are not real dangers at all, only what
you could meet with on a city street and solve with a strong
arm or a little straight talk, or'—well, I will not say what else
he said, demoiselle, but it was something that made all those
in the room to gasp, if you know what I mean, and at least a
third of them wearing coronet badges.

"'Yah!' Rusty said, 'Your Tritulaccan wenches! What
could they do at the worst but slip a steel splinter in your
back, so that you go to Heaven with the Church's blessing for
the glory of old Dossola? But the harridans we seamen must
deal with could cost a man his soul and eternal agony. Even
now I may be a lost man—a lost man.' I remember how he
said it, putting both hands to his face with a sob, and
somebody dropped a cup. They all thought Rusty taken with
wine, d'you see, and so did I, but now he began to tell a long
tale, with no sign of winishness at all in his voice.

"It was all of our voyage to the south through the Green
Islands and I swear to you, demoiselle, had I heard it before
I sailed, I would not have sailed at all, so gruesome he made

it, with escapes from storm and Tritulaccan raiders and all this only a prelude to telling of a thing he said happened in the Green Islands, where we lay becalmed one night, and he walked the deck. He said then he heard a sound like faraway singing, and the ship began to move without a wind. Going forward, he said, he saw something like pools of green fire in the water; therefore knew the ship was approached of sea-witches who were carrying her on. Would have let go the brow-anchor, he would, but all the men of the deck watch were staring over the side, so little obeying him that they even shook off the hands he laid on them. The song went to his own heart and he knew that the ship and all in it must soon be doomed; therefore, he, Rusty, who still had some part of his wits, conceived the measure of going forward to say they could have him as a willing victim if they would release the rest. This was accepted, he said. One of the demon women clambered to the ship through the rope-hangings and companioned with him all night, then bade him farewell with the word that he must come to her again.

"Demoiselle, I do tell you that never have I heard Rusty give a tale better. But when it was finished, the Ensign Glaverth took Dame Belella's hand to bid her good night, saying that he would bring his young cousin over to hear some more of Rusty's tales, and all the others began to go as well. When all were departed, Dame Belella came to sit on the hassock where the Ensign had been, staring into the fire for a while. 'Will you never become a man?' she asked her husband when he would have touched her.

"He looked at her a little. 'Have I said the wrong thing?' he asked, and was that not a strange question to put?

"'The wrong thing, yes,' she said, looking away into the fire, without as much as turning her head. 'I couldn't like it any more, even if it were not true, Rusty.' I remember that, because I did not understand and still do not.

"He did not say anything more at that time, but I noticed that people were not coming to the house so often as before during this stay of ours in port, and while we were on the next voyage, she sold the place and went out in the west to live. So I think perhaps, it was a good fortune to lose my own wife, though a great sorrow at the time, because people do change and grow apart instead of together."

A wave-crest came across the bulwarks and wetted the edge of Lalette's dress a little, so that she moved against the supporting arm. Said she (wondering why he had told her this tale); "But she must have known that he only made it up about the sea-witches."

"That could be, could be, now. Could be that she was angry with him for saying so much to a coronetted man like that Ensign Glaverth. But I think more like that just all of us want a new bed-partner now and again, and she could not bear it that he thought of it before her."

15

Charalkis; The Door Closes

I

Brog leaned back and lifted up his cup. "As human people age," he said, "the most important part of the body does gradually move northward from organ to organ, beginning with the feet, on which you will notice a baby's attention always fixed, and ending with old men who do nothing but sit still and let thoughts go through their heads. Now I have myself reached the comfortable age of the stomach, for which I give thanks."

"Yaw," said the first mate through a mouthful of food. "Ye'd put Ser Tegval lower down."

"A wee lower, yes." Brog looked at Lalette. "But do not trouble you; in my capacity, I am charged with the duty of bringing all cargo to port as safe as it left."

A smile twisted his face into the cartography of a river-furrowed mountain chain, and he swivelled round to look hard at Blenau Tegval. The first mate gulped once and said;

"Saving always captain's orders, ser cargo-overseer. Captain has rights on a ship at sea."

Lalette stood up, her body swaying with the slow drift of the slung lamp overhead, and asked permission to leave, having learned that it should be asked. The laugh began before she reached the deck, Brog's dry snicker beating time to the first mate's guffaw. She had so little lost her resentment at their remarks and the suggestion that she was spied upon that when Tegval tapped on her door in the break of twilight as usual, she cried through the wood for him to begone. But the horror of lonely hours took her before she had more than issued the words; she leaped up, opening the door and calling that she must consult him, he was to come in. This was a mistake, too; there immediately arose the question of what she was to consult on; and after a blank word or two, she could do no better than ask what the Prophet's book meant by denying reason?—when it seemed to her that only a reasonable person would read it at all.

"Ah, no," said the third mate, sitting down and taking her hand in his (which she did not mind). "It is the failure of human reason and human love that drives us to the higher love."

(Though she thought this might be true in her own case, and could even look forward with a little exaltation to the new life in Mancherei, she was unwilling to break the talk by admitting it, so) she said: "But Blenau, how can this higher love make up to us for sorrow?"

On this he somewhat unexpectedly demanded to know whether she believed in another life than that visible, and it was at her lips to say that a witch could hardly do otherwise when he saved her by hurrying on:

"Well, then, this other life itself must be Love for us, since we are its children; and since this is so, it will replace all we have lost, and more beautifully, as one does for a child. If you have lost a lover—as I think you must, or you would not be for the Myonessae—it is only that you may find a better."

(To Lalette it seemed that this was hardly more than half true, and ice-cold counsel for a smarting heart); she started to say something, but just then the door was tapped, and here was Brog, with a smile that showed all his teeth.

"Ah, little demoiselle, I thought to entertain you from being alone, but see there was no need for my trouble."

He leaned against the wall, babbling at a great rate and not without salt, seeming to take delight in Tegval's frown, which also filled Lalette with so much amusement that she felt herself sparkling at Brog's conceits on such matters as—can a fish swim backwards? The young man grew grimmer, and at last rising, said he must rest if he were to be a good officer in the night watches. Brog did not stay long after.

It was still early in the night; she lay back among the covers to consult with the book again, but after her good cheer in the company, found the volume mere gloominess and dull as could be. Wondering what her manner of life in Mancherei would be like if all were ordered by such a volume, and feeling the despair of a bird bruising its wings against a cage of circumstance, she found happiness forever elusive. This escape and that slid across her mind, but all was either dream or half-dream; and as the rising wind began to rock the ship, she fell asleep.

Waking was blended with wonder that one creak among the many from the straining vessel should have roused her; then she became fully sentient, catching the reason. That single sound had come from her own door. Her lamp had gone out. "What do you wish?" she called on a rising note, and in the black heard three waves slap the ship before there was an indrawn breath and an answer not higher than a whisper; "Dearest Lalette, I have come to be your lover."

Tegval. "No," she said. "I do not wish it."

He was close. "But you must; to refuse the gift of love is to lose all. You are of the Myonessae." (Oh, God of gods, again, she thought; do men want nothing but my body? The temptation flashed and passed to give him this and live within the confines of her mind.)

"No, I say. I will cry out." She writhed away from his couch, but he found her in the narrow space, the arm pinned her close and his head came down on her breast as he said, thickly; "But you must, you must. I am a diaconal and I have chosen you. I will tell them in Mancherei."

His grip was so strong that it paralyzed, but he did not for the moment attempt to go further. Scream? Would she be heard above the rocking wind? "No," she said, "no. Ser Brog will hear. The Captain."

"It is the watch to daybreak. No one aboard will ever know."

"No, no, I will not," replied Lalette, (feeling all her strength melting), though he did not try to hold her hands or to put any compulsion upon her but that of the half-sobbing warm close contact, (somehow sweet, so that she could hardly bear it, and anything, anything, was better than this silent struggle). No water; she let a little moisture dribble out of her averted lips into the palm of one hand, and with the forefinger of the other traced the pattern above one ear in his hair, she did not know whether well or badly. "Go!" she said fierce and low (noting, as though it were something in which she had no part how the green fire seemed to run through his hair and to be absorbed into his head). "Go, and return no more."

The breathing relaxed, the pressure ceased. She heard his feet shamble toward the door and the tiny creak again before realizing; then leaped like a bird to the heaving deck, night-robed as she was. Too late: even from the door of the cabin, she could see the faint lantern-gleam on Tegval's back as he took the last stumbling steps to the rail and over into a white curl of foam.

A whistle blew; someone cried: "A man lost!" and Lalette was instantly and horribly seasick.

II

"I will tell you plainly, demoiselle," said Captain Mül-vedo, "that if it were not for Ser Brog saying how he saw with his own eyes that this young man moved to the rail without your urging, I should have been most skeptic. As things stand, I must acquit you of acts direct. As for others, as employment of the Art, they are a matter for a court of

Deacons, and since you are bound to Mancherei, you'll be beyond such jurisdiction." He stared at her gloomily. "As captain of this ship, and therefore judge in instruction, I must ask you to keep your cabin until we reach port."

Lalette looked at the moving gullet of the first mate as he stood by the Captain beside the bed, and even this sight seemed to make her the more ill. Said Brog's voice, dry as a ratchet; "Aye. You have my word for it. The little demoiselle never touched a hand to him as he went over. But he came from her cabin."

"No more rehearsing of things known. We know all except what she will not tell us," said Mülvedo. (Her body ached all over from lying in the one position.)

"Aye." It was Brog again. "Yesterday he was all quick with life, maybe a little hasty, but a kindly, helpful young man, and now the fishes are tearing pieces of his guts out." Brog's face wrinkled in what might have been a smile, had there been any mirth in it.

She turned her face away and began to retch, but nothing came up beyond a few drops of spittle, bitter and sour.

"Not nice to think on, no," said Brog. "But nicer than the mind that would bring such a death to the lad; there's the real, black, stinking hell."

(The bird of Lalette's mind felt the bars shift in tighter, she wanted to cry and beat with her hands.) Said Captain Mülvedo; "Ser Brog, I have acquit this demoiselle of direct acts. You will oblige me by not questioning as though the matter were still to decide. If this were the Art, no jurisdiction lies in us."

"You are my captain, and I am therefore even under your orders, even as to this court of the ship," said Brog, his thin lips closing sharply. "But I am master of the cargo, of which she forms a part, and it is my province to know what kind of goods I deliver."

(Lalette had a sense without seeing it directly that the chandelier swung twice as she looked at the three and thought—the truth? But how to explain about the trip, what Tegval had done, how he had demanded the deepest fruit of love as a casual thing like a cup of water, dragging her down?) "Ah, no," she said in her dying voice, and swallowed again, turning eyes of misery toward the Captain.

He frowned (and she knew it for a frown in her favor, and knew the reason for it and hated him and herself). "Ser Brog," he said, "I now declare the court shut. This demoiselle is not cargo but a person."

Brog's wrinkles ran deeper; the three passed out, the Captain remaining till latest, to pat her hand on the coverlet. Revolt ran through her veins at kindness for the wrong reason, which was worse than hate or anger; there was no understanding in this seaman who only wanted to change bed-partners now and again, she was afloat on a sea of desires.

The daylight swung from powder to deep dusk. One knocked, and it was the gnome-like creature who stewarded for the Captain, who offered her a bowl of broth. The motion of the ship being a trifle easier, she was able to eat a little and hold it, in spite of the shadow that lay across her mind. (But I will not regret, she cried inwardly, and then one-half her mind played critic to the other and cried—no, no. Is there no surcease?) The hours slid by along a silent stream, and she was alone.

III

All movement ceased. Sickness dropped from her like a veil, and from beneath burst such a joy of spirit as Lalette had rarely known, so that she could have sung herself a song, as she almost leaped from her place to put on the new dress. There was no mirror and she had to feel the strands of her hair into the demoiselle's knot, hoping the result would not look too recklessly wild. Outside the deckhouse, shouts and confused, orderly trampings were toward, but no one came to call for her until long after she had packed everything into the small trunk, with the book Tegval had given her at the bottom. The door was tapped; Brog, followed by a man with a red peaked hat and a fur of sidewhisker, who held an annotation-roll in his hand.

"This is the Demoiselle Issensteg," said Brog (and Lalette

reflected incontinently that it was hard to distinguish an appearance of melancholy in a face from one of dissipation). "I transmit her to you. She is recommended from Ser Kimred, the residentialist at Netznegon." He handed the man in the hat a folded letter. "It is my duty to warn you that in this ship she has been confined on suspicion of man-murder through witchery. In the home country, I would have brought her before a Court of Deacons."

The dunnier bowed, as unsmiling as Brog himself, then with his annotation-roll as a wand, touched Lalette on the arm and her little trunk. "This is not Dossola, but Mancherei," he said. "Subject to the regulations of the realm of Mancherei, and the association of the Myonessae, we accept her charge and her possessions." Then, turning to Lalette; "In the name of the God of Love, come with me."

(Knowing barely the name of these Myonessae, unwilling to ask more lest she somehow tip over the razor-narrow bridge of safety) Lalette only smiled and turned to the door. A plank-way led to the dock; the sun shone yellowly upon a row of wharfside houses, whose brick looked as though streaked with wet, while at many windows there was bunting as though for a festival, but much of it faded, miscolored or torn. As she watched, she brushed against a hand which had been held out to her and was beginning to fall in disappointment. Captain Mülvedo.

"I am sorry," she said, and took the hand.

"Farewell, demoiselle. I do not believe it. If you are not accepted here, I—that is—"

He seemed at the edge of tears, a droll thing.

"Thank you. I will remember your kindness." Brog was in the rear, looking right past her (and she had the dreadful feeling that when she was gone, he would have no trouble in bringing the Captain to his own point of view on her. This was goodbye to all yesterdays.). She mounted the plank for the shore.

There was a great press of people about, the men in loose pantaloons hanging over their shoes, and all walking about and yammering as fast as they could. They seemed reasonlessly excited, as though this were a day of crisis; Lalette could hardly make out a sign of that calm assurance that seemed to be the mark of the Amorosians in her own country. They stared at Lalette, the more when two of the guards who waited at the plank with short bills in their hands and the small "city" arbalests strapped to their backs, placed themselves on either side of her at a word from the dunnier, leading across to a building with a low door, over which was a shield painted thickly with something that might be a pair of clasped hands on a field of blue.

There was a door down the hallway rightward, with a little man at a desk behind it, writing laboriously, his tongue in his cheek, as the light struck over his shoulder. The guards led Lalette in; he jumped up and threw down his quill so rapidly that a blot was left on the paper. She noticed food-stains on his jacket.

"You must not interrupt, really you must not interrupt me unannounced," he said. "You are not authorized. I am a protostylarion."

His big pop-eyes with blue white seemed to swell as they fell on Lalette; one of the guards laid a paper before him saying; "A candidate for the Myonessae, on the incoming ship from Dossola. Orders of the dunnier."

"Ah, ah." The protostylarion was no taller than she herself as he came fussing importantly around the desk to move a chair two fingerlengths for her convenience, then diddled back to his place. The paper made him frown. "Ah, ah, suspicion of the Art. This does not happen often these days, but you are very fortunate to be here, demoiselle, instead of in Dossola. Ah—you have read the First Book of our great leader and Prophet? Answer me now, the misfortune of the loss of patrimony, why do you think that came upon him?"

(Not quite sure whether he meant the character in the book, or the Prophet's own ejection from the heirship of Dossola), Lalette said hesitantly; "Why, sir, I—I suppose it would be because he tried so arrogantly to increase it."

"Admirable, admirable. Whereas if he had given of it freely to the old aunt, it had been returned to him in high measure. From which we learn, demoiselle?"

(The jargon was distasteful, but) "That we must lovingly give all we have," said Lalette, remembering.

The protostylarion bounced up and down behind his desk as he went on, prompting her replies in his eagerness, so that it hardly mattered how little she had read of the famous First Book. A porter came blundering into the midst of the collo-quy with her trunk on a hook over his shoulder. This placed a period to the examination, for now the protostylarion fussed with his hands, said "Ah, ah," two or three times more, then to the guards; "You are released."

As the pair filed out, he drew from his desk a large ledger and a sheet of blue-colored paper, pointed his quill and said: "You — swear — that — whatever — of — the — Art — you — have — practiced — in — the — past — you — will — abandon — with — all — worldly — vanities — on — reception — into — the — high — order — of — the — Myonessae," all in one breath. Then, more judicially:

"Your name is—"

"Lalette—" (should she said "Issensteg?")

"Ah, you made an evasion! The God of love demands all truth from those who come to him."

She felt a cheek-spot heat at this nagging. "Asterhax. I have given you nothing but truth. If you doubt it I will return to the ship that brought me."

"Oh no, oh no, my dear demoiselle, you must not mistake. All pasts are buried in the world of love."

"Well, I have done that."

"And they will welcome you, I am sure, my dear demoiselle. Oh, the perfect peace." His pen went scratch, scratch, skipping from ledger to paper, the head cocked on one side as he surveyed the result from one angle, then another, as an artist might look at a drawing, and his smile approved. A fly buzzed in the room.

"So. Demoiselle Lalette, you are now registered of the honorable estate of the Myonessae in the service of the God of love." He trotted around the desk to hand her the paper, with a red seal on it. "Rest here, rest here, I will seek a porter to lead you to the couvertine."

(What would he say if he knew I am a murderess? she

thought, and followed this with a quickly-suppressed flash of
anger at Tegval for having made her one.) The protostylarion
came back with a porter who grinned at her fine new dress
and picked up the trunk. "Farewell, farewell," said the little
man, waving from where he sat. "You will hardly need a
carriage, it is not far." He was writing again as Lalette
followed the porter through the door.

A little recovered from her chagrins, she turned eyes about
the street to see what this strange law of the Prophet had
made of the country that was to be her new home. The
streets seemed wider than those in most of the cities of the
ancient motherland, but the new life would have little to do
with that, nor with the height of the buildings, which mostly
gave red brick for Netznegon's gloomy dark stone. The
shop-windows were full of goods; Lalette could hardly pause
to inspect, but from the distance, they had an air of meretri-
ciousness and false luxury. All the people seemed to be in a
great hurry; Lalette began to wonder what they would do if
she put a small witchery on one of these urgent passengers to
make him stand like a post—then shuddered away from the
thought.

The porter turned a corner and they were at the gate of
what had evidently been at one time a very handsome villa,
set back deeply from the street, with a low wall in front of
it. One of the trees in the foreyard was dead and another so
yellow among the spring-green leaves that it must soon go as
well. There was no gate-tender; the porter pushed his way in
and led up to the tall oaken double door, which showed scars
where an earlier knocker had been taken off and replaced by
one in the form of a sun with spreading rays. He knocked;
after a long minute an old woman opened on a darkish hall
with a pronounced odor of javelle, and asked what was
wanted.

"I am registered of the Myonessae," said Lalette, extend-
ing her paper.

"You must give it to the mattern," said the beldame. "Set
the box there."

"Two obulas," said the porter, and as Lalette produced
her purse, shot a swift, suspicious glance at the old woman.

"No. Not in Dossolan money. Do you want me to be thrown into a dungeon?"

Lalette flushed. "It is all I have; I only arrived from there today. Can someone change it for me?" She appealed to the woman who had admitted her.

"Certainly not. It is contrary to the regulation."

The porter rather surprisingly lost his temper. "Why, you cheap whore, you cheat, you pig-sucker!" he shouted. "I should have known better than to carry for one of you Myonessae." He stamped his foot. "I'd take your dirty box and throw it in the street, if I didn't know the smell would kill half the people in town when it burst open."

A door opened on a sound of feminine background voices. There appeared a woman in black, with hair piled severely close to her head. "What is this, Mircella?" she asked.

"Demoiselle is new. She came without two obulas to pay her porter."

The dark woman reached to the purse at her belt, drew forth coins and placed them in the porter's hand. "Here. You are never to appear at this couvertine again." She turned to Lalette. "You may come in and show me your paper. It is evident that you are in need of instruction."

As they passed into the side room, light fell on the woman's face, and Lalette saw that, although it was both strong and stern, it bore the same expression of distant peace she had seen in the widow Domijaiek.

16

The Eastern Sea: Systole

The queasiness had gone from Rodvard's stomach and the illness from his head, but all his senses were more alive than jets of flame. Every rut gave him agony in the jolting mule-

cart, he could not draw away from pain long enough for
anger or fear. Yet shortly the very keenness of his hurt
anaesthetized all down to no more than an aching tooth; and
now the senses, oversharpened by witchery, began to report
the world around him. They were passing two people afoot,
then another cart, to none of which the driver made salutation.

They must be out of the village, for right overhead, branches began to go past against a sky where horses' tails slid
across tender blue. A bird lit on one of the branches and
tipped its head to look down. It seemed to Rodvard as he
gazed into the single revealed eye that he could, with his Blue
Star, read the avian thought—of food and sex, confused,
and not unlike a human's. This might only be another effect
of the witchery, but it set him thinking about his own
confusion of mind and what the butler Tuolén had said
about Star-bearers and their women; so he considered what
species of joy or completeness was to be had from these
skirted creatures, who for a spiritless complaisance would
exact a slave's devotion.

Lalette. He wondered whether her witchcraft would give
her knowledge of his infidelity of thought with the Countess
Aiella, and of deed with the maid Damaris; and if so, what
penalty would be demanded of him. Ah, no; why should
penalty be due? This was not marriage, he had taken no oath
nor meant any. Give back the Blue Star, let us pronounce a
bill of farewell, and be damned to Mathurin and his menaces,
or even to Remigorius and the cause for which all was done.

The mule's feet klopped on a bridge, the clouds were
thickening toward grey above and birds chirping as they will
when a storm is toward. No, no, friend Rodvard, he answered himself; be honorable as you hope to receive honor.
Acquiescence she gave you, aye, beneath the trees; but you
half forced her then. The night in the widow Domijaiek's bed
was no unwilling gift, but for both of them the end of life
and its beginning. A new life with Lalette the witch, holding
the sweetness of peril, not that of repose, something beyond
any connection that might have been formed with Maritzl of
Stojenrosek. Had she laid some witchery upon him to make

it so, not being herself affected? Seek her out, anywhere; discover if that enchantment were forever.

Could such things be? Witchery was something which, like death, he had no more than heard of from the world beyond his world. When he was a lad in the village among the spurs of the Shining Mountains, there was the fat old woman who had grown so dreadfully thin, all in a week, and people saying it was witchery on her. The priest came with his oils, but it was too late, and she died the next day, and no one ever found the witch, if there were one. Oh, aye, there were prosecutions of witchery in town, and now the mule-driver's wife, Lalette, the Blue Star, and he himself caught into something he did not understand and which made him afraid ... and because he had done no more than cherish high ideals and obey orders.

The pains were less, but all his muscles so immobile that they afforded no yielding to the throw of the cart, and thus piled bruise on bruise. A long ride; it must be after the meridian of the sun, though even heightened perception would not tell him if this were so, since he had lost all sense of direction in the intricacy of the turnings. The mule's feet and cart's tires struck paving stones, the movement became uneven, voices were audible and they were entering a town, so that Rodvard began to hope of a rescue—and with that hope, a fear of what would happen if there were no rescue. What did the man mean to do with him? He found no visible answer, for though it was evident that though the repulsive spouses were minded for murders, and himself not the first to fall into their clutches, it hardly seemed they would have fixed the mechanician's badge on his breast in mere anticipation of disposing of a body.

Droll to think of oneself as a body—an idea he did not remember having held before, ever. His mind achieved a wedding between this line of thought and the earlier one, or how it was when that urge toward the Countess Aiella had slipped out of merely playing a part into deep desire, it was the voice of body speaking to body. But it was not that way on the widow's bed; that night it was as though a flame sprang up, to which their bodies responded last of all. Ah,

Maritzl (he thought), with you also there might have been such a union of flames, to last forever and ever, only I did not know, I did not dare, before the Blue Star had bound me to this other.

Now a certain brightening of the diffused light reflected into the cart told him they were passing houses with snow-white walls; by this, with the time and distance, they must be in Sedad Vix city. Odors floated to him—salt water, fish, the spicy products of the south, not unpleasantly blended. The docks. Was the man going to make him a body by heaving him into the sea? To his futile angers was added that of not being able to see the old rascal's eye—now the Blue Star had recovered its virtue under the witch-wife's ministration—but there was time for little more of thinking, for the cart drew up with a cry to the mule, the driver got down heavily, his feet sounding on stones and then on plank.

He was gone briefly; Rodvard felt the covering taken from him, and with a grunt, he was hoisted to a shoulder, stiff as a log. A whirling view of pallid dockside houses, the masts of a tall ship with her sails hanging in disorderly loops; he came down with a jar that shook every bone onto what appeared to be some structure projecting from the deck, where a red face surrounded by whisker looked into his own. One eye in the face was only a globule of spoiled milk; (the cold Blue Star on Rodvard's heart told him the good eye held both cruelty and greed).

"Yah," said Redface. "The fish is cold."

"I tell you now, live as an eel. Fetch a mirror."

Redface reached out a dirty-nailed hand and pinched Rodvard's cheek, hard. "Mmmmb. A spada's worth of life. To save argument, I'll give you two."

"Ey, look at him, a proved mechanician with a badge and all. I say to you, my old woman she has done with him so he'll work like a clock, pick, pick, never mind time nor nothing. A gold scuderius; you should give me two."

They chaffered horribly over his body, while Rodvard lay moveless as a statue (thinking of how he was one, alas not cradled in light and speed like the Wingèd Man to whom he had compared Count Cleudi when Cleudi marked the resemblance between them; not upborne by spirit like the figure of the archer-hero; but a stiff corpse, subject of a sale, a carcass, a beef). He heard the chink of money passing; the one-eyed man gave an order that Rodvard was to be taken below, and someone carried him awkwardly with many bumpings down a ladder to a tight room smelling of dirty humans. He was tossed high onto a kind of shelf and left alone for a long time (thinking all the while of what the mule-driver had said about his being witched to work like a clock, and wondering whether it were true).

After a while, a doze came upon him, for which there was no emergence till the round hole in the ship's wall had ceased to give light. The place filled suddenly then with feet and words, many of the latter with a Kjermanash accent, or in that language itself. One of these persons pointed to him and there was a laugh. Rodvard tried to turn his head, and to his surprise found it would move a tiny arc, though by an effort that redoubled the agony throughout the bruised mass of his body. Yet the stirring was a joy as great as any he had ever experienced, and he lay repeating it, as the assemblage be- low—garrulous as all Kjermanash—came and went with pan- nikins from which floated an appetizing perfume of stew. Rodvard found other movements beside his head, and lay repeating them through the twinge of pain. A whistle blew, some of the men went out and up, while the others undressed noisily, put out the light and composed themselves for sleep on shelves like that which bore the young man.

For him there was little sleep, and as life flowed along ankylosed muscles, he was invaded by a sense of irrevocable disgrace, so poignant that it drowned fear. Damaris the maid . . . he had sold his soul for a copper there . . . not that he felt to the girl any profound debt as to Lalette, or that such a debt were just—but whether from the priests' teaching at the academy, or the words of Remigorius, he had somehow grown into a pattern of life which, being violated, one was cast down into a sea of life by merest impulse . . . ah, no, should it not be rather that each event must be judged by itself? . . . and no, again—for by what standard shall one judge? Impulse or an absolute, there is no third choice.

So thinking, so seeking to find a clue to conduct (or to justify his own, merely, Rodvard told himself in a moment of bitterness), he lay on his comfortless couch, aware that the ship had begun to move with uneasy tremors; and presently dawn began to flower. At the room's entrance a lantern showed a bearded face, into which a whistle was thrust to blow piercingly. All the men leaped from their shelves with a gabble like a common growl and began dressing in the greatest haste. The bearded man shoved through them and shook Rodvard so rudely that he was jerked from his shelf, coming down thump on the deck, with feet that would not hold him.

"Rouse out!" said the bearded man, catching him a clout across the headbone. "You lazy scum of shore mechanicians must learn to leap when the mate sounds."

Rodvard staggered amid coarse laughter, but having no means of protest, followed the Kjermanash, who were scrambling rapidly up the ladder. They were in open sea; the breeze was light, the day clear and the air fine, but even so, the slight motion gave him a frightful qualm. His first steps were across the deck to the rail, where he retched up all that lay on his stomach, which was very little.

"You, what's your name?" said the bearded mate.

"Rodvard—Berg-elin."

"I call you Puke-face. Go forward to the mainmast, Puke-face, eat your breakfast if you can, and then repair the iron fitting that holds the drop-gear repetend. The carpenter's cabinet under the break of the prowhouse will give you tools."

"I—I cannot use tools. I am—a clerk, not a mechanician."

"Death and dragons! Come aft with me, you cunnilingus bastard!" The mate's hand missed Rodvard's neck, but caught a clutch of jacket at the shoulder, and dragged him along the deck to where a flight of steps went up, and the one-eyed captain stood, an ocular under his arm. "Captain Betzensteg! This lump of excrement says it knows nothing of mechanic."

Sick though he was, Rodvard felt the Blue Star burn cold and looked up into an eye (brimming with something more than mere fury, something strange from which his mind turned). "Diddled, by the Service!" said the voice, between heavy lips. "When next—ah, throw your can of piss up here."

Rodvard was jerked against the steps, striking his shin, and stumbled up by using his hands. The one-eyed captain reached out and ripped the badge from his breast, tearing the cloth. "Go below, stink-pot," said he, "and tell my boy he's promoted to seaman. You shall serve my table."

"Yes, sir," said Rodvard and looked around for his route, since all the architecture of a ship was stranger to him than that of a cathedral.

"Go!" said the captain, and lifted an arm as though to strike him with the ocular, but changed his mind. "What held you from telling your status?"

"Nothing," said Rodvard, and gripped the rail of the stair-head, for his gorge began rising within.

"If you puke on my deck you shall lick it up." The captain turned his back and shouted; "Lift the topper peak-ropes!"

Down the stairs again there were not so many ways to choose from, so he took to the door to the right (hoping under his mind that this would be an omen) along a passage and into a room, where a sullen-faced lad of maybe eighteen was folding a cloth from a table. "You are Captain Betzensteg's boy?" asked Rodvard, trying to keep from looking through the window, where the sea-edge rocked slowly up and down. "I am to say you are promoted seaman."

The lad's mouth popped open as though driven by a spring, he dropped the napery and ran around the table to seize Rodvard by both arms. "Truly? If you trick me—" For one instant pale eyes flashed fury and the small down before first shaving trembled. But he must have seen honesty before him ("Born for the sea and freedom!" his thought read), and quickly thrust past to make for the door.

"Stay," said Rodvard, holding him by the jacket. "Will you not show me——?" The spasm caught him and he retched, mouth full of sour spittle.

The lad turned laughing, but without malice, and clapped him on the back. "Heave hearty!" he said. "It will come better when you come to learn the free way of the ocean; grow to love it and care nothing for landlouts. Here are the linens." He opened the midmost of a set of drawers built into the wall. "The old man takes no napkins save when there are guests aboard—a real dog of the brine, with fish-blood in his veins, that one! I am called Krotz; what's your name?"

Rodvard's telling, he hardly seemed to notice, but continued his flood of instructions. "In these racks are the silvers; he uses only the best, and be careful at dinner to set his silver bear on the table, it was given him by the syndics at the time of the Tritulaccan war for his seamanlike skill. The bed-bunk you must carefully fold in at the base, but he likes the top loose, so. Wine always with the early meals, it is here. If the weather's fair, he sometimes takes fired-wine in the evening. If he orders it so—"

The lad Krotz halted, looked sidewise out of his eyes and leaned close. "Hark, Bergelin, I am not what you would call jealous. Have you ever—that is, when he has fired-wine, he may desire to treat you as his lover."

"I—" Rodvard recoiled, and retched again.

"Ah, do not be so dainty. It is something that every true seaman must learn, and keeps us from being like the land-louts. You do not know how it can be, and he gives you silver spadas after. But if you will not, listen, all the better, when the old man calls for his fired-wine, set the bottle on the table, take away the silver bear, and call me."

Said Rodvard (no little astonished, that the emotion of which the Blue Star spoke was indeed jealousy); "No. I'll have none of it, ever."

A smile of delight so pure that Rodvard wondered how he had thought the lad's look sullen. "The cook will give you breakfast. I must go—to be a seaman."

Captain Betzensteg ate by himself. Rodvard was glad that he remembered the silver bear, but when he tried to hold forward the platter of meat as he remembered seeing Mathurin do it for Cleudi, he got things wrong, of course, and the one-eyed man growled; "Not there, you fool. The other side." The meat itself was something with much grease, pork probably, which it sickened Rodvard even to look at as the captain chewed liquidly, pointing with his fork to a corner of the cabin and declaring he would barber someone of his ears unless it were kept cleaner. That night there was no call for fired-wine; Rodvard felt a surge of gratitude for preservation as he cleared up after the meal, and made his way forward to the crew quarters in what he now had learned to be the peak-jowl.

Sickness sent him to his shelf at once, for the movement of the ship was becoming more vivid as twilight fell, but sleep had not yet reached him when there was a change of duty, as in the morning, and of those who came tumbling down the ladder, Krotz was one. He was much less the lord of the earth than earlier; no sooner was the lad in place than all the Kjermanash were after him unmercifully, with hoots and ribald remarks, pinching his cheeks and his behind, till at the last the lad, crying; "Let me alone!" flung his arms out so wildly that he caught one of the sailors a clip on the nose and sent him staggering. The fellow snarled like a tiger, all his rough humor dissolved in black bile, and recovering, whipped out a tongue of steel. But Rodvard, without knowing how or why he did so, rolled from his shelf onto the shoulder and arm that held the knife, bearing the man to the floor.

The Kjermanash fought upward; Rodvard took two or three nasty blows on the side of the head, as he clung with both his hands to the dagger, and knew with more interest than fear that he must lose in the end to the overbearing strength of the man. But just as he was giving way, a pair of hands beneath the armpits wrenched him clear and flung him against the shelves, while a big foot kicked the knife.

"What's here?" demanded the voice of the bearded mate. "Puke-face, you'll have a dozen lashes for this, damme if you don't! You to attack a full-grade seaman!"

Said Rodvard, feeling of his head; "He would have knifed Ser Krotz."

"Ser!" The mate barked derision, and his head darted round like a snake's. "Is this veritable?"

All the Kjermanash began cawing together; the mate appeared to comprehend their babble, for after a minute or two of it, he held up his hand with; "Shut up. I see it. This is the sentence—Vetehikko, three days' pay stopped for knifing. As for you, Puke-face, your punishment's remitted, but in the future, you'll sleep in the lazarette to teach you your true status aboard this basket."

He turned to the ladder, and not a word from the Kjermanash for once, but as they glowered among themselves, young Krotz came to throw his arms around Rodvard. "I owe you a life," he said, at the edge of tears.

Said Rodvard; "But I will pay for it."

"Ah, no. I—will surely buy you free."

"I did not know there was status aboard a sea-ship; you said the life on one was free as a bird."

"Why, so it is, indeed, but not for lack of status, which is the natural order of things. Are you an Amorosian?"

It nearly slipped off Rodvard's lips that he was rather of the Sons of the New Day, but Krotz' words showed how little he would find such a confession acceptable, and he did not trust the Kjermanash; and by another morning, the ship's motion told on him somewhat less heavily.

17

Charalkis: The Depth and Rise

I

It would be maybe on the fourth day out (for time had little meaning on that wide blue field) when Rodvard remarked how at the evening meal Captain Betzensteg took more than usual wine, glowering sullenly at his plate while he jabbed a piece of bread into gravies as though they had done him a harm. The last mouthful vanished, he sucked fingers undaintily and without looking up, said; "Set out the fired-wine."

Rodvard felt a cold sweat of peril. The silver bear leaped from his fingers, and it was his fortune that he caught it before it reached the floor. The captain sat with eyes down, not appearing to notice. Bottle clacked on table; the one-eyed

man poured himself a deep draught, and at the sound of the
door opening, said; "Stay."

Rodvard turned. Both the captain's hands were on the
table, gripping the winecup and he was staring into it as
though it were a miniature of his beloved. "Come here."

(Fear: but what could one do or say?) Rodvard glided to
his post in serving-position behind the chair. For a long
breathless moment no sound but the steady pace of someone
on the deck above, muted slap of waves and clatter of ship's
gear. Then the head came up, Rodvard saw how the rich lips
were working (and in that single eye read not only the
horrible lust he had expected, but that which gave him
something akin to pity, a ghastly agony of spirit, a question
that read; "Shall I never be free?" Captain Betzensteg lifted
the cup in his two hands and tossed off the contents at a
gulp, gagged, gave a growl of "Arrgh!" and, reaching up his
left hand, ran it pattingly over Rodvard's buttocks.

"No," said the young man under his breath, pulling away.
The captain jerked to his feet, violently oversetting his chair,
and with distorted face, drove his fist against the table.
"Idiot!" he cried. "Do you not know your benefit?" and
reaching to his purse, tossed clanking against the bottle a
handful of coins. Rodvard shrunk away, and giving a kind of
mewing cry as the one-eyed creature leaped, tried for the
door. His foot caught something, he took three desperate
lunges, gripped the handle as the huge fist caught the side of
his head and spilled him through onto the deck, senseless.

II

When next he knew, there was a sour smell of wine, it was
dark and dripping sounded. He could not think through the
curtain of headache; the scampering was undoubtedly rat,
but why? Where was added to why with slowly gathering
memory—still on the ship certainly, since the bare boards on
which he lay heaved with a slow and even beat.

The right side of his neck was sore, and the opposite
soreness was on his head. He thought: ah, for why am I so
punished? and heaved himself upon an elbow to find a panni-

kin of water by his side, which he drank greedily. It was dark, a kind of velvet twilight; yet not so dark that he failed to make out that he lay prisoned in a narrow passage between tall casks that rose on either hand, groaning in their lashings. The quantity of light must mean day was outside, and he had lain a long time. Now he came afoot and wondered whether he should seek the deck, but decided contrary, since someone for some reason had brought him here, and there might be perils abroad. Sleep? Ah, no. He sat down to think out his situation, but could make no sense of any part, therefore abandoned the effort, and with a tinge of regret over his lost books, let his mind run along the line of Iren Dostal's sweet rhymes until tears reached his eyes.

This could not occupy him forever, either; a profound and trembling ennui came on him, so his fingers made small motions tracing out an imaginary design. A long time; a step sounded, coming down from somewhere and then along among the casks. Krotz. He said:

"You must be careful. Oh, do not make a noise. He would hurt me if he knew I helped you. Here."

In the gloom something was thrust against Rodvard's hand which, by the touch, he knew for a dish of congealing food. "What is it?" he asked. "I was struck and lost remembrance."

"You truly do not know? I thought it was feigned when you failed to speak as he said you were to be thrown overside, and he took the young Kjermanash—." A shout sounded flatly from above. "Oh, I could hurt him. I must go." The last words went dim as Krotz disappeared among the tall columns of casks and Rodvard was left to his meditations. The food was a stew of lamb, and it tasted like candle-grease.

Dark had come before the lad did again, with a meal even worse than its foregoer; trembling and unwilling to talk. Rodvard found himself fingering round the great casks from one curve to another, counting the planks in them and thinking whether there might not be some mathematical relation in the figures he counted. A futile thing to do, he told himself, wishing he had Dr. Remigorius' philosophy, who often spoke of how a man should be complete in himself, since each one lives in a self-built cell of pellucid glass and may touch another only with, not through, that veil. Ah, bah! It is not true (he thought); I have been touched sharply enough by this very Remigorius, but for whom I'd not be in such a coil, with Lalette and Damaris, ideals thrown down, and on a mad voyage to nowhere. . . . There was something wrong with this, on which he could not put the finger—so now he fell to counting the planks again, or try to make a poem, ending the effort with an inward twitter, as though mice were running under his skin, as he waited, not with patience, for the next arrival of Krotz with his purloined food.

The lad was faithful, but always looking over his shoulder; trembling so that it was nearly impossible to get two consecutive words from him, by which it came about that there was no plan for Rodvard's escape when the word was that Charalkis Head had come in sight. The ship would lie that night in the harbor of Mancherei's brick-built capital, and what counsel now? Shifting his feet like a dancer, Krotz said he thought Rodvard might easily slip past the deck-guard into the water; but this scheme split on the fact that he lacked the skill of swimming. All was still undecided that night; a sharp sword of apprehension pricked his fitful sleep, nor were matters amended when he was fully roused by hammering over the doors of his prison.

Kjermanash voices sounded their customary cackle. A shaft of light struck down, so brilliant that Rodvard's dark-hooded eyes could scarcely bear it, and he shrank back along the cask-alley, hands over face. It was not the best means of hiding; down swung one of the Kjermanash to fix the tackle for lifting out the cargo, gave a whoop and pounced, being presently joined by other sailors. There was much laughter and excited talk in their own language; they patted Rodvard and tweaked the long-grown hair on his face, then urged him up the ladder deckward, with "Key—yip! Kee-yup!" and a sheath-knife that banged him in the crotch from behind as he climbed, blinking.

At the top he stumbled out on a deck where the mate stood, wrinkling eyes against the sun. "Puke-face, by the

Service! I thought you had been fish-farts long ago. Ohé, captain! Here's your cheating mechanician!"

Now Rodvard noticed that Captain Betzensteg was a few paces beyond, talking to a man in a decent grey jacket and a red-peaked hat, but wearing no badge of status. The one-eyed monster turned, and his full lips twisted. "Put him in the lazarette with chains, since he's so slippery. We'll have the trial at sea."

The single eye looked on Rodvard (and it said one thing only—"Death.")

The young man staggered; he cried desperately: "I appeal."

"A captain's judge on his own ship. I reject your appeal. Take him away."

Said the man in grey; "A moment, Ser Captain. This is not good law for the dominion of Mancherei, in whose authority you now stand. We have one judge that stands above every mortal protestation, that is, the God of love, whose law was set forward by our Prophet."

The captain snarled, black and sour; "This is my ship. I order you to leave it."

The man in the grey jacket had a thin, ascetic face. One eyebrow jagged upward; "This is our port. I order you to leave it without discharging a single item of your cargo."

"You dare not. Our Queen—"

"Has no rule in Mancherei. That was tried out at the time of the Tritulaccan war. Young ser, what is the ground of your appeal to our law?"

(The Blue Star was cold as cold on Rodvard's heart, but there seemed a bright shimmer like a haze in the eyes that met his, and not a thought could he make out through it.) He said; "Because the captain of this ship would be both jury and accuser."

"He lies," growled Betzensteg. "My underofficer is the accuser, for that this man refused to repair a drop-gear."

"That is a question of fact, to be decided by a court which can gain nothing from the decision," said the man in grey, calmly. He swung to Rodvard. "Young man, do you place yourself in the justice of Mancherei, to accept the rule and decision of its authority?"

"Oh, yes," cried Rodvard (willing to do anything to escape the terror of that baneful optic).

The man in grey produced a small paper scroll and touched Rodvard lightly on the arm. "Then I do declare you under the law of the Prophet of Mancherei; and you, Ser Captain, will interfere at your gravest peril. Young man, take your place in my boat."

III

Rodvard was motioned to the bow of the craft, from which floated a banner with a device much resembling a dove, but it was in the false heraldry of grey on white, and hard to make out. Spray was salt on his face; as they reached a stone dock a ladder was lowered down, and he would have waited for the grey man, but the latter motioned him imperiously to go up first.

The pierside street hummed with an activity that to Rodvard seemed far more purposeful than that of languid Netznegon, with horses and drays, porters bearing packages, men on horseback or in little two-wheeled caleches, pausing to talk to each other under the striped shadows thrown across the wharfs by a forest of tall masts. Their clothes were different. From a tavern came a sound of song, though it was early in the morning. (It seemed to Rodvard that most of the people were more cheerful than those of his homeland; and he thought it might be that the Prophet's rule had something to do with it.)

"This way," said one of the barge-rowers, and touched him on the arm. He was guided across the dock and up to a pillared door where persons hurried in and out. "What is your name?" asked the grey man, pausing on the step; made an annotation, then said to the rower guide; "Take him to the Hawkhead Tavern and see that he has breakfast. Here is your warrant. I will send archers for the complaining mate, but I do not think the court will hear the case before the tenth glass of the afternoon."

"I am a prisoner?" asked Rodvard.

The other's face showed no break. "No; but you will find it

hard to run far. Be warned; if you are not condemned unheard, no more are you released because the accuser overrode his right. The doctrine of our Prophet gives every grace, but not until every debt is paid and the learner finds by what it was he has been deceived."

He made a perfunctory salutation and turned on his heel. Rodvard went with the rower, a burly man in a shirt with no jacket over it, asking as he strode along; "What was it he meant by saying I'd find it hard to run far?"

The face composed in wrinkles of astonishment. "Why, he's an Initiate! You'd no more than think on an evasion when the guards would be at your heels."

Rodvard looked at him in counter-surprise (and a shiver ran through him at the thought that these people of the Prophet might somehow have learned to read minds without the intervention of any Blue Star, a thing he had heard before only as a rumor). "What!" he said to change the subject. "I see no badges of status anywhere. Is it true that you have none in Mancherei?"

The man made a face. "No status in the dominion—at least that is what the learners and diaconals say in their services." He looked across his shoulder. "They'll give you status enough, though, if you hold to their diet of greens and fish. Bah. Here we are."

The breakfast was not fish, but an excellent casserole of chicken, served by a red-faced maid, who slapped the rower when he reached for her knee. He laughed like a waterfall and ordered black ale. Rodvard hardly heard him, eating away with appetite in a little world of himself alone (hope mingling with danger at the back of his mind), so that it was a surprise when the rower nudged him and stood.

"The reckoning's made for you, Bogolan," he said. "Come the meridian, you've only to ask for bread and cheese and beer. Go out, wander, see our city; but do not fail to return by the tenth glass; and take notice, your Dossolan coin will buy nothing in shops here, it is a crime to take such monies."

He swaggered out. The last words recalled Rodvard to his penniless condition, and he looked along himself uncomfortably, seeing for the first time how the black servant's costume he had from Mathurin was all streaked, dirty and odorous, with a tear at the breast where the badge had been wrenched off. There was no desire to present himself to the world in such an appearance. He shrank back behind the table into the angle made by panelling and the tall settee to think and wait out his time, watching the room around him. On the floor of the place, the press of breakfasters was relaxing; maids were deliberate over clattering dishes, calling to one another in strong, harsh voices. He could not catch the eye of any to use his Blue Star in reading her thought, which might have been a pastime; and his own affairs were in such suspense and turmoil that thinking seemed little use. After a while the shame of merely crouching there overcame that of his garb, so he got up and went outside.

The town was in full tide, and noisy. There was no clear vista in any direction, the streets lacking Netznegon city's long boulevards, angling and winding instead. The buildings were set well apart from each other. Rodvard feared being lost among the intricacies of these avenues, therefore formed the design of keeping buildings on his right hand and so going around a square, crossing no streets, which must ultimately bring him safely to his starting-place.

The district was one of houses of commerce, mingled with tall, blank-faced tenements. A droll fact: there were no children in sight. In the shop-windows were many articles of clothing, so beautifully made they might have been worn by lords and princesses. He did not see many other goods, save in one window that displayed a quantity of clerks' materials, rolls of parchment, quills and books, nearly all finely arabesqued or gilded—which set him to wondering about what manner of clerks worked with such tools.

The inn swung round its circle to present him its door again. It was not yet the meridian, therefore he crossed the street and made another circuit, this time reaching a street where there were many warehouses with carts unloading. Round the turn from this was a house of religion, with the two pillars surmounted by an arch, as in Dossola, but the arch was altered by being marked with the device of a pair of clasped hands, carved in wood. A man came out; like the one who had rescued Rodvard from the ship, he was dressed in grey. The look of his face and cant of his head were so like the other's that Rodvard almost spoke to him before discovering he was heavier built. The grey clothing must be a kind of uniform or costume.

A wall bordered the grounds of this building, with a cobbled alley, which had a trickle down its middle. Rodvard followed it, pausing to look at wind-torn placards which lay one over the other, proclaiming now a festival for a byegone date, the departure of a ship for Tritulacca, a notice against the perusal of the latest book by Prince Pavinius, or a fair for the sale of goods made by certain persons called the Myonessae, a new word to Rodvard. The alley at length carried him to face the inn again. He wished for a book to beguile the time, but that being a vain desire, went in to seek his former place. Not until he sat down did he see that the nook opposite him was occupied.

It was a little man, hunched in a long cloak, so old that his nose hooked over his chin, making him look like a bird. Before him was a mug of pale beer; he was deep in thought and did not look up as Rodvard sat down, but after a moment or two sipped, smacked his lips and said; "Work, work, work, that's all they think of."

Said Rodvard (glad of any company); "It does not do to work too heavily."

The gaffer still did not elevate his eyes. "I can remember, I can, how it used to be in the Grand Governor's time, before he called himself Prophet, when on holy days we did not labor. And we going out on the streets to watch processions pass from Service with the colors and silks, but now they only sneak off to the churches as though they were ashamed of it, then work, work, work."

He drank more of his beer. Rodvard was somewhat touched by his speech, for though he was hardly one to defend Amorosians to each other, it was just these processions in silks while so many were without bread that bore hard on Dossola. He said; "Ser, it would seem to me that no man would worry for working, if he could have his reward."

The old man lifted his eyes from his mug (Rodvard

catching behind them a feeling of indifference to any reward but calm) and said; "Silence for juniors, speech for seniors."

One of the maids approached; Rodvard asked for his bread and cheese and beer, and drew from her a smile so generous that he looked sharp (and saw that she would welcome an advance, but the thought at the back of her mind was money). The ancient shivered down into his cloak again, not speaking till she was gone.

Then he said; "Reward, eh? What use is your reward and finding money to spend when it buys nothing but gaudy clothes and a skinfull of liquor, no credit or position at all? Answer me that. I tell you I would not be unhappy if we went back to the old Queen's rule, and that's the truth, even if they send me to instruction for it."

"Ser, may I pose you a question?" asked Rodvard.

"Questions show proper respect and willingness to be taught. Ask it."

The food came. Rodvard nibbled at his cheese and asked; "Ser; is it not better and freer to live here where there is no status?"

"No status, no," said the old man, gloomily. "And there's the pain, right there. In the old days a man was reasonable secure where he stood, he could look up to those above and share their glory, and we had real musicians and dancing troupes as many as a hundred, who made it an art, so that the souls of those who watched them were advanced. Where are they now? All gone off to Dossola; and now all anyone here can do is work, work, work, grub, grub, grub. It is the same in everything. I can recall how joyous I was when I was a young man in the days of the Grand Governor before the last, and received my first commission, which was to carve a portrait bust for Count Belodon, who was secretary financial. A bust of his mistress it was, and I made it no higher than this, out of walrus ivory from Kjermanash, as fine a thing as I ever did. But now all they want is dadoes for doorways. No art in that."

"Yet it would seem to me," said Rodvard, "that you have some security of life here, so that no man need go hungry if he will labor."

"No spirit in it. Will go on, men working like ants till one day they are gone and another ant falls into their place. No spirit in it; nothing done for the joy of creation, so they must have laws to make men work."

He went silent, staring into his beer, nor could Rodvard draw more words from him. Presently a young lad with long, fair hair came peering down the line of booths until he reached this one, when he said that the old man, whom he addressed as grandfather, must follow him at once to the shop, where he was wanted for carving the face of a clock.

18

Decide for Life

I

It was like no court Rodvard had ever seen. Behind a simple table sat two of the men in grey, their features calm and strangely like each other. At the end, one with an inkpot and sheets of paper before him wrote down Rodvard's name as it was given. The guards at either side carried no weapons but short truncheons and daggers at the belt. The burly mate was already in one chair, looking truculent, with a pair of Kjermanash sailors beside him, one of them a fat-faced lad, unhealthy of appearance. A man of negligent air, richly dressed, occupied the end of the table opposite from the writer. There were no other spectators and the proceeding began without ceremony when one of the Initiates asked simply what was charged against Ser Bergelin.

"Mutiny," said the mate. "I gave the rat a task to do, which he flatly refused."

The well-dressed man said; "It is Dossolan law that cases of mutiny at sea be tried by the captain of the ship, who bears judicial powers for this purpose; else mutiny would spread through a ship. I would have your writer here record that I make formal demand for the body of this criminal, in accordance with the treaty of amity and respect between your nation and the Queen, my mistress."

One of the grey men said calmly; "Be it recorded. Record also that the treaty declares none shall be delivered before the adjudgment of guilt, for though we be all criminous, it is not love's desire that men shall exploit each other for anything but sins determined as such by the word of human law."

(The well-dressed man's eyes said utter disgust.) His lips said; "How can there be an adjudgment before trial? It is to try him that we demand him."

The second Initiate spoke. "This young man has placed himself in the protection of the domain of Mancherei. Before he is delivered for trial there is required proof of a wrongdoing that would merit sentence. Is there such proof?"

"Why, damme, yes!" said the mate. "I saw the fellow do it; I heard him refuse my order. Here are two of my crew to say as much." He swept a hand toward the Kjermanash, who began to cackle at once, but the first Initiate merely nodded to the writer, who laid the pen down and clicked at the pair in their own tongue. When they had answered, he said; "They declare it is true that Ser—" he consulted his sheet "— Bergelin was ordered to repair a mast, and he refused."

The Initiate looked at Rodvard (and not a thing could he read behind those cold eyes, though they seemed to pierce him through), saying, "The evidence is sufficient for a trial unless you can contradict it."

Said Rodvard; "I could not make the repair. I did not know how."

The Initiate; "That is a question for the trial to determine; no reason for not hearing the case."

The mate guffawed. Cried Rodvard, in despair; "But sers, this captain—I pray you . . . it is not for this . . . he is . . ."

"You shall clearly speak your trouble; for it is the will of love that nothing is to be hidden."

Rodvard felt the rosy flush light up his cheek. "Well, then, it is not for any failure of duty that this captain pursues me, but because I would not be the partner of his unnatural lust."

With an exclamation, the ambassador of Dossola brought his hand down on the table, and the hard-faced mate gave a growl, but the Initiates were as unmoved as mountains. One of them said; "No lust is more natural or less so than another, since all are contrary to the law of love, and the soul in which love runs full tide may and should give to this unreal world of matter all that it desires, without imputation of sin. Yet we do find that if the wrong cause for this trial has been stated, there is a basis of appeal to our law. We would hear of this further."

He signed; the writer spoke to the Kjermanash, while the mate glared venom at them, his glances darting from one to the other. The seamen seemed hesitant, especially the fat young one, to whom the writer chiefly addressed himself. Though Rodvard could not understand a word, the voice-lilt told clearly enough how the tale was going. Now the lad began to catch at his breath and sniffle, saying a few more words. The mate's head turned slowly round (hardest murder staring from his eyes), while his hand slid, slid toward belt and knife—

"No!" cried Rodvard. "He's going to kill him!" The mate leaped snarling to his feet, bringing out the knife with the same motion, but Rodvard's shout had quickened the guards. One stepped forward, striking with his truncheon, while the other seized his man from behind, arm around neck. A roar from the mate, squeaks from the Kjermanash, and with a crash of heavy bodies, the big man was down and firmly held, cursing and trying to wring a broken hand. One of the Initiates said serenely; "This is an act of self-accusation"; then to the writer; "Do these also accuse?"

"Yes, Brother. The lesser one says that he has been this captain's catamite and that Ser Bergelin was cabin-keeper to the captain and must have been solicited to such purpose, for this was his custom with all. They say further that an order was given to throw Ser Bergelin into the sea. Further, they say they were instructed as to what they should report on the repairing of the mast."

"Love is illumination," said the Initiate. His companion; "Our decision is that this mate shall pay a fine of ten

Dossolan scudi for ruffling the peace of this court; but for having brought false accusations against one under the protection of the Prophet, he shall be submitted to detention of the body and instruction in doctrine until such time as the court shall release him."

The mate gave a yell. "I protest," said the well-dressed ambassador, "against the condemnation of one of our gracious Queen's subjects on perjured evidence and as the result of the actions of one who is not only himself a criminal, but a provocator of others."

"Your protest is recorded. We declare the business of this case has been dispatched." The two Initiates rose as though their muscles were controlled by a single mind, but as the Dossolan rose also and the guards frogmarched their prisoner out, one of them looked at Rodvard. "You will remain, young man," he said.

II

They sat down again. One of them said; "Be seated," and the pair stared at him unmoving with those impassive eyes. The inspection lasted a good three or four minutes; Rodvard itched and hardly dared to squirm. One of them addressed him:

"You bear a Blue Star."

(It was not a question, but a statement; Rodvard did not feel an answer called for, therefore made none.)

"Be warned," said the second Initiate, "that it is somewhat less potent here than elsewhere, since it is the command of the God of love that all shall deal in truth, and therefore there is little hidden for it to reveal."

"But I—" began Rodvard. The Initiate held up his hand for silence:

"Doubtless you thought that your charm permitted you to read all that is in the mind. Learn, young man, that the value of this stone being founded on witchery and evil, will teach you only the thoughts that stem from the Evil god; as hatred, licentiousness, cruelty, deception, murder."

Now Rodvard was silent (thinking swiftly that this might be true, that although he was no veteran of this jewel, it had never told him anything good about anyone).

"Where is your witch?" said one of the Initiates.

"In Dossola."

"It will be impossible for you to return there with the case of today's court standing against you, and the mate of your ship in our detention, by our necessary action."

"Perhaps, in time——" began Rodvard.

"Nor can you well bring her here," said the other Initiate. "The practice of witchery is not forbidden among us as it is by the laws of your country. But we hold it to be a sin against the God of love, and it is required that those found in witchery undergo a period of instruction in the couvertines of the Myonessae."

(A wild wave of longing for Lalette swept across him, drowning the formless regret of leaving behind the Sons of the New Day—a new life—an empty life— "No spirit in it," the old man had said.) Before Rodvard could think of anything to say, one of the Initiates spoke again:

"All life in this material world is a turning from one void to another, and shall be escaped only by filling the void with love. And this is the essence of Spirit."

(A jar like a fall from a height told him that he was facing men who could follow his thought almost as clearly as he could that of others, and Rodvard half thought of how the butler at Sedad Vix had said it was possible to conceal one's thoughts; half wondered what these strange men wanted with him.) The strong, resonant voice went on; "It is not the thought of the mind, but the purpose of the heart for which we seek; for the mind is as material as the world on which it looks—a creature of evil—while the other is arcane."

Said the second Initiate, as though this matter had now seen settled; "What is your profession?"

"I am a clerk. I was in the Office of Pedigree at Netznegon."

"Here we have no pedigrees. Soil-tillers are needed; but if you lack the skill or desire for such labor, you may serve in

he commercial counter which places for sale the products of
he Prophet's benevolence."

"I think I would prefer the second," said Rodvard (not
really thinking it at all; for tillage and commercial clerkship,
he held to be equal miseries, yet the latter might offer a
better chance of release).

The Initiates stood up. "We will inform the stylarion at the
door, who will find you harborage and instruct you where
you are to report for work. You must give him your money
of Dossolan coinage, which he will replace with that of ours."

"But I have no money of any coinage, none at all," said
Rodvard.

The two stopped in their progress toward the door and
turned on him faces which, for the first time, were struck
with frown. One of them said severely; "Young man, you
have evidently been under the control of the god of Evil.
Unless this financial stringency disappears, we shall be required to order that you take doctrinal instruction; and it
were better if you did so in any case. The stylarion will give
you a warrant for new garments and your other immediate
needs, but all must be strictly repaid, and within no long
time."

They left. Rodvard thought their final remarks a very
strange pendant to the generosity they had otherwise shown;
and wondered unhappily whether he would ever see Lalette
again.

III

The lodging assigned was in a room over the shop of a
tailor named Gualdis, at a corner where three streets ran
together. The man had a fat wife and three daughters, one of
whom brought from a cookshop on the corner a big dish of
lentils and greens with bits of sausage through it, from which
they all ate together. The girls chattered profusely, curious as
so many magpies about Rodvard and how life was lived in
Dossola, for they were too young to remember when Prince
Pavinius had turned from Grand Governor to Prophet and
the Tritulaccan war began.

Rodvard liked the middle one best; called Leece. She h
thick and vividly black eyebrows that gave her eyes a spar
when she laughed, which was frequently. (The Blue Star te
him that behind the sparkle crouched a kind of dumb qu
tion whether he might not be the destined man, and t
thought of being sought by her was not unpleasant to hi
but she turned her head so rapidly and talked so much th
he could make out no more.)

After he had been shown to his bed, the usual sleeplessn
of a changed condition of life came to him, and he began
examine his thoughts. He felt happy beneath all, and dou
ing whether he were entitled to, searched for some bac
ground of the sense of approaching peril which had held h
the night Lalette came to his pensionnario door, and ag
when he spoke with Tuolén the butler. But it was nowhe
all seemed well in spite of the fact that he was more or les
prisoner in this land. The common report had it that this w
not an unusual experience, that Amorosian agents circulat
all through the homeland, recruiting for their own purpos
especially those with any touch of witchery, and he thou
that might be true. The Initiate on the ship had taken h
very readily into protection, and if he were like those in t
court, must have known that Rodvard bore a Blue Star.

Yet it seemed to him that these Amorosians were so w
disposed toward each other that one might do worse to li
out a life among them, in spite of a certain unearthlin
among their Initiates. Now also he began to look ba
toward Dossola and to understand why it was that Ma
cherei should be so hated, most particularly by the upp
orders. For it seemed that if he could but return, persua
Remigorius, Mathurin and the rest how the people of t
Prophet lived among themselves, the Sons of the New D
might fulfill their mission by striking an alliance in Ma
cherei. No, never (he answered himself); that would be to s
the son above the parent, the colony over the homeland, a
politic would never permit it.

Yet was it not cardinal in the thinking of the Sons of t
New Day that to hold such a thing wrong was in its
wrong? The evil in the old rule was that it set one man abo

another for no other reason but his birth. Was not Pyax the
Zigraner, with his odd smell and slanted eye, entitled to as
much consideration as Baron Brunivar? Why not then, up with
the standard of Mancherei and its Prophet? For that, what
had Pavinius found so wrong in this place that he had
deserted the very rule he founded?

Rodvard twisted in his bed, and thought—of course; I
have been slow indeed to miss the flaw. For though there
were no episcopals here, the Initiates surely filled their office.
If freedom from tyranny were won only by making episcopals into judges, then it was only a viler slavery. Was life,
then, a question of whether spirit or body should be free?
But on this question Rodvard found himself becoming so
involved that he went to sleep, and did not wake till day
turned behind the shutters.

Leece brought him his breakfast on a tray and wished him
a merry morning, but when he would have spoken to her
said she must hurry to her employ. (Her eyes had some
message he could not quite read; if the Initiates were right,
it would be a gentle one, and kindly.) His mind was more on
her than on his new fortune as he went forth, and he missed
a turning in the streets, so that his task began badly with a
tardy arrival.

The building of his toil, like so many in Charalkis, was new
and of brick, with mullioned windows along the street front
and a low, wide door at one side, through which carts passed
empty to pick up bales at a platform within. Rodvard entered
to see a row of clerks on stools sitting before a single long
desk and writing away as though for dear life. A short, round
man paced up and down nervously behind them, now and
again speaking to one of the writers, or hearing a question
from another.

This short man came over to Rodvard and looked up and
down his length. "I am the protostylarion," he announced.
"Are you Bergelin, the Dossolan clerk? You are in retard by
a third of a glass. The fine is two obulas. Come this way."

He led down to the inner end of the desk, where under the
least light stood a vacant stool. "Here is your place. For the
beginning, you have the task of posting to the records of

individual couvertines from those of the general sales
ships. Here—this is a ship's manifest from a voyage
Tritulacca. Three clocks from the couvertine Arpik, as y
see, have been sold for eight reuls Tritulaccan. You will o
a sheet for Arpik, on which noting this fact, one sheet
each couvertine, then place a mark here to show that
matter is cared for, not pausing to translate—yes, Ivrigo?"

The interrupter held his ledger in hand and diddled fr
foot to foot, as though being held from a cabinet of ease. "(
Ser Maltusz, I crave pardon, but I cannot carry throu
this posting according to system until I have a ruling
where falls the sea-loss in such a case."

"Hm. Let me see—why, stupidity, look there! It is plai
stated that no offer had been made on the said lost bal
They were therefore couvertine goods still, and not regard
whether the loss were caused by piracy or not, it must
there." He turned back to Rodvard. "Do not try to transl
into our money, for that is the function of another. You
expected to finish this manifest by evening."

"I have never done this—"

"Work is prayer. There is the lamp."

19

Two Choices

I

The stern-faced mattern's name was Dame Quasso; s
told Mircella to show Lalette to a small brown room ang
by a dormer, where a bed with one blanket, a chair and
chiffonier were the only furniture.

"The dress-room is down here," said the servant, pointi
"The regulation is that all demoiselles stir themselves toget
at the ringing of the morning-bell, so that the day's tasks m
be assigned."

"Why?" said Lalette, sitting down on the edge of the bed
so glad to hear a voice without malice or innuendo in it that
he words hardly mattered).

The eyes were round and th mouth was round; a series of
ounds. Said Mircella; "It is the regulation. . . . You must
dress your best for evening. It is the day of the diaconals."

"Ah?"

"Oh, some of them are quite rich. We will have roast meat
or supper. Wouldn't it be nice if one of them would take
ou way up in the mountains?"

Lalette felt her heart contract. "What do you mean?" she
asked. "I am from Dossola, and this is all new to me."

"Why, the diaconals. Those learners who are in the second
stage, almost Initiates, so they can't be married, and once a
month they come—"

"Mircella!" came Dame Quasso's voice, impatiently.

"I must go. You won't have to work today. You never do
on the first day."

Lalette thought: what trap am I caught in? It was a
diaconal that Tegval said he was, and that he had chosen me,
that horrible night when—when—. A fierce surge of anger
burned through her at the widow Domijaiek, who had babbled so of love and God, yet brought her to this dubious
esort; and once more, as when she stood in the mask-
maker's parlor, there was the feeling of being hemmed in by
metal walls. But before her fury could rise to the performing
of the black witchery already forming at the back of her
mind, the door was tapped and a toothless old man brought
in her chest and said Dame Quasso awaited her attendance.

The entrance broke a spell; Lalette was inwardly assuring
herself there was some mistake, the thing might be better
han appearances, while the mattern began in the most ordinary way to ask her what work she had done or might be
fitted for. At last Dame Quasso said:

"I do not know what you Dossolan girls are trained for by
your mothers, except marriage to counts. No one of you can
earn the worth of her clothing. You know nothing; but I will
place you with the stitchers who work on linen till you have

learned something better. You will find your witchery of lit
value here. I suppose the charge is justified?"

Lalette stamped her foot (all the fury returning at t
treatment). "Madame," she cried, "as I was brought up,
girl sold into prostitution had already earned the worth
her clothing and something else beside."

There was a silence, in which the cool, hard eyes did
change, nor the face around them (and Lalette had t
sensation that if she looked into them any longer, she wo
drown). Dame Quasso said; "Sit down. . . . We have had gi
like you before, and always they make me doubtful of th
who admit you to the company of the Myonessae. Nevertl
less, it is our task, who conduct these couvertines, to see t
you are instructed to a better way of life. Listen attentive
there is in this domain of Mancherei and in our honora
order no question of prostitution, which concerns those w
sell for money what they should give for love. But it is t
wise ordinance of our Prophet that they who would attain
the state of Initiates shall not marry before quitting tl
material body for that life which is the God of love. F
marriage is viewed with approval by the old churches
though it were something to be desired. Yet it is but a licer
to serve the god of Evil, in whose armory no weapon is
potent as the propagation of further mankind into this bod
world, which he wholly rules. Therefore it is ordered tl
when one who has reached the diaconal estate is overcor
by the desires which the god of Evil has placed in all flesh,
shall seek out the Myonessae, choose one, and cohabit wi
her for as long as they both will. It is a matter of free choi
and no compulsion. Yet during such time, the diaconal is r
allowed to continue his studies, thus standing in danger
never becoming Initiate, but of dying and being reborn ir
some ugly form, as a serpent or an insect."

Said Lalette, nipping a lip in her little white teeth; "A
what of us, who merely satisfy the lusts of these men?"

From severity, the mattern's face turned to astonishme
"Why, this is the very service of love, that we offer o
bodies, not in exchange for the sustainment a man gives
and the satisfaction of our own desires, but in the name

the love of God, that all may benefit by learning the vanity of earthly wishes."

"I was not told of this, and I do not think I like it."

Dame Quasso's face turned stern again. "Very well," she said in an iron voice. "There are some who will not accept instruction. I will have the account made up of what ʼou owe for the passage here. When it is paid, you may have ι porter take your box wherever you please."

(Where, indeed? And how pay? Panic mingled with the ιnger that boiled anew in Lalette's mind.) "Ah," she said, ʼyou talk of love and holiness, and—" then burst into tears, ʼeaning forward with her hands covering her face. The mat-ʼern came around and placed a surprisingly gentle hand on the ʒirl's shoulder.

"My child," she said. "It is not I nor the Initiates of Mancherei that place you under hard compulsion, but this material world, in which the god of Evil has all power. All you have learned, all you have gained through witchery is straight from hell. Return to your room; meditate what I have said until supper, when some of the diaconals will come, and see for yourself whether it is as sour a fate to be of the Myonessae as you now think."

II

Rodvard had no meal at noon (lacking money), his eye-balls ached from toiling under lamplight, and the others had finished their eating when he reached the Gualdis' shop. The dame's voice was not very pleasant (the Blue Star told him she hoped he was not going to be as much trouble as— something he could not make out). But Leece and Vyana, the oldest daughter, reheated for him some of the stew in a casserole, and made to entertain him by asking him about his work. (When he told them it was casting accounts for the Myonessae, there was something behind Vyana's eyes that came to him as a shapeless whirl of fear and desire, but he could neither draw her thought more clear, nor cause the subject to be pursued.)

Now the talk turned to Dossola, and especially to Count

Cleudi, for the whole family became much excited when the learned Rodvard had actually seen that famous person in th flesh and even worked for him. It took him several momen to realize that here in Mancherei he need not withhold h tongue, for these people thought the Count as great a villa as did the Sons of the New Day. Rodvard related the tric Cleudi had played on Aiella of Arjen (keeping his own nan out of it for a reason he did not quite know), whereupo Leece asked innocently what a "mistress" might be, and th elders laughed.

His own room was very small, with the window right ov the bed and only space for a garderobe, a cabinet and on chair. The next morning the girl brought his breakfast ver early, and it needed no Blue Star to see that she wanted t talk, so he made her sit on the chair and took the tray acro his knees, as he asked why Vyana had been so strange abo the Myonessae the night before.

"Her sweetheart is a learner who has now become diaco nal and wishes to join the sisterhood. But father and moth want her to marry in the usual way." She leaned close and i a voice that was little above a whisper said; "You won't tel will you? ... But we are afraid he'll bring an Initiate t persuade them, and then he'll find out that father and moth really believe in the old religion, and he'll send both of the away for instruction, and all three of us will have to go in the Myonessae, and I don't want to."

(So many questions whirled in Rodvard's head that h could not find words fast enough; and all his senses wer tingling with the sudden nearness of Leece's red lips, th swelling breasts and the message that darted from her eye saying she was pleased with the same nearness, but not a Damaris the maid, she held herself high and....) He sai rather stupidly, not thinking of his words; "And why not? would think—"

She leaned back again; (the eyes went dead) the thic brows came together. "Ah, but you do not think like woman. We—we—want—"

"What, charming Leece?"

She flashed a smile which accepted his tiny apology an

announced they two would play the game so set in motion. "We want to be loved for ourselves, here in this world. There! I have said it. Now, when you make your fourth-day report before the stylarion, you have only to complain that I am out of the law of Love, and they'll send me somewhere for instruction, and you won't have to be bothered with my questions about Dossola."

"Defend the day! But tell me, Leece, is it contrary to the law not to be Amorosian?"

"Oh, no, you don't understand. It isn't that hard, really. Only the Initiates have to see that people don't do wrong things, and doing something wrong always begins with thinking, so they send people away for instruction when they begin to think the wrong way."

She rattled this off like a lesson learned. Rodvard said;

"But who decides whether the Initiates themselves are right?"

"Why, they have to be! They learn everything through the God of love, and one of them couldn't be wrong without the others finding it out. That was how they found out that the Prophet was falling under the power of the god of Evil, when he tried to change everything and had to leave us."

Rodvard picked at the bedcover for a moment (deciding it was as well to change the subject). "But tell me—why can't your Myonessae be loved for themselves? I am only two days here, and know so little about your customs."

"By the diaconals who choose them, you mean? Ah, no. All the Myonessae know they are only second choice. The diaconals have already chosen the service of the God of love first."

"Then the Myonessae are jealous of the church—or of your God of love?"

"Oh, no. Women think more spiritually than men. You must go to a service with me and then you'll understand." The corner of her mouth twitched slightly; she reached over to touch his hand. "I must go," she said, and was gone.

This was the beginning of a custom, by which she came to him each morning to be his instructor in all that concerned Mancherei. Once or twice fat Dame Gualdis wheezed up the

stair and smiled through the door at the two, wishing them
good morning as she went past on some errand, real or
pretended; she seemed to find it decorous that the girl often
sat on the edge of Rodvard's bed. Their conversation never
seemed to fail, and they took delight in minor contacts, as
when he showed Leece the fashion of sitting wrestle he had
learned as a lad, with each opponent gripping the other's
right elbow and only that arm engaged. Leece was so nearly
as strong as himself as to make the contest a true one (and
she was as greedy as he of the almost-meeting of bodies, as
the Blue Star told him. She would go a long way with him, it
said, perhaps all the way if pressed, but felt a little fearful of
her own desires, and would want him as a husband in
permanence. When she left, he would think of Damaris the
maid as he dressed, and how she also had sat on his bed, and
the end of that meeting, sweet and terrifying, how she had
killed his Blue Star, and how he would surely have been
trapped into some regular connection with her, had not circumstance ordered his flight from Sedad Vix. At this it
seemed to him, walking the street to his daily toil, that there
was nothing in the world so precious as that jewel and the
use to which it must be put, and he must reach Dossola
again, and by no means do the thing that would rob the Blue
Star of its virtue; and then he thought of the penalty Lalette
had promised, which lay at the back of his mind like a dark
cloud of dread. But as he took his place on his stool, the
thought came that he had already earned whatever penalty
there was. It was not credible that the accident of having the
Star's power restored by the old woman in the hut would
disannul what he had to bear; nor was it likely that the
restoration would hide his action from one possessed of the
witch-powers of the far-away girl to whom he was bound.
But why was he bound to Lalette? Now the sweetness of the
touch of Leece and the desire of her body ran through him
like a liquid fire, and he felt as though he were running
across a bridge no wider than a knife-blade over a yawning
chasm, toward a goal hidden in mist, and all his inner organs
were wrung.)

"Bergelin!" said the protostylarion. "You will remember that this work is given to you as a charity, which it will profit you not to abuse."

20

Inevitable

I

Another girl was already before the mirror in the dress-room, running a comb through fair hair; taller than Lalette. She looked over her shoulder at the newcomer with an expression not unlike that of a satisfied cat and went on with her task, humming a little tune; Lalette felt that she was being asked to speak first. "Your pardon," she said, "but I have just come. Can you tell me where the soap is kept?"

The tall girl surveyed her. "We use our own," she said, "but if you have not brought any, you may take some of mine tonight. In the black-dressing-box, there on the table— that is, if you do not mind violet scent."

"Oh, thank you. I didn't mean . . . My name is Lalette" (again the hesitation, a momentary question whether to say "Bergelin" here, but that was all dead and gone, she would never see him again) "Asterhax."

"My name is Nanhilde. We don't use second names in the Myonessae unless we have been married. Have you, ever?"

"I—"

"Oh, you must get rid of old-fashioned prejudices in a place like this. I used to think that being married was something I wanted so much; but it isn't really. It only chains you to some man, and next thing you know, you're sewing jackets and raising brats for him. You wait till you're chosen; he'll want to marry you and give up being an Initiate. They always do, and if you say yes, you're lost, not your own mistress any more, and he'll always blame you."

Lalette had been washing her face. Now she lifted it from the towel in time to catch the middle term of the series. "But are you—are we of the Myonessae prevented from having children, then?"

"You are a greenie, aren't you? Of course not; only we don't have to snivel around any man for their upkeep. There's a couvertine for that. I have one there now; the diaconal who fathered him on me had his miniature painted and I'll show it to you. Hurry with your dress and we'll go down together. Old quince-face doesn't like anybody to be late."

She took Lalette's arm and guided her along a hall already powder-grey with dusk, to the stairwell, where the racking note of a violin floated in a funnel of light. Below, it was all so different that Lalette had seen it in the morning, or even at noon, when she had eaten a rather gloomy meal of pulse and one apple, while the others around her chattered in a subdued manner under the eye of Dame Quasso. The whole place was now gay with lamps and someone had hung spring branches among them, under which girls were gathered in excited little groups, some of them talking to young men, the ruffles of their dresses vibrating, as though they too had caught the mood of animation. Among the moving heads Lalette could see how the double doors of the eating-hall were flung wide; at its entry the mattern stood, talking with a white-headed man dressed in grey, whose expression never changed. Dame Quasso beckoned; as Lalette worked her way in that direction, a voice floated past, ". . . I told her he already said he would choose me, and I don't care if I do lose my place, I'm going to ask for an Initiate's trial. . . ."

The eyes looked down into hers from a height. "This is our newest member, called Lalette," said the mattern. "She is from Dossola, where she was accused of witchery, and she is somewhat troubled in mind."

A long gaze. The grey man said; "It is because she feels compelled and has not learned the wonderful freedom of the service of the God of love. My child, witches find it harder than anyone else to forget the material self, but once they do so, attain the most surely to perfection."

(Perfection? Lalette wanted to cry that it was no desire of hers.) She said; "The material self? I don't really care what I eat—or where I sleep."

The grey man said; "Do not think in mere terms of nourishment, which is a means of maintaining the material body we despise. In love, we serve the soul."

(Lalette felt her inner gorge rising toward forbidden anger.) "I am not sure I understand."

"Do not be troubled. Many fail to understand in the beginning and to many, perfection comes after a long struggle in self-denial."

The rebecks and flutes broke out, all in tune. Dame Quasso offered her arm to the grey man and Lalette looked around to see other pairings, two and two, moving into the eating-hall. She herself was suddenly left unattended, to go in with the blonde Nanhilde. The taller girl leaned close and said; "Nobody."

"What do you mean?" said Lalette.

"Nobody. Not an obula tonight," replied Nanhilde.

II

"Listen," said Leece. "Oh, hear. I am not ignorant. If you really desire that I should come no more, I will not. I am not one to intrude."

"Lovely Leece," he said, "it is for you, not I," (yet knowing it was for himself) and drew her hand to his lips, folding her fingers round the kiss he placed in the palm.

She looked at him intently. "There is a cold breeze," she said, and stepping to the door, closed it before she ran across the room with little quick steps to throw back the covers and slip in beside him. The black brows brushed his cheek.

"If you hated me and really wanted to get rid of me, let me ask you, what would you do? How different would you behave toward me than you are now doing? You tell me that talking with you here in the morning gives you pleasure and is a help to you. Why do you wish to stop it then, if I am willing to come? And if you are thinking of any damage to me, why surely that is my concern."

As her arm came around his neck and their lips met in the long deep kiss, he closed his eyes, not daring to look into hers, for this was no Damaris the maid (and it was not that he dared not, but that he would not). They came shuddering from the contact. "Ah, no," he cried and drew her close again and for a third time. But then she said suddenly; "Three is enough," and without another word slipped from beside him and was gone.

All nights were now turned into a prelude to the mornings, and all days to a prelude for the evenings, when one of the other sisters would talk with them and gently jest at them for a pair of lovers, until Rodvard and Leece went out for a stroll under avenues of plane-trees, where lights flickered through the leaves in the warm summer air. The elder Vyana or the younger Madaille often accompanied them on these journeys, laughing a great deal as they conversed on matters of no importance, for it was as though he and Leece had signed a treaty never to show anyone outside how deeply they were concerned with each other. In the mornings, when the subject turned to themselves, there were checks and uncertainties in their words; yet it was a topic they could not avoid. Rodvard would often leave his breakfast uneaten, the better to lie beside her, kissing and kissing, with now and then some little thing said.

"You must not love me," she whispered one morning, turning her burning face from his; "not in the human way."

"Why not, Leece? I love—this," and kissed her again.

"Ah, so do I. But to love, to love—it would be falling into the hands of the Evil god for me to love you or you to love me, before you had been to instruction and accepted the doctrine of the Prophet. Do you understand?"

He did not (nor, when he broke the rule he had set on himself and looked into her eyes, could he read behind them any illumination). "I am not sure I want to be an Amorosian," he said gravely, "but if you say I shall not love you, I will try not to. Only—"

She hugged him close then, and her lips sought his to end this, and to say without words that this commerce of theirs was a pleasure for its own sake and might be brought to destruction by any talk of a deeper relation—or so he reasoned out her action, that night, as he lay in the hour between waking and sleep. The pleasure of it was so sweet that he dared do nothing to change the pattern; though when she tried to tell him of the strange religion of the Prophet, he would change the conversation to the mystery of their mutual attraction—in the midst of which a vertigo of kissing and clasping would come upon them and there would be silence for a long time. The door was always closed now; sometimes the footsteps of Dame Gualdis could be heard outside, but after the first time, when Leece slipped from the bed in panic, they paid no attention, for the mother neither knocked nor entered. Only when the steps sounded, Leece would gently hold his hand to make him cease fondling her breasts, which she now allowed him freely to do at all times, lying with dark lashes on her cheek and lips half parted.

She would not let him go further than this, nor did the cold Blue Star speak of any willingness to do so. When once, with senses reeling, he would have pressed the matter on, she said no, someone might come, there was no time, and made other excuses, though she kissed him as she said it, and caressed him with curious fingers. Yet it had become part of an unspoken agreement between them that he should ask for no more, only kiss her and be as bold as she permitted; and it was she who ultimately brought the matter into words.

"If we were married, you could have me whenever you wished." She said it half regretfully (and he did look this time, catching behind her eyes something like a color, something that spoke of a desire in her, though somehow not of the same kind as his own).

By the convention into which they had fallen, he must now clasp her eagerly and say, "Ah, Leece," and kiss her for a long time, before saying; "Yet if we did marry, and the mixture proved imperfect, consider how we might hate each other."

"I like to kiss you," she said simply. "Vyana cried last night. She saw him in the afternoon, and does not know what to do."

"Feel my heart beat," he said, placing her hand over it. "It would seem to me that she and her lover are really meant for a perfect union. Could she not enter the Myonessae and be chosen and persuade him to marriage afterward?"

.The girl went stiff in his arms, looking at him with eyes wide in astonishment. "Why," she cried, "that would be deception and sin—leading him from the service of the God of love to Evil. Oh, Rodvard, never say such things."

There was a true trembling in her voice and he felt the moisture of a tear, where her face was pressed into the crotch of his neck. (It did not seem to him that a chance remark was a matter for such fervor, for as he knew religion, it was a guide, and the world would go mad if one tried to observe its commands in every particular.) But all this was only the background of a flicker of surprise across his mind, as he left her face and kissed her closed eyes. "Leece, Leece," he said, "I didn't mean—" and did not know what more to say.

"Oh, Rodvard, I could not bear it if you deceived me like that."

"Do you think I am trying to?" (Kiss.)

"I do not know. No. Ah, we must not do this. It leads us into the hands of Evil. Rodvard, Rodvard, you must, if you want me. . . . Oh—" The word died into lips moving without sound, on which his lips closed, her breath began to come fast, she let his seeking fingers linger a moment at her breasts and slide past, he could not see her eyes, but without the intervention of his amulet, he knew that this was the moment—but at the very point of sliding from the crest, Leece flung herself gasping from his arms, and with a sob was gone.

Next morning his breakfast was left outside the door.

III

The linen stitching was very tedious. Five or six of them, all novices like herself, sat in a circle and went round the edges of napkins, drawing three threads, stitching them home, drawing three threads, bringing them home again, while the mattern or Mircella or one of the older girls read slowly from the First Book of the Prophet, pausing now and again to make exposition of the meaning of a passage. Talking was discouraged. At noon there was always the same meal of pulse with fresh greens or fruit, but in the evening sometimes a piece of meat.

Every fourth-day they all marched in procession to the house of religion and there was a service, not like those in the Dossolan churches, with their flowers and music, but merely a discourse, such as Lalette had first heard at the conventicle in Netznegon, with everybody embracing each other afterward, and prayers of grace pronounced by an Initiate. This took place at noon; after the service, no more work was done on these days.

After dinner and on the free afternoons, all were at liberty except for such matters as personal laundry. Most of the girls walked two and two for a while in the garden, where tall alleys of hollyhocks divided the vegetable plots on which some of the Myonessae labored during the day. Going on, out into the street was not forbidden, but not encouraged. Neither—as Lalette quickly discovered—was it very pleasant, for although these people of Mancherei had no badges of status, which at first seemed a very strange thing, everybody seemed to know at once that she was one of the sisterhood. This was all right as to older people, but in the half-twilight, young men would call out to her, or what was worse, sidle alongside her on the pave and try to make conversation, or offer a glass of wine.

She found their insinuation so infuriating that the second time this happened, with the fellow almost directly making an insinuation, only the memory of Tegval kept her from putting a witchery on him then and there. Dame Quasso had been walking in the garden that night. As Lalette came hurrying through the gate, she looked so long and intently that it seemed she must somehow have caught part of the Initiates' trick of thought-reading, and to Lalette's other troubles was added the fear of being known for a murderess.

On this night of all, the blonde Nanhilde would choose to come to her room for a talk, babbling against the clerks of account, who had allowed her far less than she deserved for some broideries she had done; "—and they gave 'Zina just

double my price. I know what it is; she slips out of here o
fourth-days and gets drunk with some of those clerks and let
them do anything they want. She's awful."

Lalette (upset, and wanting to talk about anything but
this); "But how can she keep the mattern from knowing
about it?"

"Oh, she is careful. A girl has to be in this place. She
always gets back before bedtime, and her sister in town says
she spends the afternoons there."

Lalette sighed. "I thought, when I came here——"

Nanhilde said; "What did you expect to be different?"

Lalette's hands fluttered. "Is there no way we can escape
from the overwhelming lusts of men?"

"A girl in the Myonessae can do very well if she does not
fear herself."

Lalette burst into tears.

21

Midwinter: The Return

I

"Make up this account for closing," said the protostylarion
handing Rodvard a dossier which bore the endorsement
"Approved to expel the subject from the Myonessae for
contumacious refusal to accept any choice—Tradit, I."

Rodvard dragged weary feet to the bench, for his night
had been sleepless, with this matter of Leece reaching
crisis. All week, she had striven to pretend in the presence of
others that nothing was changed, but would neither bring his
breakfast, nor allow him any opportunity to speak with her
alone in the evening. A crisis—the sleepless night began when
he had refused to walk with her and Vyana under planes still
clinging to their last leaves, then felt unhappy over the look
of a friend betrayed that came into her eyes. A crisis; for

that look was a trap as grim as the one the witch had set for him. He did not really want the dark-browed Leece (he told himself), overall, at the price of permanent union she set upon her body. It would have been, it was, enough merely to talk with her and be gay companions, as he was with the other sisters. Only the moments when a contact of lips or body sent a devouring flame along his veins were different. Yet there was now upon him a compulsion to find the next move in the game and carry it through, as though he were involved in a complex dance and dared not miss a pace.

What is this, then? (he asked himself). Am I a mechanician's instrument, or so weak I am not my own master? Is it that I owe her a duty, and by what sanction am I held hereto? The priest at the academy might have had an answer for that. He would have said that the sanction was of God, "who sends us all peace, so that even those misguided men who say there is no God must make an inner peace, through a claim to be true to some image of the Ideal, which they call themselves. So that God is not balked, but enters in them unawares, and they only make their own path harder by reaching Him through devious ways instead of simple." He could remember the argument accurately, and how its force had once struck him. Thus the priest, then; but if the sanction was of God, did God (Rodvard now asked himself) urge him to this pursuit of Leece? No matter what; he knew that when he reached the Gualdis' house that night, the intricate pavanne would continue, and he a part of it as before.

Leave then. No. Not in this land, where he was a public prisoner, required still to report on every tenth day, an irritating routine. For that matter, leave for where? Not Dossola, with the prosecution hanging over his head; not any other place. Dance out the dance.

The protostylarion's step roused him from reverie. He opened the dossier and with a feeling of vertigo, perceived that it was from the couvertine Lolau: "—on the account of the Myonessan Lalette Asterhax."

II

Without a knock the door opened, Leece slipped in an stood with her back to it, looking down. Rodvard bega hastily to make good his jacket-laces.

"It was my fault," she said in a thin voice, then hurriedly "What I did was contrary to the law of love. Do you war me to bring your breakfast in the morning?"

Her eyes were veiled, but one could guess what lay behin them (and one must—one must tread the right measure) "Yes."

"You are still angry with me."

He ran across the room and seized her in his arms, so sh let her dark head slide down against his neck. "What can say?" kissing her ear and the side of her neck (yet at the sam time feeling a revulsion almost physical, and all the time th thought of that other was at the back of his mind, no coming forward because he dared not let it).

A sudden tenseness was in her grip; she flung her hea back and looked at him (out of eyes that spoke distrust) "Rodvard! What is wrong?"

"Nothing. We must hurry and go to supper or they wi miss us." A rivulet of perspiration coursed down his spine She kissed him long and hard (with the doubt still there) an was gone.

Afterward it was the tall Vyana who went to walk wit them. Leece took his hand; all gay, but casting glances tha seemed to show an unasked question in her mind (so tha Rodvard wondered whether she might not have some part o the Blue Star's gift). He said to Vyana; "Tell me something If you were in the Myonessae, how could I come to se you?"

Her face fell sober. "I am not a Myonessan yet. But if were, it would not be easy unless you became at least learner. The Myonessans have no contacts with the oute world save those they make themselves."

"A strange rule," he said, not daring to push the matte further lest he betray his thought.

Now Leece spoke, trying to justify the regimen under which the girls lived, but Vyana, being so near to the sisterhood, was doubtful, and Rodvard heard both of them with only part of his mind, considering what he must do. There was no question but he must do it, ah, no; the expelled of the Myonessae, he knew well, were shut away in gloomy prisons for "instruction", it might be for years. The couvertine Lolau was—

"—do you not think so, Rodvard?" said Leece's voice.

"I am sorry. I was thinking of a thing."

All her attention and affection suddenly rushed at him; she pressed his hand hard. "I was only saying—" and in spite of that warm grip, his mind went off again under the babble. The Blue Star would perhaps let him make his way in, if the light were good—and they reached the door. Leece squeezed his hand again, possessively; he knew she would have sought a corner and kissed him, but he managed to avoid that, with a certain shame picking at him.

Inside he went rapidly upstairs, then stood tingling in his own room as outer steps went to and fro. His mind toiled at details—the lock of the street-door was a heavy one, usually turning with a grating sound, he must have a story ready to tell if someone woke and asked him questions. But before he could work out a tale the small sounds died to a single series of pat, pat, pat, and he had a moment of dreadful fear and excitement mingled that it might be Leece, coming to him that night.

This was his turning-point in life (he thought) and the choice was being made from outside himself. The steps went past; Rodvard released his breath, sat down and, trying to use up the time until all should be asleep, began to repeat to himself Iren Dostal's ballad of the archer and the bear. But at the third stanza a rhyme somehow eluded him, and he nearly went mad trying to recall it, while at the same time the other half of his mind went round the problem of Leece-Lalette, Lalette-Leece, without once making a real effort toward the plan he must have. Then he tried to solve how the line of duty might be considered to lie, according to one or another system of philosophy; but all this yielded was

the unsatisfactory conclusion that he did not know whe
duty or even true desire lay, only what he was going to
Now he began to count boards in the floor, as he h
counted the cask-staves of the ship, merely to pass time; an
time passed. He cracked the door ajar, heard someone snor
and reached the odd thought that even the loveliest of gi
sometimes snore. Tip, tap, and he was down the hall to t
stairs. A board creaked there; he paused. The key grat
even more harshly than he had anticipated, and again he sto
breathless a minute, then was in the street.

A sense of freedom swelled through him as he looked
at the winter stars—this must be the right line, the glorio
line, hurrah! even though the adventure failed. A silent stre
down which advanced in the near distance a cloaked coup
picking their way along with a light-boy before. The chec
ered gleams from the window of his lantern caught t
tree-trunks and half-reflected from the dull surfaces, seem
like weary fireflies. A one-horse caleche went past, its for
dimly outlined against the darker shadows beneath the branc
es. Step on, Rodvard, the way is here. He stumbled in t
dark over the edge of a cobble, turned a corner and anoth
wondering how the glass stood, and reached the couverti
Lolau at last.

He remembered it as the building he had passed on his fir
day in Charalkis, with a foreyard in which a dead tr
stood. The lodge-box held no porter; its window was broke
Rodvard thought—now this is somehow the model of t
Myonessae, if I could trace the resemblance, as his fe
clicked on the pave up to the door, where one light burn
behind a transom in a fan of glass. Summing his force,
knocked. No answer. He knocked again.

Far in the interior a step sounded, coming. The door w
thrown back to show a fat beldame with a robe gather
round her, whose hand trembled slightly with palsy.

"What is it?" she said. The light was above and behind he
he could not see her eyes to use his jewel.

"I am from the office of account," he said (dependi
upon sudden inspiration), "in the matter of the Demoisel
Asterhax."

"A poor hour to be coming," she grumbled. "Ay, ay, the Lalette. I will call the mattern. They will take her in the morning."

She moved aside to let him enter, and as she did so, the light caught her face. (His glance, quickened by emergency, caught in those muddy eyes a green flash of mingled hate and greed.)

"Wait," he said, and touched her wrist. "Perhaps it is not needed to rouse anyone." (That covetousness—if he could use it.)

"What do you mean?"

"It is a simple matter; not official accounts." He fumbled out a coin or two and pressed them in her hand.

The fat face moved into a leer. "Eh, eh, so that's the story. Want to take her, do you? And poor Mircella will be blamed, maybe sent for instruction. It should be worth more."

(Money again; he experienced a moment of panic.) "I am from the office of account," he repeated. "I am to take her there to close her reckoning. You will have the perquisite of her possessions."

"He, he, and you the best perquisite. It should be worth more."

"Sh, someone will hear us." He found another pair of coins. "This is all—if not, give back the rest and call your mattern."

He turned; she clutched his arm, grumbling in her throat (and he could see she did not believe him in the least, but would be satisfied if given a story to tell). "Come. Come."

Another stair-journey through a silent house, this time upward. The place had the indefinable perfume of many women. The guide shuffled along in a dark almost complete; Rodvard heard the chink of keys, then a tick against the lock and the door opened.

"Strike a light." Rodvard felt a candle pressed into his hand; being forced to give his attention to it, Lalette saw him first when the light flared, he heard her gasp and looked past the little flame to see her standing with disheveled hair, so lovely beyond the imagined picture that he could not resist

running across the room to kiss her astonished lips. She mu
have been sitting fully dressed in the dark.

"Rodvard! How did you come here?" The fat woma
shuffled in the background, and he:

"No matter now, it can wait. We must go quickly."

She stared at him like a sleepwalker. "Where?"

"Hurry."

There were no more words between them at this time
place. Lalette turned in the feeble light to make a packag
but the fat woman said; "Nah, my perquisite," so she on
snatched a cloak. The beldame addressed Rodvard; "No
you use your knife on the lock to show where it was picke
then leave it. Then they know my story is true, a man w
here."

He hacked at the brass plate that held the keyhole for
moment, and fortune favored by letting one of the screw
come loose with a snap, and the fat woman clawed his ar
to indicate that was enough. She led the way down the sta
Rodvard could see no eyes, and he and Lalette were sudden
out the door.

III

She turned to face him under the dead tree.

"You do not want me any more. How did you find m
Where did you come from?"

(He thought: out of one pattern-dance of compulsions an
into another.) "I do want you or I would not have come.
could not help it. Did you not receive my letter?"

"I suppose you have some story to cover your utter dese
tion."

"I swear I left with Dr. Remigorius a letter for you, tellin
how I was called to Sedad Vix on the most urgent of affai
and then things happened. I will tell you."

"Then it is true. You are one of the Sons of the Ne
Day." (The eyes were hidden, but the tone told clearly ho
deep was her anger and despair.)

"I have come for you," he said, simply.

She uttered a bitter little laugh. "It is somewhat late, n

friend. I am one of the licensed whores they call Myonessae, and now an attainted criminal."

"I know—and so am I for bringing you from there."

She took three steps in silence. "Where are you taking me?"

"A tavern." (He had not thought, this was part of the plan he had been too excited to make.)

"Do you lodge in it?" (The voice was so small that he knew something lay behind the words.)

"I have been working in the office of account, and learned of your trouble there," he said, inconsecutively.

She turned toward him in the dark street, where far down, someone walked with a light, the hand on his arm trembling a little. "Oh, Rodvard—they would have put me in that prison for instruction and then turned me into the street without an obula."

"I know. See—that is what we are looking for."

An inn it was, a palpable inn, beyond the corner, with light streaming from its windows. They entered through the public-room where a table of men with mugs before them all turned their heads like sunflowers. One of them whispered behind a hand, and there was a snicker. A lugubrious person in a dirty apron came to the inner door and said yah, he would give them welcome for the night. Supper? No, said they both, and a small girl with her hair in tight braids showed them to a room where there was only one chair and a bed where they would sleep together for the first time since the night in Dame Domijaiek's room, now in a far country and long ago. (Rodvard thought: she is wearing her hair down as an unwedded girl, and that is why they snickered.) She sat on the edge of the bed, tossing her head back.

"Rodvard," she said, "you have been unfaithful to me."

"No!" (He answered in reaction merely, and the thought that crossed his mind was not of the maid Damaris, but of Leece, now perhaps herself sleepless, and waiting for the dawn, when—) "Your Blue Star is still bright."

She did not move, only crossed her eyes in a spasm of pain. "I think perhaps it was another witch. I know one put a spell on you. Did you know I saved you from it? You can go to

her, if you wish; even take the Blue Star. I do not want it any
more."

"Lalette! Do not talk so."

He stepped to her on the bed, slipped his arm under both
hers where she supported herself, leaning backward, and drove
her down, his lips seeking hers. She met him passively, neither
giving nor avoiding. "Lalette," he breathed again.

Now she twisted in his arms. "Ah, men think there is only
one way to resolve every problem with a girl. It was that I
wished to get away from. I will go back."

He released her then, and lay beside her, unspeaking for a
moment. Then:

"And be sent for instruction and then turned out? It was
that I came to save you from."

"Oh, I am grateful. I will not go back, then, and you
can have what you have bought."

(There was a torture in it that he should at this moment
think of Maritzl of Stojenrosek.) He double-jointed to his
feet and began to pace the floor. "Lalette," he said, "truly
you do not understand. We are in real danger, both of us, and
cannot afford bitterness. I have not been in this country long
enough to know its laws, but I know we have broken more
than one; and they are very intent after both of us, you as a
witch and me with the Blue Star, even though they say
witchery is not forbidden here. Now I ask your true help, as I
have helped you."

"Ah, my friend, of course. What would you have me do?"

She sat up suddenly, with a tear in the corner of her eye
(which he affected not to notice), all kindliness; and they
began to talk, not of their present emergency, but of their
adventures and how strangely they were met there. He gave
her a fair tale on almost all, except about Damaris and
Leece. She interrupted now and again, as something he said
reminded her of one detail or another, so that neither of
them even thought of sleeping until the candle burning down
and a pale window spoke of approaching day.

"But where our line lies now, I do not know," he con-
cluded.

Inconsequentially, she said; "Tell me truly, Rodvard, about

the Sons of the New Day." (Her face was toward him as she spoke; he was astonished to catch in her eye a complex thought, something about feeling herself no better than the group she considered thieves and murderers.)

"Well, then, we are not murderers and steal from none," he said (as she, remembering the power of the jewel, lowered her head; for she had not told him of the fate of Tegval). "We are only trying to make a better world, where badges of condition are no more needed than here in Mancherei, and men and women too, do not obtain their possessions by being born into them."

"That is a strange thing to say to one who was born into a witch-family," she said. "But no matter now. What shall we do? I doubt if we can reach the inner border before they set the guards after us, and with the case of this captain against you, you cannot now return to Dossola. Or can you? We might get a ship that would take us to the Green Islands. I have a brother there somewhere."

"Who's to pay the passage? For I have little money. Much of my gain has been withheld to pay for the things I needed when I came."

"And I no money at all. But did you come here from Dossola by paying? Can we not offer service?"

He (thought of the one-eyed captain and the service demanded then, but) took her hand. "You are right, and it is the only thing to try," he said. "Come, before any pursuit fairly starts."

They crept down the stairs, hand in hand, like conspirators. At the parlor Rodvard sacrificed one of his coins to pay for his night's lodging. (The thought of Leece and what she would be doing at this hour was in his mind as) they stepped into a street from which the grey light had rubbed out all the night's romance to leave the city drab and wintry.

A milk-vendor met them with his goats and gave a swirl of his pipes in greeting. There were few other passengers abroad, but more began to appear as they drew near the harbor area; carters and busy men, and hand-porters. Presently they were among warehouses and places of commerce. Beyond lay the quays and a tangle of masts. Here was a tavern, opening for the day; the proprietor said that a Captain 'Zenog had a ship at the fourth dock down, due to sail for the Green Isles with the tide. The place was not hard to find, nor the captain either, standing by the board of his vessel, strong and squat, like a giant beaten into lesser stature by the mallet of one still stronger.

"A Green Islands captain, aye, I am that," he said. "I'll take you there on the smoothest ship that sails the waters."

Said Rodvard; "I do not doubt it. But we have no money and wish to work our way."

Bluff heartiness fell away from him (and the glance said he was suspicious of something). "What can you do?"

"I am a clerical, really, but would take other labor merely to reach the Green Islands."

Lalette said: "I have done sewing and could mend a sail here and there."

The captain rubbed a chin peppered with beard. "A clerical I could use fair enough, one that could cast accounts." He looked around. "Most of you Amorosians, though—"

Rodvard said joyously; "I am not of Mancherei, but Dossolan, educated there, and can cast up an account as easily—"

"There'd be no pay in it. The voyage merely," said the man quickly.

"We will do it for that," said Rodvard, and touched Captain 'Zenog's hand in acceptance. The squat man turned. "Ohé!" he shouted. "Hinze, take these two to the port office and get them cleared for a voyage with us."

22

The Law of Love

I

(For a moment after the man had spoken, Rodvard felt as though he were falling.) He looked at Lalette (and saw the same black fear was in her also), but the step was taken, they could only hope to carry matters through at the port office. Hinze was a thin man in a sailor's jacket, who looked over his shoulder back at the captain as he led them down the cobbles to a brick building that Lalette remembered all too well. "You will find it a good voyage. The ship is tight as an egg, but the food not too good," said he.

There was a doorman in his coop, who directed Hinze down a hall, whereupon the girl clutched Rodvard's arm and said; "I do not like this. I—"

(A silly remark, he thought.) "We cannot run away now," he said. "It is the only chance"; and Hinze was back to say that the protostylarion would entertain them at once, there could be only a moment of waiting. They looked at each other apprehensively; Lalette leaned against a wall and closed her eyes, and a man came down the hall to call them in.

Rodvard led the way into a room where a little man sat behind a desk with lines of disobligingness set round his mouth. He said; "You wish to leave the dominion of Mancherei for the barbarous Green Islands?"

"It is because of a family matter," said Rodvard. "My wife and I—"

The protostylarion looked at Lalette's hair, down in the maidensweep, then quickly at Rodvard and back to her face. Wrinkles shot up the middle of his forehead. "Wife? Wife? What is your profession. Where is your certificate of employ?" He came up out of his seat (like a small bear, Rodvard thought), peering the more intently at the girl. "Ah, I have it! I know! You are the one I registered for the Myonessae. The Dossolan; and a witch, too. Guards! Guards!" His voice went treble; two or three armed men tumbled into the room.

"An inquiry!" said the protostylarion, flinging up his arm to point at the couple as Hinze shrank back. "These two for an inquiry! I accuse her of being a runaway Myonessan!" The face was distorted (the thought behind it one of the purest delight and triumph). "Be careful with her; she is a witch!"

Rodvard was gripped above the elbow and jerked stumbling to the door, catching only a glimpse of Lalette's despairing face. Outside, people stopped and goggled as the two were hurried along and into a carriage, with a guard beside each. "I am sorry," began Rodvard, but one of the guards said; "Close your clack; not talking among prisoners." (His eyes spoke a brutality that would have taken pleasure in a blow.)

They came to a structure with a battlemented gate, like a small fortress; an odor of sewage emanated from it. A pair of guards brought forward bills in salutation to those entering. Rodvard and Lalette were swung into a gate-house, where a man lounged at a window—an officer by his shoulder-knot. One of the guards said; "These two are in for an inquiry. Authority of the Protostylarion Barthvödi. He says to be careful of the woman, she's a witch."

The officer looked at Lalette appreciatively, then seated himself at the desk and drew out a paper. "Your names and professions," he said.

Rodvard gave his; Lalette checked over the profession (wishing to cry out that she would not give it, wishing to defy the man). The officer looked at her. "You are warned," he said, "that I am diaconal, and your witchery will be wasted on me."

"Oh," she said, and half-choking; "Myonessan."

"Which couvertine? ... The more trouble it is to obtain the information, the harder it will be with you."

"Lolau."

The officer turned to one of the guards. "Go to the couvertine of Lolau and inform the mattern that she is to come here tomorrow morning at the fourth glass for an inquiry in the matter of Demoiselle Lalette." He addressed the other guard. "You wait here while I draw the proclamation calling for information on this Bergelin, then take it around."

(Rodvard thought of Leece, and wondered what she would say in answer to the proclamation), (Lalette of facing Dame Quasso again.) Another pair of guards came in to take them to stone cells, set in the wall of the fortress. Rodvard saw Lalette vanish into one and heard the door clang behind her, then was himself thrust into another. There was a stool and straw on the floor, an archery-slit for the only lighting. The place stank, the origin of which odor was a bucket beneath the archery-slit. He sat on the stool and tried to think, but the turmoil of fear held him so that he could do little more than run around back and over his own conduct like a mouse, to ask where he had stepped wrongly and what else he could have done to make things come out other than they were. This was the morning when Leece ... and he would have been bound to her for life.... No, that could not have been the right path. Farther back, then? When he asked that, he went off into a train of reminiscence in which thought almost ceased.

His throat was dry, there was no water in the cell. Nor did he seem to have near neighbors, all being silence around, save that somewhere a tiny drip of water increased his thirst. Would he be able to hold anything back tomorrow morning at the inquiry, where an Initiate would surely question? Round the circuit of his failure his mind ran again, and slid off into a consideration of present circumstance. He rose, going to the iron-bound door, but even the small trap in it would not open from his side. Alone.

Not for the first time. How like the imprisonment on the ship this was, and how dark the prospect had loomed then! Out of that he had risen, but to what? A choice between Leece and this. A wave of misery swept across him, and then he thought of Lalette, and her misery equal to his own, and maybe more.

But this was no help either, and he began to examine his prison, finger-breadth by finger-breadth, for something that might take his mind away from this procession of regrets and anxieties toward a future he could not know. There were only accidents of the wall at first, in which he tried to see pictures and carvings, making up a tale for himself, like those in the ballads. This had not gone far when he came to a trace of writing which looked as though someone had tried to wipe it out, for there were only a few words to be read:

"Horv ... in the month ... only for lov ... God."

A cryptic message, indeed; he tried to imagine the tale behind it, and how the love of which these Amorosians forever gabbled had brought someone to this cell. This caused him to ask himself whether it was really love for Lalette that had brought him there; for that matter whether he loved her, and what love was; and to none of these questions could he find a satisfactory answer, because he kept comparing her with Maritzl and wondering whether the emotion were the same. But this in turn brought a deep weariness; he flung himself on the straw to rest and work the matter out; and so doing, fell into an uneasy slumber—product of his sleepless night—in which he dreamed that the world was ruled, not by the God he had been taught to believe in, nor disputed by the two gods of whom the Amorosians spoke, but by three demons, who sat in a closed space with smoke pouring from their mouths, and decided what penalties should be exacted for witchery.

A key grated; he woke to see the trap being pulled back from without, and a voice said roughly:

"Here's your banquet, my lord. The sweetmeats come with the dancing girls."

A plate was thrust through, with a pewter mug of water. On the former were some vegetables, cold and sticky, and no table utensils, but Rodvard was in a mood of hunger that forbade him to be over-nice and he ate, saving part of his water to cleanse his fingers after the meal. It was hardly done before the trap opened again, and the outer voice demanded; "The tools, pig-face. The administration doesn't give souvenirs to its guests."

Rodvard passed the dishes through and seated himself again. Time ticked; the light that had been fading when he woke was all gone, he had slept so much that he could do so no more, and the uncertainty of his lot held him from consecutive thought. Somewhere outside there was a thin cry and a sound of feet. Then quiet again, but for the briefest space; and now another key grated, in the main lock of his door. It was flung open; in the space stood a small man and a dark, with no cap. Behind him, a smoky torch held by another showed this first visitor to be holding a naked sword, that dripped, plash, plash, on the stone.

"You are Bergelin?" he said. "I call myself Demadé Slair. The revolt has begun. Have you the Blue Star safe?"

II

Questions whirled in Rodvard's mind, but the larger of the pair said; "Hurry," and gripped him by the elbow like the guard who had brought him in, dragging along the corridor.

"Wait!" said Rodvard, resisting. "There is another—"

"We must hurry," said Demadé Slair. "You do not know how desperate a business this is. We have had to kill."

"No. I will not leave her. She is my sweetheart; my witch."

"You have her here? Of the two of you, she is the more important! Where is she?"

"At the third cell here, I think."

Without another word Slair counted off. "The torch, Cordisso," and began to try keys from a chain of them. The big man advanced the torch, but the place held only some babbling, furtive creature with white hair and idiot eyes. The next cell was empty. Slair swore furiously. "You are sure your doxy's here?"

"She was brought in with me."

He tried another door. It was she, rising surprised from the floor in a whirl of dresses. Rodvard pushed past the small man to grip her by the hands. "Come, and quickly."

She made small uncomprehending sounds. Rodvard put an arm around her and drew her toward the door. Reverse of the stair by which they had been brought in; in the torchlight Rodvard saw a pair of feet at the base. A dead man, one of the guards. In spite of the hurry, he paused to unbelt the fellow's dag, and rushed with the rest, feeling more a man again now the lost knife was replaced.

At the outer gate stood two more men, hoods pulled over their faces. They saluted Demadé respectively and led across the street to where a carriage stood, pushing Lalette into the back seat. There were three horses, one in front of the pair, according to the Mancherei fashion. One of the hooded men cracked his whip, and they were off at a bumping pace, as Demadé Slair said; "It is as well you were placed in arrest and proclaimed this afternoon. We should not have known how to find you otherwise."

"Who sent you—Dr. Remigorius?"

A shadow winked across the man's face, even in the dark. "The High Center; I say the revolt has begun and they are in rule. But you shall be told everything soon." He would say no more; the carriage bumped across cobbles, and they were at the dock, with a man holding a candle-lantern by its side. Slair leaped down without offering a hand to Lalette and sprang across the plank of a ship with "Hurry!" Already, as she and Rodvard reached the deck a whistle was blown, and men were moving rapidly among the ropes. They followed their guide's beckoning down a ladder to a cabin; he set the lantern on a table.

"Let yourselves be placed, and hear me carefully," he said. "It is of the utmost moment to the cause and everything that you are not caught or even held back. If the guards come aboard, if we are stopped by a galley as we leave the harbor, you are strictly to go down the ladder leftward of this cabin. At its base is a pile of bales of goods, of which one is hollowed out to take a man, with a flap at the edge that can be pulled to from inside. Insert yourself and pull the flap."

(A thrill more of excitement than apprehension shot through Rodvard; the thought of being as important as this to the great enterprise.) He said; "If this ship's invaded, they will likely have an Initiate or at least one of their diaconals with them, and from the mind of anyone aboard, he will be likely to know where the hiding place is."

Slair grinned. "That has been thought of. No one knows of this hollow but me. I made it and can take care of myself."

Lalette said; "And I; what shall I do?"

Slair frowned. "You are a problem, demoiselle. We came for friend Rodvard and his Blue Star, imagining you were still in Dossola, and there's no preparation." He put an index-finger on his chin. "You have the Art. Could you not—"

She raised a hand. "Ah, no. Never." (In the flash of her eye Rodvard saw how she was thinking of some witchery on a ship, something terrible and sickening connected with it.)

"Of course," said Slair. "Against an Initiate, it would miss nine times out of ten. And concealment's a weak resource. No, the problem is one of hiding you in plain sight; that is, to let them look but not know your identity. . . . Ah, I have it; let your hair down and the hem of your dress up to show an ankle; be one of those travelling strumpets who call themselves sea-witches."

Lalette said steadily; "How will this deceive one of the Initiates?"

Demadé Slair made a twisting with his mouth. "Why, demoiselle, these Initiates are not magicians; they can read no more than thoughts and not all of those. All women have in them a trifle of the strumpet; you have but to think yourself one, be one with your mind. It would be a rare Initiate to tell the difference."

(Lalette's mind beat frantic wings; the bars were there again, whatever route she took led to the same cage); (and Rodvard caught enough of her thought to know how deep was her trouble.) "Is there not some better plan?" he asked.

"No time; see, the ship is stirring." Demadé Slair stood up. "So now I must leave you." The door banged behind him.

Lalette said; "This is a second rescue—from one prison to another, each time. I thank you, Rodvard." (Her eyes flashed a dark color of anger, he knew what was stirring in her mind, but also that if he mentioned it directly, there would be a flash.)

He said; "Lalette, let me implore you. I will not quarrel with you about whose making this trouble is, or how we seem to go from one difficulty to another. But if we can work together, this escape shall be better than the last. I did not leave you at the couvertine."

"Oh, I am grateful," she said, in the tone of one who is not grateful in the least, turning aside her head. "If you had only—"

(He had wit enough not to carry this line on.) "Do you know anything of this revolt?" he asked.

She turned again. "Ah, I cannot bear if that I should never have a thought of my own while I am with you. Will you give me back the Blue Star?"

"No! It is all our lives and fortune now, and the fate of many more important than we."

"I am not beautiful and brilliant like those girls of noble houses; but even so, would like to be wanted for myself, and not what I can bring."

Outside, the first harbor-swell caught the ship; she turned her face again, queasy at her stomach. They slept in shut-beds on opposite sides of the cabin.

23

Netznegon: Return to Glory

I

The skies were filled with glory, the new day rising. The man who called himself Demadé Slair explained, leaning against the rail at the waist of the ship, in the blue-and-gold morning, a day anointed with white in the form of a circling seagull.

"It's an intricate tale," he said, "of which the sum is that we are unlikely to see queens in Netznegon again. But I'll begain with Cleudi's plan for having the nobles gather taxes in their seignories. They would not have it."

"Something like that seemed to be happening when I was at the conference of court," said Rodvard.

"They say there was a scene to remember when Florestan told the old bitch there was no more money," Slair went on with a laugh. "She beat him about the head with a slipper and for days he wore a patch over one eye."

Lalette said; "She is your queen." (She wanted to cry out, to say something that would drive this man to fury.)

Rodvard drew her hand toward him, but she pulled it away; Demadé Slair said; "I crave your pardon, demoiselle; truly. I did not know you were so royalist. . . . Then Brunivar fell. You heard of it?"

Rodvard said; "I have had little news, buried in Charalkis; only that there were troubles."

"Attained of treasons, and sent to the throat-cutter. The case was pressed by the Duke of Aggermans, very violent against him, no one altogether knows why."

"I think I could find a reason."

"No doubt, with your stone. But d'you see the situation that left? With Brunivar gone, there's no regent-apparent in the case of Her Majesty's death, which may fall any day. I think it was you who sent word to the Center that Florestan expected the regency in his room. Very like he would have had it, too, but for the tax matter; but the regency question furnishing an excuse the nobles summoned a general assembly of all the estates, and once they were met, they began to consider everything."

"And the revolt?"

"Oh, it began in the west—at Veierelden, with some of the army and not with our party at all. Brunivar's people joined, setting forward the name of Prince Pavinius, and how he was wrongfully set aside from the succession, and had long since abandoned being an Amorosian. They even persuaded the old man to come out of Mayern and raise his standard. Most of the nobles have gone there with what troops there are, but I don't know how much fighting there has been. Neither side's very anxious for war. The important thing is that the great assembly was left in session with the nobles out of it, and you can see what that means."

"Not quite. Enlighten me."

"Why our party in the majority and Mathurin in control of everything."

Rodvard turned a face of utter astonishment. "Mathurin? How—What—? I might have thought Dr. Remigorius—"

Slair laughed again, a sharp bark. "Bergelin, for one who can see the thoughts in a head, you are the ignorantest man I have seen—or one of the cleverest." He shot a quick glance of suspicion at Rodvard. "You truly did not know that Mathurin was the head of the High Center, the major leader of the Sons? As for Remigorius, the less you mention him, the better. Some connections are not quite healthy."

"I did not know," said Rodvard slowly (trying in his mind to re-assort the tumbled building-blocks of his world). "But I? The Blue Star's a treasure, but why send a ship for such a mouse as I am?"

"Answer your own question, friend Bergelin. Look, here's Pavinius; the court; our party with its control of the great assembly; maybe some of Tritulaccan tendency, and a few Amorosians—all opposed to each other. You are the only man we know can untangle where the true loyalties lie and discover whom we can trust."

"But surely, this is not the only Blue Star."

"The only one we can be sure of. We know the court butler Tuolén had one; perhaps there is one or more in Pavinius' party."

"You say 'had.' Does Tuolén have it no longer?"

Slair looked sidewise (with something a little savage in his glance). "An accident befell him. You know Mathurin."

Said Lalette; "If I understand what you mean, you had him killed. But this would not affect the Blue Star itself."

"Not if we could find the heiress. And there's another question also; suppose we have found her, does she know enough of the Art to make the Star active? True witches are very hard to find, with the episcopals so bitter against the Art on the one hand, and the Amorosians draining so many off to Mancherei on the other."

"My mother—" began Lalette.

"Oh, Mathurin followed that line up long ago. She could instruct, but would she? I think not for our party; the last I heard she had followed Cleudi and the court out to Zenss. You two are our mainstay."

Rodvard (thinking of the witch of Kazmerga, and thinking also that it would be little good for the Sons of the New Day to have commerce with her) said; "It should not be hard to trace Tuolén's heiress. I was in the Office of Pedigree myself once."

"One more reason why you're a figure. I'll conceal nothing; most of those who can read the old hands, or trace the pedigrees, are either fled with the court or little trusty. We dare not place reliance in them; and it's a matter of hurry with the armies in the west both anxious to do us harms, and even the Tritulaccans calling out new troops."

A whistle blew; men moved among the ropes, the ship changed slant. Rodvard said; "What you say is very strange. I would like to know—"

"Ah, enough of politics for now. I must make my apologies to this lovely demoiselle for having spoken unthinkingly." He offered his arm to Lalette. "Will you honor me?"

Rodvard was left standing; and not for the only time either, in the next three or four days, for Lalette formed the habit of walking with Slair along the deck, she laughing and both of them talking of trifles in a manner that seemed to Rodvard inane and pointless. Of an evening the girl would hardly speak at all, of if she did so, it was in a flat voice, shunning his eyes, so that he could tell little of what she was thinking; at night, she shut herself in her lock-bed before undressing. This became so intolerable that at last he rose one night and tapped on the door of her bed.

"Open," he said, and over the noise of the thuttering rigging, heard her say faintly, "Rodvard, no."

"Open I say," he cried again. "You must hear me."

There was a silence of seven breaths, and then he heard her spin the lock.

"Lalette," he said, "why do you treat me so?"

"Have I treated you worse than you have treated me?"

(He fought back an impulse to a retort that would bring angers.) "I do not know that I follow all you mean."

(There was only night-shine from the window, she emboldened at knowing he could not learn her fullest thought.) "Will you still say you did not cheat me? Now that I know you were always one of the Sons of the New Day. Tuolén had an accident—and the doorman at your house—and how many more? I used to believe in some things before you trapped me."

"No trap," said he, jerking back so violently he struck a beam and gave an exclamation. "No trap. You cannot make a new world without destroying some of the old, and some suffer unjustly for every gain."

In a small voice she said; "I feel—used."

"Lalette," he said gravely, and not taking offense. "Listen to me. We of the Sons of the New Day are truly striving for a better world, one in which there are such things as honesty and justice for everyone. But this much I have learned, and not from Dr. Remigorius, that any such effort is a swimming against the world's stream, and must be paid for. You feel used? Myself no less. But I like to think of myself as used for the betterment of men—perhaps by God."

His voice was a little unsteady at the end, and now it was her turn to be silent for a moment. At last she said; "And how do you know the use is for betterment—not someone's personal pleasure in ordering others? What you say is not too different from the teaching I heard at the couvertine. Only there they would say that God uses no earthly vessels."

"Do you believe that?"

"Ah, I do not know. I only know that I am tired, and alone, alone . . ." The words tailed off, he heard her shift in the darkness of the bed, and then the intake of a sob.

"Lalette, don't cry." He bent over, wiping a tear from her face, then as it was followed by more, fell to kissing her eyes. "I love you" (for the first time since that night on the roofs). "Lalette, Lalette." More and more he kissed, from eyes to lips, and she gripped her arms around him (because he was the nearest anchor in a shifting world), and his kissing turned to passion (as she had known it would, and what did it matter?) (But she was only a recipient, and to Rodvard it was a relief and an agony. In that moment he wished it had been Leece.)

II

It was after sunset bell when they came upstream to Netznegon city, its gated towers rising dark against the west like the worn teeth of giants. Rodvard stood near the prow, hearing the measured cry of seamen at the sweeps; through all he felt the golden note of glory returning. Dossola (he murmured to himself)—Dossola strong and fair, how shall I contribute to your greatness and so find my own? He felt himself making a poem of it, but in a rush of emotion so

ntense that he could not bring the rhymes quite true, nor the
rhythm neither, quite; and when he tried to pause and think
consciously of how the verses should go, the emotion vanished, and the dark city was only a tumbled pile of stone.

The bridge leading to the southern suburbs blotted out the
prospect; little white cakes of ice came swimming like ducks
down the stream, and the ship swung to its quay, the one
around the curve. There were lanterns there and a little
group waiting; they must have been seen from the walls, and
the word passed through to meet them. Someone hallooed to
Rodvard from the stern of the ship; Demadé Slair was
waiting there with Lalette, muffled close in her long cloak.
(Rodvard thought: we are come back to Dossola, both of us,
as naked as when we left it, but at least with more hope.)
Said Slair:

"It would be as well to hurry. It does not do to be on the
streets too much at night these days."

(The back of Rodvard's mind recognized that he had given
Lalette no more than a priest's argument that night in the
lock-bed, and wished that he had found a better, since she
must see the defect in this one. But what? How educate her
to the ideal?) The plank was flung. Five or six men were at
the other end, one of them in a provost's cloak, but the shoes
were not like what they should be, nor did the doublet seem
to belong to the uniform. A longsword bulged out the cloak;
the eyes flicked past Rodvard to rest on Lalette. Demadé
Slair identified himself and shepherded his charges past a
dark shed to the quay-side street. A man was there with a
horse; Slair spoke to him, he swung himself into the saddle
and rode off.

Said Rodvard (to say something); "That provost seemed in
an inquiring mood."

Slair; "This was no provost. The general assembly has
abolished that hateful order. What you saw was a people's
guard."

Rodvard; "This is a different Dossola."

Slair; "It will be a better one."

Lalette said; "Where are we going?"

"To the guest-house of the nation, that used to be the

palace of Baron Ulutz, who has fled to join Pavinius. Th
man has gone for a carriage."

The conversation winked out. Around a corner of th
street somewhere in the dim, there was a shout that came t
them only as the confused "Yaya!" of many throats, followe
by a crash of glass and then another shout. "What is it?
Rodvard looked at Slair.

"Some of the people, doubtless. You should know; ther
are many debts being paid these days." He shrugged.

Lalette stirred; (without the Blue Star's intervention Rod
vard knew that she would find in this wild lawlessness th
case against his new day). He said; "Is there much of thi
from day to day?"

The man's voice was indifferent. "Enough. It is mostl
Zigraner moneylenders who suffer."

Round the corner came a carriage with a single horse, th
messenger riding ahead.

"You will report to the office of the committee at th
second glass in the morning," said Slair to the rider. Th
fellow's chin was badly shaven; he leaned from the saddl
and said; "Well, friend Slair, I will do the best I can, but i
will be hard to ride more messages so early, for Mousey her
is nearly done, and she's my livelihood."

Rodvard now noticed that the horse was drooping wit
weariness, but Demadé Slair said; "If you lose one, there'
another. The people's business will not wait. Be on time."

The man got slowly down and patted the neck of th
horse. "Friend Slair," he said, "I am as much for the peopl
as anyone, but there's more to this than livelihood. This is m
friend." The tired horse sniffed at the hand he put up.

Slair surprisingly burst into laughter. "Go, then, with you
friend. I'll be your warranty if you are late."

The carriage had wide seats; Lalette huddled down in th
corner, so that Rodvard was barely touching the edge of he
cloak, and Slair sat facing them. Beyond the corner, wher
the turbulence was, figures were visible at a little distanc
and torches moving, but nobody said anything in the vehicl
(because, thought Rodvard, there was so much to say).

Presently they turned in at the gate of the wide-flung Ulutz palace, where some statue on the entrance-pillar had been thrown down, leaving broken stone across the cobbles. There were lights in the building, but no doorman. Demadé Slair led the way, and straight up the wide flight of marble steps to a tall-walled room, where he struck light to a candle. A huge bed stood in the corner, and one of the chairs had been slit, so that the material of the upholstery flowed upon the carpet. "I bid you good-night," said their guide. "There's a kitchen below-stairs where you can have breakfast, and a messenger will call for you in the morning, friend Bergelin."

When they were alone, Lalette sat in the good chair with her hands in her lap, and looked at her feet. "Rodvard," she said at last.

"Yes?" (His heart jumped hopefully.)

"Be careful. You are not so important to them as you think. If you were—gone, they might make me give the Blue Star to someone else."

"Could they compel you to put the witchery on it?"

"No. But they might find another witch . . . Rodvard."

He went over to her, but at his touch she made a small gesture of dismissal, as though to rebuke him for bringing something childish into a moment of utter intensity.

"I am afraid, Rodvard. Don't let them do that to me."

He stepped away from her. "Ah, pest, you are shying at shadows. I am a member of the Sons; and even so you have the Art."

"Yes. I have that."

She only undressed to a shift, and wrapped it close around her, sleeping on the far side of the bed. The water was very cold.

24

Speeches in the Great Assembly

I

It was the old Hall of Presence. The throne stood as before, its dark wood bright with jewels, and the jewelled star bright above it, so that Rodvard felt at his back almost a palpable emanation of Dossola's high fame. Before him, chairs had been swung out from the walls into the space where all had once stood to hear judgments pronounced from the throne, as in the great days of King Crotinianus; and other chairs brought in, not consonant with those already there. He himself occupied the seat once reserved to the Announcer, two steps up; a board was placed for him to write on, since this was to be the pretence for his being there. To the right, another step up, was the place once occupied by the Chamberlain, which Mathurin would presently take. It also had a board.

Rodvard looked out across the hall, now filling with men, most of whom bowed to the throne on entering, in the ancient form. Very few were badged with coronets, and it seemed to Rodvard a cause of hope and pleasure that this was so. There was a solid group of legists; some merchants; and a few men from the lesser orders, though not as many as he had expected. As he watched, the Episcopals came in, six of the seven at once, not looking around at the fall and sudden rise of chatter that attended their entrance. They moved to places in the premier row of chairs; legist badges began drifting toward them as straws on a stream will be drawn by a log.

Mathurin came in. He wore his servant's black and badge of low condition as though they were robes and a crown, strutting visibly. He did not bow to the throne, but walked straight up to the Chamberlain's place, sat down, bounced up again immediately and slapped his palm on the board for attention. As the buzz of talk died reluctantly and men took their places, he watched with tight lips; when only two or three whisperers remained, he struck the board again and said; "There is a new matter of utmost importance before the assembly of the nation."

A solid-looking man who bore the coronet badge stood up into the dramatic pause and said; "I am the Marquis of Palm. There is an old matter for which this assembly was called that I shall never cease to urge. No regent-apparent has been—"

He was allowed to say no more. A chorus of angry babbling covered his voice, and Mathurin slapped sharply. His voice rose; "I am only the writer before this assembly, and will place before it whatever is desired; but it does not seem to me that it wishes to hear your proposal, Ser Marquis. The more since the matter of which I speak is so great that it overrides every other. I have to say that the nation, already threatened by exterior enemies, is now called upon to face a worse danger, one that will call for all our exertions. It is this: the leaders in whom we have most trusted have turned traitor, and are conspiring with the enemies of the people."

Now there were more babblings, and angry cries, such as "Cut their throats!" with a couple of fists brandished aloft; but Rodvard noticed that all the outcry came from one section of the hall, behind the Episcopals. One of the latter began fanning himself rapidly. Instead of quieting, the tumult augmented as Mathurin stood sweeping his eyes across it with a half-triumphant air. At last he raised a hand.

"I will tell you the worst," he said, "not in fine words but brutally, for this is a brutal thing." He shuffled a handfull of papers. "No, wait, I will begin with the tale of how this knowledge reached us.

"At Drog, below the pass that leads through the Ragged Mountains to Rushaca, there is an inn. Some eight days gone there came to it a carriage, bearing one of the ladies of the court, oh, a beautiful lady, all dressed as though for a ball. She came from the north, from Zenss, where the court is, and as the road leads to Tritulacca ultimately, her actions roused some suspicion in the mind of the innkeeper. He is a true patriot, and thought she might be carrying wealth away out of the country in violation of the decree against it; watched her, and noticed that she was very careful of a certain casket. The innkeeper thereupon summoned people's guards, who seized the casket and broke it open. They found no money, but they found—this."

Mathurin drew from his papers one that seemed to be of parchment, and waved it aloft, so that all could see that it bore at its foot a huge blue seal, star-shaped, the sign-manual of the chancery of the realm. There were sharp intakes of breath and stirring among the chairs; the Episcopal who had been fanning himself stopped. The sturdy man who had described himself as the Marquis of Palm stared aloft with his mouth open and a frown on his face.

"Shall I read it to you? No, not word for word, for it is written in Tritulaccan, and with the stupid, decorative court phrases that try to hide real meaning." (Rodvard thought: he has more orator's tricks than I ever would have imagined.)

Pause. "Here it is, then: a missive, signed with the name of Count Cleudi, himself a Tritulaccan by birth, to Perisso, Lord Regent of Tritulacca, but bearing as proof of genuineness, the seal of our Gracious Majesty, the Queen. The substance of it is that while without doubt the rebellion of her cousin Pavinius, aided though he is by the Mayerns, will soon be put down, the war is likely to be long and wasteful. Her gracious majesty therefore consents to the proposal of the Lord Perisso, made in the name of true religion and the old friendship between the two houses, that he shall join the army of Dossola with not less than sixteen shars; and in return for this, it is graciously conceded that Tritulacca has a just claim to the city and province of Sedad Mir. And some of these Tritulaccan shars shall pass to the war by way of Netznegon city, to suppress certain disorders there. The rats! There is no dealing with such people!"

"Shame!" shouted someone almost before he had finished, and now all over the hall men were on their feet and shouting, but among other cries there was one of "Forgery!"

Mathurin seemed to be waiting for that moment. "Forgery!" he cried, his voice going up almost to the cracking-point. "If you think it is forgery, look at it yourself," and threw the paper outward, as one might the caught hunted animal to the dogs. "Will you call it forgery when I tell you also that the whole Tritulaccan fleet has been placed on war standard? The nation is betrayed!"

Now the tumult seemed completely out of hand, men moving from place to place confusedly or trying to say something (and in every eye Rodvard could catch there was nothing but mere fury, which expressed itself in a color of maroon). Mathurin looked out on the scene, making no effort at control; but from the first row there rose a tall old man with white hair and a face set in a habitual expression of benevolence, who raised high his white staff of office, by which Rodvard recognized him as the Arch-Episcopal, Teurapis Groadon.

Eyes caught the staff; voice after voice was abstracted from the uproar until only a few still tried to speak, then two, then none. The Arch-Episcopal waited until there was a silence broken only by a cough; Mathurin pressed Rodvard's shoulder to read the eyes, but the old man only cast one swift glance at the dais before turning to address the assembly.

"Ser writer," he said, "and you, lords and estates of the realm, this is not a pleasant thing that we have heard. There may be some question of the authenticity of this message, or it may have been written merely to deceive; a document from the hand of the heretic Pavinius, who would make himself the equal of God. Yet I will not deny that we must behave as though it were true; for if we do nothing, and it proves to be so, it will be too late. And for myself I fear it is true; for it is given to the spiritual estate to discern the machinations of the powers of evil. There is before us, then the question of how, joying in the protection of God, we can circumvent the machination of the Enemy, who has made man and women naturally good, into instruments of evil.

"Let us therefore prayerfully address ourselves to the question of how the realm may escape this trouble. In an emergency equal to this, in the reign of King Cloar with Queen

Berdette the First, the assembly of the realm set aside their rule in favor of their daughter, with her husband, the great King Crontinianus, of glorious memory. But now there are no heirs female, and of heirs male, only Prince Pavinius. Thus we seem faced with the hard choice of accepting him, and so swelling the soul to preserve the body, or of adhering to the Queen's will and saving the soul through bodily submission to Tritulacca. But I do not think God demands of us such submission, for our God is a God of joy.

"We are here met in the high assembly of the realm, which I hold to represent what of the power material has failed to protect its own; and the power spiritual is fully represented. Therefore, though such a step has no basis in law or custom, I say let us set up a regency in the time of a living Queen. It should have members of lords and estates to show forth the source of its authority; and since the true enemy is that power of evil which has led our good Queen astray, I humbly offer to preside."

He sat. There was a rumor, almost of agreement, but with a little edge in it that left Rodvard glad the Arch-Episcopal had ended so, for all the rest of what he said might have led them to agree, and it seemed to Rodvard that a regency with lords and Episcopals on it would be only the old rule again. Mathurin jerked his finger toward one of the brown legists, who had risen and was waiting for attention.

"I am the kronzlar Escholl," said the man. "I will say that this proposal of a regency in the time of a living ruler has good support in law and custom, though it is not generally known. It is now over eight quadrials of years since King Belodon the Second was killed at Bregatz during the Zigraner wars, and few remember that only three weeks before his death, it was determined that he had gone mad, and the barons set up a council of regency. We may, I think, assume a like madness in the Queen's Majesty, since her offer to Perisso is clearly contrary both to the law of the realm and true religion. His claim to Sedad Mir is based on descent in the male line, since it is well known that the last Count of that seignory wrongfully dispossessed his sister, who survived him to pass on her rights to the crown of Dossola."

The bright morning light struck through the window, fairly on the speaker's face (and as he took his place, Rodvard caught from his eye a quick gleam of greed and lust for power, altogether surprising in one who had spoken so dry and calmly). He touched Mathurin's arm to mention this, but now half a dozen more were on their feet to speak, and the writer before the assembly shot his finger at a man with a merchant's badge, in the group that had made the tumult when the Marquis of Palm was shouted down.

"I protest!" this one bawled. "I am called Brosen Zelitza. We are the assembly of the nation, and therefore already regents in our own right. Why vest the regency in a council? Why should Episcopals have the temporal power as well as the spiritual? If no one else dares to speak, I will tell you why; it is because they are sold—sold to Tritulacca. They wish to have the power to complete Cleudi's contract, and their objection to it is only a sham." (The voice had a curious dynamic quality that seemed to stir the very bones, but in Rodvard's mind, watching the face, there grew only a picture of something with teeth, he could not make out any mind or thought.) "—by the rule of these Episcopals and their mercenaries of the priesthood the old customs of Dossola were set aside, and it is forbidden that women shall use the Art. So Dossola is being made a half-nation like the savage Kjermanash, with women in bondage, unable to defend—" (The voice was stirring them, excitement in the hall, with movements and the scratch of a pushed-back chair.) "—corrupt priesthood, refuge of scoundrels and bastards," (Rodvard swept the line of the Episcopals, and though they were turned so he could catch no eyes, every pose told of rising indignation.) "—who cannot define the God they profess to serve—"

"Stop!" The Arch-Episcopal was on his feet again, staff upraised.

"Ah, the sword bites, does it? Conspirator! Plot—"

"Stop!" The voice that was accustomed to dominating the vast recesses of the cathedral was thunderous.

Up leaped Mathurin. "My lord Episcopal," he said, "this is

the great assembly of the people, where each may speak in turn. When you have heard him, we will hear you."

The Arch-Episcopal swung round (and from his eyes Rodvard could catch the flash of anger clearly enough, but that was not the sole emotion, and the rest was veiled). "I will never hear blasphemy," he said. "As the highest officer of government remaining loyal to the realm, I declare this assembly dissolved. All who love God and Dossola, follow me."

Amid a renewed outburst, catcalls and shouts of approval mingled, he lifted his staff high and strode toward the door, followed by the others of his class. A good half the legists came behind. The nobles stood, but hung hesitant, looking toward the strong Marquis of Palm; and then, seeing him sit, some returned to their seats. Of the merchants some followed, but the little knot where the shouting started remained in their seats.

When the procession had passed, Mathurin said; "The session for this day is closed." He turned toward Rodvard (and the latter saw in the smiling eyes that everything had gone exactly according to plan, and Zelitza was a good man).

II

Rodvard left the Hall of Presence alone, more than a little prideful at being a partaker in great deeds at last, and wondering what the old companions at the Office of Pedigree would say, who had so looked down on and baited him, when they knew he was one of the writers before the great assembly of the nation. Silver spadas were in his pouch; the new clothes were neat; it was the finest day of winter.

He felt he must tell someone of his delight in all; lifted his head as he strode, and so striding, inadvertently trod on the heel of one before. The man turned to show a face as young as his own and a clerical badge. His hands were hunched beneath the edge of his jacket.

"I beg your grace," said Rodvard.

"No matter," said the other.

"I was thinking. Did you know that the great assembly is going to make itself a regency in the place of Queen Berdette?"

"No." A pause. "Well, now the Tritulaccan Count will find him a better bedfellow. Perhaps we'll have this Prince Pavinius."

"The Episcopals left the assembly."

"Oh." Another stop to the conversation, step, step to the corner, side by side. The encounter glanced around (with discomfort in his eyes at having nothing to say). "Have you seen the new representation at Leverdaos? It is called 'The Maid's Problem' and Minora is playing."

25

Interview at the Nation's Guest-House

I

Lalette lay curled on the bed, half propped by pillows under her armpit. Demadé Slair had unbelted his sword to sit down; it leaned against his chair. Mathurin sat in the one by the table, the candle throwing his sharp profile into strong silhouette. Rodvard shifted in the damaged chair, whose lost stuffing made his seat uneasy.

"And that was all?" said the writer to the assembly, pinching his lower lip. "Nothing more from Palm, nothing more from the other Episcopals? Pest, Bergelin, you are less useful than I had expected."

"There was the legist who spoke," said Rodvard. "I think he is a man to beware of. His thought was so ruthless and desirous of power that he would ride down anything."

"You mean the kronzlar Escholl? That is of some use at all events," said Mathurin. "We need more like that, whether as allies or enemies. Things must be stirred; too many people are careless of who wins." He stood up and began to pace the floor slowly, head thrust forward a little, hands behind him. "Listen, Bergelin, I will be wholly frank with you. We held a meeting of the High Center this afternoon, following the session."

Rodvard said; "Are the names of its members still a secret, except for yourself?"

Mathurin gave a snort. "They will not be long, for things have so fallen out that the High Center and the Council of Regency will be one. You will have guessed that Brosen Zelitza of Arjen is one, there's the best speaker in Dossola. General Stegaller; he's in charge of the recruit bureau technically, but is really organizing what will be a people's army. It may surprise you to know that your old friend Mme. Kaja is a member; a wonderful woman for handling matters of detail, and we have to have one of her sex because of our position about the Art, but I could wish it were someone beside her, she's so religious." Lalette made a little sound; Rodvard caught sight of her face (and knew she was about to burst into one of her angers).

"Will no one tell me what has become of Doctor Remigorius?" he asked (hoping to forestall the outburst).

Mathurin's pacing stopped. "I forgive you and will tell you, but if you wish health, you will not mention him again. Rat, spy, tool; he has fled to his employer, Prince Pavinius— but he will not live long, so no more of him."

(Lalette thought: these are the creatures round my husband, my man—if he is my man, and not merely using me and my Blue Star.)

"It was decided—" Mathurin began, but before he had finished, a mouse slipped from under the edge of the bed, and ran rapidly across the floor as though on tiny wheels. Slair's arm flashed up and out with the scabbarded sword like a striking bird; blade and beast together arrived at the center of the carpet and the mouse twitched once and died. Demadé Slair picked up the small corpse and stood looking at it.

"Poor creature," he said, "I ask your pardon. Now your children in the hole will starve for lack of the food you went in search of."

Rodvard was astounded to see a tear glitter at the edge of the swordsman's eye. "Ah, bah!" said Mathurin. "Will you defend vermin, Slair? You'll have use enough for your steel when the new decrees are passed."

Rodvard stirred. "What decrees?"

Mathurin turned (with his back carefully to the candles, Rodvard noted, so that his face was dark). "There's to be a new court, to try special cases; it was what I was about to mention when interrupted. Treason against the people and nation. You will be writer to it; more important than the sessions of the assembly." He turned to Lalette. "There is also a part for you; you are one of the keys now."

Lalette said unhappily; "In what way?"

"As versus these Episcopals. They spread venom; represent the greatest danger we now have to face. Pavinius? I give him a snap of the fingers; he is too nice, with his Mayern foreigners and western herdsmen. The Tritulaccans? Nothing by themselves, they had never beaten Dossola in the former war but for the revolt of Mancherei, Mayern help and the treason of the Kjermanash chieftains. The court? Now sold to Tritulacca, and destitute by its own action. But the Episcopals are still not out of credit with the people, who have been lulled by their solemn mummery. We drove them from the assembly of the nation this morning, good. But now they may join Tritulacca in the name of what they call true religion."

"But what have I to do with the Episcopals?" asked the girl.

"Child, fool, use your Art. Not to the death; they'd only fill the office with another man, but paralyze, cripple, drive idiot. The Arch-Episcopal Groadon, notably. His loss would hurt them most."

Lalette sat up. "Ser Mathurin, you do not by any means understand this matter of the Art. Groadon is protected by the holy oils, and nothing I can do will bite on him."

"It is you that do not understand. I do assure you that if Groadon be taken in a moment of anger, as today, or other violent passion, neither his oils nor any other thing can protect him from your ministrations. Be assured, we will provide the occasion."

Lalette's mouth twitched. (She wanted to cry; "Not for any reward or punishment you can give!" but) it was a moment before she said; "Am I the only—witch in Dossola?"

Mathurin made a grating sound. "No. I'll be open; we are pressing the search. Have found three others—aside from those who claimed the Art, but could witch nothing more consequential than a frog or chicken. One is an old beldame who has nearly lost her wits, and can be made to understand nothing. One's a young girl—witch enough, but never taught, did not know the patterns, and besides, she ran away. One we caught, not found—she was in Chancellor Florestan's pay." He drew a finger across his throat. "None of them heiress to a Blue Star."

"I am not sure I can follow all the patterns myself," said Lalette. "I have used the Art—so little."

Mathurin looked at her sharply, "Hark!" he said. "I see your slowness, but you more than another should be on our side; as witch and woman. The Art has almost died out; driven down by priest and Episcopal. There are likely many with the right inheritance who do not know it. Never taught. Yet it's a woman's defence. We have the butler Tuolén's Blue Star, for instance. But where's the girl can bring it to life? We do not even know her name."

He whirled suddenly and flung out an arm toward Rodvard in an oratorical gesture. "Bergelin! I remember; that was the other matter. You were in the Office of Pedigree; know its secrets. Forget the great assembly for the time; that's under control. Until the new court's set up your task is seeking out Tuolén's heiress. I'll give you an authority."

"It may be somewhat harder than you think," said Rodvard.

"I did not say it would be easy. I said it would be done," said Mathurin. "Slair, let us go."

II

When they were out, he turned to look at Lalette. She had sagged down, with her face in the pillow, and now without moving, she said as before; "Rodvard."

He went across the room and put an arm around her. "What is it?"

"My mother. She is with the court, and she knows the patterns. If that man takes her, he will have her throat cut."

(The fate of many thousands, and the guarantee of the future, with the Art not in the hands of ignorant peasants, but women of intelligence and good will—balanced against one lie. But how to say it?) He said; "Has she shown so much concern for you?"

Lalette twisted under his arm. "If she had, would I know it? You hold me a prisoner—you and your Dr. Remigorius, who does not deliver letters, and your Mme. Kaja, who will sell me, and your Mathurin, who wants to cut my mother's throat. I never knew what dirt was till I knew you."

(Rodvard felt the blood beat at his temples; he wanted to strike her, to make a fiery retort.) He released her, stood up, and began to walk the floor. (No: no. A quarrel so entered could never be composed. Look beyond it, Rodvard; see how the world would be without her. Somewhere perhaps there was another who would have more response for an interior fidelity deeper than any single act; would not drive him from her side with bitter words when . . . He thought of Maritzl of Stojenrosek; and by this route came again to the high purpose. No. It was mere selfishness to let his own thought, his own problem, stand first; the very thing he had wished to bring her to see. Keep the peace.)

A small sound made him turn. She was just settling into place among the covers, and her face turned toward him. "Oh, Rodvard," she said, "help me. I can't do it. The Episcopal."

Nothing more was said on the subject, but that night they slept in each other's arms.

26

The Court of Special Cases

I

Punctual to the hour, as Rodvard and Lalette sat at breakfast with the woman who cared for the kitchen and a Green Islands buyer of northern wools, there arrived a messenger bearing the authority signed by Mathurin to consult all documents and registers in the Office of Pedigree, even those hitherto held under ecclesiastical seal. For Lalette also, a note; the Arch-Episcopal had declared himself in seclusion for prayer, and she would be notified further. Between them that morning there was a truce to contention; they walked for a while in the gardens among dead rustling leaves, and she kissed him sweetly when he left.

On the way to the Office of Pedigree, Rodvard thought of Asper Poltén and the rest when he walked in with an authority to examine the sealed registers, but this small triumph was denied him. Poltén was nowhere to be seen, and in the distributing office was only an old, dry, dusty man Rodvard remembered as having seen once or twice with some document close to his nose. He held Rodvard's paper in the same manner, sniffed as though it had an unpleasant odor, and shufflingly led the way to the sealed strongroom, which he unlocked with a creaking key. There seemed fewer people than usual in the halls.

The sealed files themselves showed the search likely to be a long one; mostly old, written in crabbed hands, and largely concerned with the illegitimacies of persons now forgotten, or convictions of witchery in cases that now had no meaning. Of the specific line of Tuolén there was no trace that morning, and the older records of families having Kjermanash blood were so badly kept as to indicate a long search.

At noon, Rodvard went to a tavern and lingered over his mug to savor the gossip of the town, but that was something of a failure, too, for there was none of the high excitement over the doings of the great assembly he had expected. The only group he overheard specifically were three or four merchants at a table, rather gloomily discussing the rise in the price of wool caused by the troubles in the west, and the fall in the price of southern wine, which kept coming in from oversea and could not be dispatched to the disturbed seignories. Nobody said a word about the Episcopals; the only time the court was mentioned, there was a little growling over the name of Florestan.

In the afternoon, Rodvard began by setting aside the registers that had to do with the three northernmost seignories, Bregatz, Vivensteg and Oltrug; but the task was so wearisome and his mind so occupied with other topics that he put them away early. It seemed to him, as he summoned the caretaker to lock the room, that there was nothing in the world as dear or desirable as Lalette, if he could only somehow reach an agreement with her, all troubles would vanish away. As he walked back toward the Ulutz palace, he thought that if they could only sit down in the clear winter air after last night's storm all coils would be unwoven.

But she was not in the room when he arrived, and when he found her, it was on a bench among the garden alleys, wrapped in a cloak and laughing at she talked to Demadé Slair. The swordsman leaped up at his coming. "Hail dauntless dompter of the written page!" he said, in a tone which was that of banter between friends, but with something in it that made Rodvard look sharply at the eyes. (Clear as speech, the thought came through; "And this long-legged booby who has never handled a weapon in his life will lie with her tonight while I'm alone.")

Rodvard said, a little unevenly; "I have made a beginning. Are there any tidings?"

"Not in the assembly," said Slair. "Much discussion of how

to raise troops for the people's army, and a report by General Stegaller. The decree for your court."

"My court?" said Rodvard (thinking of the Queen).

"That of judgment in special cases." (The eyes had gone blank.) "You'll be writer to it, as Mathurin to the assembly. If there's anyone you have a grudge against, name him for trial."

He laughed; so did Lalette (and as Rodvard caught her eye, he saw in it a color of regret that he could not be as gay as the swordsman, and a wave of dislike for the man who had rescued him from Charalkis prison contracted his veins). "I think I saw in the library a book by Momoroso that I have never read," he said. "I will see you before table, Lalette."

II

"The session will recess," said the kronzlar Escholl. He rose and swept the courtroom with his curious lacklustre eye, that never seemed to be settled on anything. "I will go over the evidence with you, Bergelin."

The legist on his right, the Zigraner, frowned; he on the left leaned his chin on his hand and his elbow on the table. The accused, a man with a coronet badge, iron-grey hair and heavy dewlaps, looked disconcerted. Rodvard gathered his papers and followed the president of the court to the little room in rear.

When they were there; "What have you found?" asked the legist.

"I think he tells the truth," said Rodvard, "when he says he has given no help to the Queen's party or Pavinius. When you asked him that, however, there was something like fear—perhaps for his brother. It was not clear."

"Ah." The legist placed his fingers together and studied them. "Bergelin," he said, after a moment, "you are to remember that this is a special court of inquiry. We are empowered to handle not only direct treasons, but matters which the ordinary law holds criminal. Such acts dissipate the resources that of right belong to the nation. You tend to be narrow. Let us return."

As they came in, one of the guards nudged the prisoner forward again. The jurist president frowned on him portentously. "Kettersel," he said, "a brief examination of the record shows no evidence of your giving aid to either of the two destituted persons who claim to rule the realm of Dossola. Unless my fellow-jurists disagree, of that you are acquitted." He glanced at one and the other; the Zigraner gave a somewhat unwilling nod, the third legist had only an absent expression. "But in pleading innocence of giving such aid, you are answering a charge that has never been brought. If you say you are not guilty of garroting people by night in King Crotinianus' Square, we will find you innocent of that also, and so through a list of possible crimes, did it not waste this court's time to agree with you that you have committed none of them. But you are charged with treason to the nation, which in its essence consists not of any specific act, but of a point of view, which may be proved by a number of actions, in themselves bearing an innocent appearance until they are assembled with each other. I take it my fellow-jurists agree."

He looked again, and again those in the lower seats nodded.

"Kettersel," he said, "answer me. You have a brother with the court?"

The man cleared his throat. "I have answered that. He is a capellan in the Eagle Shar of Her Majesty's lancers." (The shadow of worry was behind the man's eye; now deepened, and very surprising in such a person, whom one would have expected to be concerned about gold scudi or the fidelity of his mistress.)

"The nation's lancers," corrected Escholl. "Kettersel, are both you and your brother married?"

"Only him; the Baron."

"Has he daughters?"

"No. Only a son."

"If your brother should fall in the fighting, where would the inheritance lie?" (Now the fear was at the front and perfectly sharp; it was a fear of being left penniless.) Kettersel said slowly (and lying); "I am not sure; would have to consult the Office of Pedigree. There is a cousin, I think, to whom the income would fall. The title and the estate would pass to the son, of course."

"How old is the son."

"Twenty-four."

"I see." The jurist president moved his lips (and Rodvard observed that the man before him was perspiring with the effort to keep some thought down; a thought which came to the watcher dark as sin and midnight). "Is your nephew married?"

"To one of the Blenau family."

Rodvard signed; without appearing to see him the jurist president said; "Kettersel, you are engaged in concealments. It is useless. What is the trouble between you and your nephew?"

The man's self-control split apart suddenly. He flung at Rodvard a glance of purest venom and burst out; "The damned young puppy is trying to have his own father killed so he may have the title for his whore of a wife. There is no reason, none at all, why he should take a command in the Eagle Shar. He is an old man, taking the task of that young bastard in the lancers, where all the fighting is."

There was a little murmur in the courtroom. The jurist president said; "Why did he accept the charge?"

(It was the wrong line; Kettersel's eyes were perfectly clear.) "To spare his son, I suppose. My nephew was appointed earlier."

Rodvard coughed. Kronzlar Escholl said; "Where are your nephew and his wife now?"

The man paused (and in that pause the thing came through; it took Rodvard a minute or two to realize what it was). "I heard of them last at Landensenza."

Rodvard stepped up to the jurist's seat, with one finger on the paper to maintain the fiction, and whispered; "His true concern is not his brother, but because he wishes to lie with his nephew's wife. I think she may have refused him, but he still believes it may be done somehow if the nephew can be killed before his brother."

Escholl put a finger beside Rodvard's. "That is correct, after all," and turned to the prisoner. "Kettersel, your con-

cern for your brother does you the greatest credit. It is
evident that you have been in correspondence with him, but I
think my brother jurists will agree when I pronounce you
guiltless of true treason and order your release."

The two jurists wagged their heads silently and in unison,
like those toys with flexible necks which children play with
during the winter festival.

"We will hear the next case."

27

Winter Light

I

As Rodvard left the courtroom, Demadé Slair fell into
step beside him (The man was determinedly, if coldly,
friendly; how to shake him off? instead of leading him home
to Lalette and another of those conversations in three, where
Rodvard felt himself so much hearing a language he did not
understand that he always ultimately fled them for a book or
the outer air.)

"Escholl is one of our best," said the swordsman, kicking
at the skin of a fruit, "but there's a judgment I failed to
understand."

"Which one? The merchant who was confiscated for bringing wool-carts past the Mayern camp?"

"Ah, bah, no. He had money, the nation needs it; that's
crime enough. I spoke of the baron's brother, the noble Kettersel."

"No more did I understand it," said Rodvard. "As dirty a
character as I ever saw, but the kronzlar let him go and
praised him."

"Oho!" said Slair. "It begins to come clear. What's the
tale?"

"Why, he was after his nephew's wife—whether for her

money or her body the most, I am not sure, but he wants both." (He could not resist adding); "And it's a poor task to break up a couple at any time, for it destroys two people's chance of happiness for the temporary pleasure of one."

"Not always," said Slair, avoiding his eyes. "But I am interrupting. Is there more?"

"His only fear is that the Baron will die before the son, and so the right of remarrying the girl will pass to another family. I did not tell the kronzlar because it was not clear enough, but I think he was planning murder. Yet Escholl let him go."

Slair laughed. "Bergelin," he said, "do not lose your innocence; it may save your life some day, for no one will ever believe you are subtle enough to be dangerous. I said Escholl was one of our best; depend upon it, he thought more deeply than you, and without any witch-stone to help him. Why, it is precisely because Kettersel has murder and rape at the back of his mind that he was let go. For exactly the opposite reason, the court will condemn Palm as soon as there's a pretext for a trial. Mathurin has arranged it so."

"I am innocent again and do not quite understand the reason."

"Yet you will dabble in high politic! Hark, now: are not all of the noble order enemies to the New Day by constitution, by existence? Are not all their private virtues overwhelmed by this public fault? The true villains among them will sooner or later dig their own graves and save us the trouble, bringing discredit on the whole in the process. But when you have one like Palm or the late Baron Brunivar, he's dangerous; sets people to loving the institution because they cannot hate the man, and so must be pulled down by force.... For that matter, we need something to stir the people, make them fight for their liberty."

"This seems a hard way," said Rodvard, (trying to resolve the torsion in his mind).

"It is a hard life, and hardest for those who avoid battle," said Demadé Slair; and Rodvard not replying, they walked in silence. (Would this new system somehow produce men of better heart and purpose? For he did not see how the hardness could be justified else. And now his mind fell to wagging between man-system, system-man, and he decided that the justification of the system would be that it produced better men generally, and not merely a few of the best. No, not that either, for that was to confuse politic with ethic, and each was itself a system; for the one would make men good without regard to their happiness, and the other make them happy without regard to their good. . . . Or what was good? Where was the standard? By the system of Mancherei—)

"Will you go on to the quays?" said Slair's voice, suddenly, and Rodvard found himself three steps beyond the entrance to the Palace Ulutz.

"I am weary tonight," said Rodvard. "Perhaps because I am so innocent that this affair of spying upon the minds of my fellows is somewhat unpleasant."

He extended his hand to bid goodnight.

"Oh, I am going with you," said the swordsman, and as he caught Rodvard's glance of aversion, "I cannot bear to be without your company." His face went sober as he quick-stepped beside Rodvard's dragging feet up the entrance-walk. "This is Mathurin's arrangement, also, in case it troubles you. Did you not notice those two men who followed us from the court at half a square's distance? There will be another outside tonight. People's guards."

(A tremor of peril.) "But I have—"

"Done nothing but your duty to the nation. True; and for that reason precisely it is needful to guard you like an egg sought after by weasels. Do you think that the fact you bear a Blue Star is a secret? There are not a few persons who may be brought before the court that would rather conceal an assassination than what they have in their minds. You and I may have a fight on our hands." His face lighted with pleasure at the prospect.

II

They paced slowly through the dead garden, along a walk so narrow that shoulders sometimes touched. Lalette could hear the tiny tinkle of the chain that bound Slair's sword to his hip when that touch came; she knew he was stirred, and the rousing of emotion was not unpleasant to her. Beyond the slate roofs of the town the sun was sinking redly through striations of cloud; all things lay in a peace that was the peace of the end of the world. He turned his head.

"Demoiselle," he said, "what will you give for news?"

"Oh, hush," said she. "You spoil it. For a moment I was immortal."

"I ask your grace. But truly I have news for you, and it should please you."

"Sit here and tell me." She took her place on a marble bench beneath the skeleton of an espaliered peach against the wall.

"You will not have to use your Art against the arch-priest Groadon. Does that not please you?"

"More than you know. What is the reason?"

"He has fled; slipped through the watch set on his palace and gone—whether to hell, the court or Tritulacca, no one knows."

"I am glad." She looked straight before her for a moment. "Ah, if things were better ordered."

"You are not as pleased as you might be."

"Oh, I am. But Rodvard—"

"What has he done? I'll—"

"Oh, it's no fault of his. You will tell no one?" She laid a cold hand on his warm one. "He has found who the heiress of Tuolén is, but does not know whether to tell Mathurin or not."

"Who is she?"

"A child, thirteen years old. She lives at Dyolana, up in Oltrug seignory. But I do not know how long Rodvard will keep the secret. He feels a sense of duty."

"Why should he not? What withholds him from telling?"

"I would have to teach her the patterns and everything. I do not wish it." She shivered slightly. "And to be a witch—"

The rising shades had drowned the sun. A silence came on the garden, so utter that Lalette felt she could hear her own heart beat, and Demadé Slair's beside her. The trees stood straight; the ruins of the flowers did not stir. In that enchanted

stillness she seemed to float without power of motion. He
leaned toward her, his arm close against her back, his other
hand crept over her two.

"Demoiselle—Lalette," he said in a voice so low it did not
break the quiet. "I love you. Come away with me."

Her down-bent head shook slowly; tears gathered behind
the almost-closed eyes.

The arm around her back slid slowly beneath her own
arm, the hand groped to close slowly around one soft breast;
as though it were by no volition of her own, her head came
back to meet the kiss. The tears ran down her cheek to touch
his; he drew from her and began to speak rapidly in a voice
low and urgent:

"Come with me. I will take you away from every unhappiness. We can go beyond finding. I am a fighting man, can
find a need for my service anywhere. It does not matter; we
can forget all this entanglement and make our own world. I
have money enough. We can go to the Green Islands, and
you will never have to use the Art again. Oh, Lalette, I
would even take you to the court and join your mother. Do
you wish it?"

Her lips barely moving, she said; "And Rodvard?"

He kissed her again. "Bergelin? You owe him nothing.
What has he done to you? And now he will tell Mathurin
about the heiress of Tuolén, and there will be no more place
for you—execpt with me. I will always have a place for you,
Lalette, now or a thousand years from now. Or do you fear
him? I am the better man."

Now her eyes opened wide on the first star, low in the
darkening sky, and with one hand she gently disengaged his
clasp from her breast. "No," she said in a voice clearer than
before. "No, Demadé, I cannot. Perhaps for that reason,
but I cannot. We had better go in now."

III

"Friend Ber-ge-lin! Friend Ber-ge-lin!" the voice from below-stairs brought back to a consciousness of unhappiness the
mind that had lost itself in the sweet cadences and imagined

worlds of Momoroso. Rodvard sprang up and threw open th
door.

"What will you have?"

"Someone to see you."

Down the hall another door closed. It would be the littl
old man who asked so many questions and went almos
a-tiptoe, as though always prepared to look through a ke
hole. From the stairhead, Rodvard could see in the evening'
first shades a figure covered with a long cloak, someho
familiar, but the face hooded over.

"Beg her to come up," he called. The figure mounted wit
one hand on the bannister, in the slow manner of the ol
Near the last step his mind clicked; he was not surprise
when in the room the hood fell back to show Mme. Kaj;
Face cold as ice, he remained standing. She came across th
room in a whirl of skirts, with both hands out.

"My de-ear boy," she said.

With the hangings at the windows, it was too dim to te
how far her sincerity went. "I am more than honored to hav
one of the regents—," he said, and let it hang.

"Oh, you are the most necessary of all," she said, an
frou-froued to the best chair. "I hope you have forgiven m
It was so-o-o necessary; someone had filed an informatio
with the provost that I was part of the New Day, and it wa
such a help. Isn't it to-o bad about the Episcopals no
cooperating? But there are so many of the priests on ou
side."

She had seated herself where her face was in the shadow.

"Madame, why have you come?" he asked brutally.

There was a silence in the darkening room. Then: "T
help you," said the voice that, though it might no longer sing
had not lost its silver in speech.

"I will make a light."

She stirred. "Do not. It is better so ... I know—you ar
thinking of the Blue Star. Do you imagine that I fear you
using it? No."

He sat quietly (noting with the back of his mind how th
dubious nicety had dropped from her voice, and thinking tha
this was the woman who had been taken into the Hig

Center). Once more she seemed to gather her forces. "Rodvard Bergelin," she said, "do you know why I am in the High Center?"

"I . . . think so."

"I will tell you. It may be that in my ancestry there is a strain from one of the witch-families. It may be because I sincerely serve God. I do not know. But it has been given to me to be able to trace certain secrets of the heart." Her multitudinous bracelets jingled as she lifted a hand to her breast. "Not as you do with the Blue Star."

She was silent again, and he (unable to restrain an impulse toward malice) said; "Your success in understanding Dr. Remigorius was—as great as my own."

"Rodvard, you are so-o unfair." She dropped for a moment into the old manner, then seemed to shake herself. "I know. Your—witch will never forgive me. Not that I brought the provosts, but that I came in that day when you were on the bed. I do not care; she brings an evil Art into our New Day."

"Do you think so?"

"Rodvard, hear me. This witch, to whom you are affected, will one day be the end of you. I have seen her but little, yet I know—it is your nature to give offense, and hers to take it. Sooner or later it will happen that she will find something not to be borne and put a witchery on you that will strike like lightning."

(This clipped him close; with a certain convulsion round the heart, he remembered Lalette's occasional sudden rages.) "Well," he said, "what would you have me do?"

"Bid her farewell. Both of you can find partners better suited."

Rodvard came to his feet and walked across the room slowly (thinking in little flashes of sweet Leece and Maritzl of Stojenrosek). Mme. Kaja sat immobile.

"No," he said. "Better or worse, I will not give her up for anything."

Mme. Kaja also stood. "Forgive an old woman," she said, and gathering her cloak around her, slipped out the door.

28

Embers Revived

I

"We will hear the next case," said the kronzlar Escholl.
The people's guard opened the door to the room of the
accused and called, "Bring her in," while a sharp-faced countryman stepped forward from the rear of the court, two more
guards behind him. The countryman had a merchant's badge
and so quick an eye that Rodvard gazed at him, fascinated to
see what it would tell, and was therefore unprepared when he
turned his head to see the accused.

It was Maritzl of Stojenrosek.

A Maritzel pale behind her red lips, still even when she
moved, and much changed. (How? Rodvard asked himself
and could find no answer but in a certain lessening of fibre
that was expressed around the mouth, though the breathtak-
ing thrill of her presence was still so much there that he
swallowed.) The craggy-faced prosecutor stepped forward. "I
present an accusation of treason against the nation on the
part of the Demoiselle Maritzl of Stojenrosek, mistress of
Count Cleudi, the foreign traitor. I call the innkeeper of
Drog."

("Mistress of Count Cleudi?" and Drog?) The sharp-faced
man stood forth. Maritzl turned to look at him, and as her
eyes turned back, they fell on Rodvard. She started (and
before she looked down again he caught from them an arrow
of purest and most astounding hatred). "Tell us your story,"
said the jurist president.

"I keep a good house," said the man, twisting his cap in his
hands, "and I have to be careful to preserve its reputation,
because—"

The prosecutor touched his arm. "Give your condition
first."

Head bobbed. "Thank you, friend. I am keeper of the inn Star of Dossola at Drog, on the road through the Pass of Pikes in the Ragged Mountains, and mine is the largest inn there, with three upper rooms beside the general chamber." (Maritzl was looking at him again, not now with hatred, but weariness of the world, and the thought that he, Rodvard, was as dreary as any part of it.) "It has never been necessary for the provosts to come to my place except when I called them. Now when this woman came into my inn, I knew right away that something was wrong. Late at night it was, and she in a three-horse coach with a driver, and that seemed strange—"

The prosecutor halted him again. "Explain why you thought something was wrong."

"Look at her; she comes evidently from the court and bears the marks of it." He jabbed a finger at the girl, but it was Rodvard she looked at (a long slow glance, in which was some decision to make a desperate appeal). "When I saw her, I think to myself, as a man often will, that this is not the place for a court woman to be, not with the court in Zenss. So I think this is a good one to watch and perhaps I will learn something, and while she is supping—she sat apart from the coachmaster in the high dining room, she did— while she was supping, I served her myself and marked how there was a little casket she kept beside herself and touched her hand to, even while she was eating."

(Her face now outwardly held the appeal, but a plan was building in her mind; he could see it grow stone by stone, but not clearly what it was, because little hate-flashes kept jagging across the picture.)

"So I said to her that if her casket was that precious, I ought to hold it in the strongbox of the inn, there being so many wandering soldiers about. When I said this, her ladyship—" he grinned a vulpine grin to show this was intended for a joke "—said no, she would as soon lose her life as the casket, which being so small, I think it must have in it something besides jewels. So I said to myself, here is some mystery, but if anyone can unlock it, it is my friend Khlab, that was a provost of the court at Sedad Vix till it was broken up. So while her ladyship was at the dessert, I slipped out to find my friend Khlab, and let him walk past the door to look at her. The minute he saw her—"

"One moment," said the prosecutor, and addressed the court. "I present the former provost Khlab, now a people's guard." He motioned to a man behind, who took the innkeeper's place. "Tell your story."

"Yes, your—friend. I saw her through the door as I went past and I knew her at once for Maritzl of Stojenrosek because I had seen her before. She is the one Count Cleudi brought to Sedad Vix to be his mistress after the spring festival. I told this to friend Brezel, and he said if she was as close as that to Cleudi, she had no business in Drog. So we went in and under pain of the sword, made her give up the casket. It had some jewels in it, but underneath the lining was the letter."

"The letter is here," said the prosecutor, handing up a parchment, partly torn, but bearing the unmistakable blue star seal. "It is a document already famous, in which Cleudi beseeches the aid of the Tritulaccans in return for cessions of territory. Most treasonable matter."

"Hm-hm," said kronzlar Escholl, looking at it as though he had never seen it before. The Zigraner jurist craned his neck. (Her plan was complete now;) she took one step forward and in a low urgent whisper said; "Rodvard, help me."

(It was an entreaty, and as though she knew of the use of the jewel, she was projecting a promise behind the entreaty; and the plan was behind the promise. But it was as though that "Help me" laid a compulsion on him.) Rodvard turned round, as Escholl was handing the parchment to the third jurist. "Your pardon, kronzlar."

A frown. "Very well, I will see it."

Rodvard stepped to the bench and whispered: "She is thinking of some sort of plan, I do not know for what. I think I could find out, if I could question her alone. I knew her in the old days."

"I see."

Escholl addressed the court. "This is perhaps the foulest piece of treason in the history of Dossola; and we have proof that the message is no forgery in the recent march of the Tritulaccan shars over the southern border, and the delivery to them without a battle of the castle of Falsteg. It is evident that the accused had full knowledge of the contents of this letter, and is therefore guilty of taking part in a vile conspiracy against the nation. But this court is required to follow every treason to its source, not merely to establish individual guilts. We will postpone this matter for inquiry, and pass to the next case."

II

Rodvard sprang up as she was led into the room, hurrying to get her one of the comfortless chairs from the row against the wall. The guard leered at him (with a thought so nasty that) Rodvard's tongue stumbled as he said; "She wants to—tell me something in private." The guard laughed, glanced at the barred window and slammed the door.

Maritzl said; "Rodvard, I do not want to go to the throat-cutter."

"What can I do?" said he.

Her hand clenched, fingers entwined in fingers. "Take me away. You are the writer to this court. Can you not make an order or something for my release to be transported else-where?"

(This was the plan, but it was not the whole plan; and yet under the magic of her presence, the words seemed to count more than what lay behind them.) "It—it would be very difficult," he said. "The order would have to be counter-signed, and—"

"And you are a writer!" A note of scorn in her voice.

"You mean—I should forge the signature?"

"Why not? This regency of yours is hopeless. I have been confined, but even I know that. How many shar of soldiers do you order? Enough to fight the court and all Tritulacca?"

(Now it was Rodvard's turn to be uneasy, for he had

asked himself these questions.) "The people will rise," he said.

"Have they risen yet? Where are their weapons? How many leaders do you have who can set a battle in order? Pavinius will never fight with the Tritulaccans; they'll compose." (Now genuine black anger jutted from her eyes.) "All you can do, here in this little dream-world, is lay the ground for vengeance on yourselves." She was near enough to reach out a hand and touch him. "Take me away. I do not want to go to the throat-cutter, and I do not want you to, either."

"And you would have me betray . . .?"

(Her eyes flashed a resolve;) before he could say more, she was out of her chair, arms around his shoulders, cheek caressing his head. "Ah, Rodvard, I will make it up to you."

He stood up in the circle of her arms; her head tilted back, the long lashes lying on her cheek over veiled eyes. (Mistake, he thought, a sudden rivulet of cold running down his spine. It cannot be true, you were hating me a moment ago; I think I see your plan now.)

He held her off with rough hands on her shoulders. "You are Cleudi's mistress," he said.

The liquid flesh changed to brass, the eyes snapped open as she shook herself free. "Yes, I am Cleudi's mistress," she cried. "And whose fault is it? I was a good girl once; I would have given you everything and remained good, no matter what I did for you. You did not want me."

She was down in the chair again, crying through her fingers. "You are too much like him," she said, and he (wrung by the thought of that fair neck delivered to the executioner) laid a hand on her shoulder and said; "I will do what I can." Now kronzlar Escholl must be persuaded, if possible, that though there had been treason, it was treason done for love and could be passed over.

III

Rodvard came in late, and had had no supper save some bread and cheese caught at an inn with the two people's guards who accompanied him, Demadé Slair having left long before. Lalette was arranging her hair before the mirror, with a candle on either side, and did not turn round. (At the sight of her lifted graceful arms, a wave of tenderness swept over him.) "Lalette," he said, almost lilting the word.

"Good evening." She still did not turn, and the voice was formal.

He hurried across the room in long steps and turned her around. "What has happened?"

There was an impatient movement. "Don't. You will spoil my hair. Nothing."

"Lalette, there is something. Tell me."

She kept her eyes away from him. "Nothing," and then, as he merely stood, waiting in burning intensity; "A small thing, truly. You need not be troubled. Only I know now who it was you were unfaithful to me with."

(He was hot and cold together.) "Who says I was unfaithful?"

" 'Will you come with me now?' " she quoted. "Rodvard, you may be able to read some of my thoughts, but do not forget why. Is she a witch, too? She must be, or my Blue Star that I lent you would be dead. Or did she give you another before you shared her with Count Cleudi?" (She wanted to hurt him as she had been hurt, to make him regret and feel that no regret in any fashion could replace what had been lost.)

"Shared her with Count Cleudi?" (He could feel honest indignation now.) "Lalette, who are you talking about?"

"I am glad you saved her life," said she, still not looking at him. "It is a pity my hair is dark and my skin muddy. When these troubles are over, you can have a good time with her on the estate. It is in 'Zada, isn't it?"

(The indignation no longer needed to be pushed; all he could think of was how he had rejected the shell of that Maritzl once desired.) He said; "Lalette, I swear to you that I have never been with Maritzl of Stojenrosek, if that is the one you mean. I swear that I never will, I don't even want her."

(The accent of sincerity was making her doubt, but the bitterness persisted beneath, she had only lost the line somewhere, and was not yet ready to release him.) "If you are really in love with her, you may go. Only I'll not be one of your—casual contacts."

(He was invaded by despair of making her understand, with or without the fullest tale of the maid Damaris and the witch of Kazmerga.) "Why," he cried, "it would seem to me that it is asked of any pair who live together to protect each other from casual contacts by one means or another. But this is merely not true. Will you listen to every talebearer who tries to split us apart for reasons of his own?"

She lowered her head (melting a little, knowing he knew of Demadé Slair's desire, if not of her own temptation). "There are some tales you might have borne to me yourself instead of letting me learn them by hazard. Why did you betray me by telling Mathurin of the child of Dyolana, Tuolén's heiress?"

Now he took her strongly by the shoulders. "Lalette," he said; "I never told him. You accuse me of being liar and betrayer, do you think I am a fool as well? If Mathurin knows of her, he has learned it through some other source; you are the only one I told."

(Suddenly and dreadfully, she knew where that other source was—that night in the garden, when she herself told Demadé Slair, Mathurin's voice and sword.) She moved close, putting both arms around him in a convulsive gesture. "Oh, Rodvard," she said, "I am afraid. He is having her brought here, and will make her a witch himself—that little girl."

She began to cry then. That night, as they sought and received from each other whatever comfort passion could give, she touched him and said; "It is true. I am a witch and your partner. The great marriage."

29

No and Yes

I

"You helped me so much before," said Lalette.

The widow Domijaiek contemplated her tranquilly from among the husks of characters who never lived. "Yet you are again in need of help."

"The Myonessae. I could not—"

"You could not give up the desires of this false, material world for the God of love. However, it is not necessary to agree with everything that is done under the rule of the Prophet, and when the mattern and the diaconals tried to force you to an advancement for which you were not ready, they were also submitting to the rule of Evil. It is asked only to take steps we are prepared for."

"Yes," said Lalette.

"I do not know whether I can help you. Let us examine circumstance. Are you still stricken by lack of money?"

"I had not thought of it. Rodvard touches the fees of the court where he is writer. Our needs are small."

The widow's smile was approving. "That is an element of progress. But he receives these fees because he uses the witchery of the Blue Star, does he not?"

"Yes."

"Then that is an element contrary to progress and very dangerous."

Lalette looked at the floor. "I know. Everything seems to be a danger. I am so afraid of Mathurin. He keeps those guards around Rodvard, but I think they are more like jailers."

"One thing you must not do is let fear enter your heart; for it will breed fearful things. Remember that all in this false material world is only the reflection of your thoughts. Have you any word from your mother?"

"Yes. A man brought a note. She wants me to escape and join her at the court."

"Do you wish to go?"

"I would like to see her again. . . ." Lalette looked up to see Dame Domijaiek watching her attentively, though she remained very quiet, and under the pressure of that silent scrutiny, the girl moved. "She is under Count Cleudi's protection. And I told you about Demadé; he is very kind and gay, and I think he is in love with me, but—"

"Go on."

"He told Mathurin about the little girl, the heiress."

"He was also trying to do the best for you, in his own way. Do you want to go? Or would you rather stay with Rodvard?"

In a small voice, Lalette said; "I think I would rather stay with him. Is it wrong?"

"Not if it is done in love and good will, rather than for any hope of gain. Have you asked him to take you away from the city?"

"No. This—regency is so much to him."

The widow stirred. "You will find help, child. Come to me again when he makes a plan."

She stood up, but before the words of farewell could be pronounced, the door was flung open and the boy Laduis burst in, crying; "Mother! I was at the market, and—"

"Laduis, we have a guest."

He looked embarrassed and made to Lalette the bow of a miniature courtier. "Oh, I remember you," he said. "You are the Princess Sunimaa, only you are not cold any more. I am glad to see you." He turned again. "Mother, everybody at the market is excited. They say there has been a battle in the Ragged Mountains, and Prince Pavinius has beaten the Tritulaccans and taken three of their generals, and the rest of them are all running away."

II

She had gone quietly to sleep; Rodvard had to rouse her with the finger-touch behind the right ear that wakens without shock. Even then, she tried for a moment to draw him close until he whispered; "We must hurry."

Beyond the window there was only cold wintry starshine and little enough of that; but Rodvard had hoped for snow or rain. Lalette gathered her smallest of bundles; he led along the balcony three windows down, to where thee trellis was, and stepped off backward into night, resting a moment on each step before taking the next. Lalette's dresses almost made her stumble on the last steps; she sank into his arms with a little gasp at the bottom. They had carefully worked out the matter of getting over the garden-wall, from the barrel to the shed-roof, the shed-roof to the wall itself.

It was too late for the bracket-torch on the back street to have remained alight. As soon as she was down, they dodged shivering past the plane-trees, across, around a corner and into the appointed alley. Something jingled; the man said; "Are you the travellers?"

"Dame Domijaiek's travellers," said Rodvard, as agreed, and; "Here is your horse and your let-pass," the other.

Rodvard got up first; the man, whose features remained indistinguishable, helped Lalette up behind and gave them a farewell in tones not unfriendly. Rodvard had seldom followed the maze of streets toward the northwest quarter, but it was fairly easy to maintain direction, and there was only one gate leading to the Archer's Highroad. The horse walked, and Lalette felt so sleepy that it was almost agony to keep her place.

There was no one moving on any street and hardly a light at any window. Once a wrong turn led into a blind alley, but that did not hold them back long, and now they were in the shadow of the gate, with a sentry barring the path with a pike and another holding up a lantern.

"This is a fine hour to be leaving the city," grumbled the first.

"All hours are fine when one must go," said Rodvard, and produced his paper; this was the moment of test.

The sentry puzzled over it a moment, looked back at them, to the paper again, and said; "Pass friends." As he turned back to the sentry-cachet with his pike-bearing companion, Rodvard caught a fragment of words ". . . won't be too glad to see that couple," and wondered what the paper had said.

As they reached the far end of the bridge, where the ancient stone leopard stands, he urged his mount to trot, but the pace was too fast for Lalette, she had to beg him not to. They moved for a long time through a space without figures until, like a conjurer's trick, trees and houses began to appear in grey outline around them, and then slowly to take on color. The road turned leftward, and the river was beyond, with ice on it. Lalette said; "Rodvard."

He did not turn his head. "What will you have?"

"Can you forgive me?"

"For what?"

"Taking you away from—everything. Your new day, the work."

"There is nothing to forgive. I had to go."

They were silent again, and in that silence the sun grew behind streaked clouds. Lalette was so tired and sore that she felt she must say something about it, but just before endurance reached its limit, they came to the famous bridge of boats at Gogau, with its inn on the opposite bank, and Rodvard said; "Let us rest here and take refreshment."

He helped her down and inside to a seat, still without words, and a round-cheeked innkeeper came to them with a good morning. After he had gone, Rodvard said:

"No . . . I do not know quite what I wished or what I wish now; but I am sure it is not to be compelled to use all I have in Mathurin's way. . . ."

He stared across the room away from her, and she (grateful that he was not looking to read her thought with the Blue Star) said; "Do you think he can make his regency stand?"

"I do not know, but I think not in the long run. If Prince Pavinius has beaten the Tritulaccans so badly . . ." He touched the jacket where the cold stone lay. "This is not me, and I'll not be ruled by it, no more than you by your gift of witchery."

She shuddered slightly. "It is a gift I never wished."

Now his face showed trouble. He stood up and paced the floor, then turned to the inn portal, where after a moment she joined him, looking out. The sun had daunted down the clouds, picking everything out in winter's white gold; beneath them the river hurried past, carrying little pieces of ice against the black boats. At last he said; "Somewhere I have lost the line. . . . I suppose that the most we can do is try to use the lesser evil to overcome the greater, forgiving what we can. . . . It is I who ask you to forgive me."

She put an arm around his waist. "You do not need to. I think I love you."

For an enchanted moment they stood so. Then Rodvard's hands went to his neck, and with a swift motion, he drew out the Blue Star, over his head and holding it in his hand, glanced at the stream and then at Lalette.

"Yes," she said. It made only a small splash where it struck the water.

Epilogue

In view of the speed with which the low-hung clouds were driving past the window, there would evidently be no business with ducks that day. Hodge helped himself to more coffee.

"I wonder what happened to them afterward," he said.

"Does it matter?" said Penfield. "When an emotional problem is solved, the others become unreal."

"You don't consider poverty a real problem?" asked McCall.

"Only in a social and relative sense. Go look at the natives in the hill-country of any Latin-American state. They live on rice, beans and fifteen cents a day, and remain quite happy."

Hodge said; "I agree that poverty is a minor matter in this

particular case. But it seems to me that you're assuming too much when you speak of the emotional problem of that couple as solved. It's not like a sum in arithmetic, with a simple answer in definite figures. There are all sorts of sub- and side-problems involved, to which no definite values can be assigned. For instance, isn't the memory of the girl, Leece, together with one of Lalette's outbursts of temper, going to produce an explosive mixture at some point? And aren't they keeping a good deal from each other?"

Penfield's long face was thoughtful. "There are secrets in the background of every union," he said. "Even secrets as black as the murder by witchcraft, and as inexplicable as the failure and recovery of the Blue Star. But it seems to me that they are like the disagreements of parties in a politically stable state. Once the essential agreement to abide has been reached, any difficulties can be resolved or compromised. Another thing—these people have a capacity for . . . well, close attunement to each other. More of it than we have. What puzzles me—" he took a pull at his cigarette "—is a certain preoccupation with sex."

McCall laughed. "Since it was the product of all three of us, that probably came out of Hodge's mind somehow. Persons of your age and mine . . ."

Hodge said; "I don't know where it came from, but I think I can explain it. It goes with religion, which is so often an outgrowth of sex—or a substitute for it."

"What really interests me," said McCall, "is what happened in a political sense."

"Well, the short-range developments seem fairly obvious," said Penfield, "and long-range ones are always unpredictable."

"I wonder if it really exists," said Hodge, as Penfield had the night before.

Penfield got up, went to the window, and looked out at the scudding clouds. "I wonder if we do," he said.

About the Author

Fletcher Pratt was born in 1897 and died in 1956, only four years after *The Blue Star* was published. In a long and fruitful collaboration with L. Sprague de Camp, he produced a number of fantasies which were distinguished by wit, sophistication, a sense of humor, and a delightful and lively imagination—books such as the "Harold Shea" trilogy, comprised of *The Incomplete Enchanter** (1941), *The Castle of Iron* (1950), and *Wall of Serpents* (1960); and novels like *Land of Unreason* (1942), *The Carnelian Cube* (1948), and a bookful of modern-day Runyonesque stories: *Tales from Gavagan's Bar* (1953).

On his own, Pratt lived to produce only two works of epic fantasy. Both are long, intelligent and carefully plotted novels laid in imaginary medieval worldscapes. Of these two, *The Well of the Unicorn* (1948) is perhaps the best known.

But *The Blue Star*—in some ways the more thoughtfully conceived and more brilliantly worked out—is almost completely unknown. This novel was never published in a magazine, unlike the majority of Pratt's fantasy fiction. The one and only other edition of the book was published—together with two other novels (*Conjure Wife*, by Fritz Leiber and *There Shall Be No Darkness*, by James Blish)—by Twayne Publishers, Inc., in 1952 in a fat omnibus volume under the title of *Witches Three*.

---

* In the Spring of 1976, Ballantine will publish *THE COMPLEAT ENCHANTER: The Magical Misadventures of Harold Shea*—a giant volume that includes both *The Incomplete Enchanter* and *The Castle of Iron*.

Pratt was a writer of unusual skill, who found more excitement in the interplay of ideas in action than in the familiar sort of swashbuckling heroics. He was a born story-teller in the grand tradition—the sort of man who read Norse sagas in the original, adored Eddison's *The Worm Ouroboros,* and read collections of obscure national mythologies for pleasure. As de Camp points out in an article on his late friend, "Pratt stories move right along. Something is always happening. His writing is full of novel conceits, flashes of wit and interesting turns of phrase. The settings are lush and vivid."

Such a man was Fletcher Pratt. Such a book is *The Blue Star.* I commend both to you, with affection.

—LIN CARTER
Hollis, Long Island, New York

MORE S-F
from
🅱️🅱️
BALLANTINE BOOKS

VOYAGE TO A FORGOTTEN SUN
Donald J. Pfeil   **$1.25**

**THE BEST OF PLANET STORIES #1:
STRANGE ADVENTURES ON OTHER WORLDS**
Leigh Brackett, Editor   **$1.25**

STAR TREK LOG THREE Alan Dean Foster   **$1.25**

A MIDSUMMER TEMPEST Poul Anderson   **$1.50**

STAR TREK LOG FOUR Alan Dean Foster   **$1.25**

WHEN HARLIE WAS ONE David Gerrold   **$1.50**

FARMER IN THE SKY Robert A. Heinlein   **$1.50**

THE BEST OF HENRY KUTTNER With an
INTRODUCTION by Ray Bradbury   **$1.95**

DECISION AT DOONA Anne McCaffrey   **$1.50**

▼ Available at your local bookstore or mail the coupon below ▼

🅱️🅱️ **BALLANTINE CASH SALES**
P.O. Box 505, Westminster, Maryland 21157

Please send me the following book bargains:

QUANTITY	NO.	TITLE	AMOUNT
	24338	Voyage to a Forgotten Sun $1.25	
	24334	The Best of Planet Stories #1 Strange Adventures on Other Worlds $1.25	
	24260	Star Trek Log Three $1.25	
	24404	A Midsummer Tempest $1.50	
	24435	Star Trek Log Four $1.25	
	24390	When Harlie Was One $1.50	
	24375	Farmer in the Sky $1.50	
	24415	The Best of Henry Kuttner $1.95	
	24416	Decision at Doona $1.50	

Allow three weeks for delivery.   Mailing and handling   .50
Please enclose check or money order.   **TOTAL**
We are not responsible for orders containing cash.

(PLEASE PRINT CLEARLY)

NAME..

ADDRESS...

CITY....................STATE..................ZIP............

BB 26/75

An extraordinary extrapolation of the future, in the tradition of The Andromeda Strain and The Terminal Man.

THE SPACE MERCHANTS

FREDERIK POHL & C. M. KORNBLUTH

Imagine a world run by Madison Avenue, where the account executive is king and his audience just a mass of helpless serfs living by the law of the singing commercial!

That's the amazing but possible world you'll find in this sardonic and fascinating satire about a society manipulated by advertising!

THE CRITICS RAVE!

"A novel of the future that the present must inevitably rank as A CLASSIC!"
—The New York Times

"Very entertaining . . . Anyone who's ever considered the power of advertising in present day life will read this BRILLIANT satire with absorbed enthusiasm!"
—Chicago Tribune

"Distressingly ACCURATE predictions . . . dramatically CONTEMPORARY."
—Boston Phoenix

"In The Space Merchants we have SOME OF THE BEST SATIRE OF OUR TIMES!"
—Denver Post

$1.50

▼ **Available at your local bookstore or mail the coupon below** ▼

BB BALLANTINE CASH SALES
P.O. Box 505, Westminster, Maryland 21157

Please send me the following book bargains:

QUANTITY	NO.	TITLE	AMOUNT
....	24290	The Space Merchants 1.50	....

Allow three weeks for delivery.
Please enclose check or money order.
We are not responsible for orders containing cash.

Mailing and handling .50
TOTAL _____

(PLEASE PRINT CLEARLY)

NAME...

ADDRESS..

CITY......................STATE..................ZIP...........

BB 22/75

THE BEST S—F IN THE UNIVERSE
from
🅑🅑 BALLANTINE BOOKS

LEST DARKNESS FALL L. Sprague de Camp $1.25

ALPHA 5 Robert Silverberg, Ed. $1.25

STAR TREK LOG TWO Alan Dean Foster $1.25

THE TEXAS-ISRAELI WAR: 1999
Howard Waldrop & Jake Saunders $1.25

STELLAR 1 Judy-Lynn del Rey, Ed. $1.25

DARK STAR Alan Dean Foster $1.50

THE QUESTOR TAPES
Dorothy C. Fontana $1.25

THE HOUNDS OF SKAITH (STARK #2)
Leigh Brackett $1.25

MAJOR OPERATION James White $1.25

▼ **Available at your local bookstore or mail the coupon below** ▼

🅑🅑 **BALLANTINE CASH SALES**
P.O. Box 505, Westminster, Maryland 21157

Please send me the following book bargains:

QUANTITY	NO.	TITLE	AMOUNT
	24139	Lest Darkness Fall $1.25	
	24140	Alpha 5 $1.25	
	24184	Star Trek Log Two $1.25	
	24182	The Texas-Israeli War: 1999 $1.25	
	24183	Stellar 1 $1.25	
	21796	Dark Star $1.50	
	24236	The Questor Tapes $1.25	
	24230	The Hounds of Skaith (Stark #2) $1.25	
	24229	Major Operation $1.25	

Allow three weeks for delivery. Mailing and handling .50
Please enclose check or money order. **TOTAL**
We are not responsible for orders containing cash.

(PLEASE PRINT CLEARLY)

NAME..

ADDRESS..

CITY......................STATE....................ZIP..........

BB 13/75

WHAT HAUNTING LULLABY
LURED AMERICA'S
LEADING BRAIN SURGEON
TO THE CASTLE
IN TRANSYLVANIA?

A
MEL BROOKS
· FILM ·

YOUNG FRANKENSTEIN

A NOVEL BY
GILBERT PEARLMAN
BASED ON THE SCREENPLAY BY
GENE WILDER & MEL BROOKS
PLUS: 16 PAGES OF FABULOUS PHOTOS
FROM THE SMASH 20th CENTURY-FOX MOVIE!

$1.50

▼ Available at your local bookstore or mail the coupon below ▼

BB **BALLANTINE CASH SALES**
P.O. Box 505, Westminster, Maryland 21157

Please send me the following book bargains:

QUANTITY	NO.	TITLE	AMOUNT
....	24268	Young Frankenstein 1.50	

Allow three weeks for delivery.   Mailing and handling   .50
Please enclose check or money order.
We are not responsible for orders containing cash.   **TOTAL** _____

(PLEASE PRINT CLEARLY)

NAME...

ADDRESS..

CITY..................STATE...................ZIP...........

BB 21/75

INCREDIBLE S-F
from
🅑🅑
BALLANTINE BOOKS

STARMAN JONES Robert A. Heinlein	**$1.50**
NORSTRILIA Cordwainer Smith	**$1.50**
FARTHEST STAR Frederick Pohl & Jack Williamson	**$1.50**
A FUNERAL FOR THE EYES OF FIRE Michael Bishop	**$1.50**
THE MAN WHO AWOKE Laurence Manning	**$1.50**
WARM WORLDS AND OTHERWISE James Tiptree, Jr., with an INTRODUCTION by Robert Silverberg	**$1.50**
MORE THAN HUMAN Theodore Sturgeon	**$1.50**
CYCLE OF FIRE Hal Clement	**$1.50**
THE TAR-AIYM KRANG Alan Dean Foster	**$1.50**

▼ Available at your local bookstore or mail the coupon below ▼

🅑🅑 **BALLANTINE CASH SALES**
P.O. Box 505, Westminster, Maryland 21157

Please send me the following book bargains:

QUANTITY	NO.	TITLE	AMOUNT
	24354	Starman Jones $1.50	
	24366	Norstrilia $1.50	
	24330	Farthest Star $1.50	
	24350	A Funeral for the Eyes of Fire $1.50	
	24367	The Man Who Awoke $1.50	
	24380	Warm Worlds and Otherwise $1.50	
	24389	More Than Human $1.50	
	24368	Cycle of Fire $1.50	
	24085	The Tar-Aiym Krang $1.50	

Allow three weeks for delivery. Mailing and handling .50
Please enclose check or money order. **TOTAL**
We are not responsible for orders containing cash.

(PLEASE PRINT CLEARLY)

NAME...

ADDRESS..

CITY...................STATE....................ZIP...........

BB 25/75

WINNER OF THE NEBULA, HUGO, AND JOHN W. CAMPBELL MEMORIAL AWARDS!!!

Rendezvous with RAMA

Arthur C. Clarke

The book for all readers! Richly imaginative... compelling... powerfully evocative of the mysterious universe... based on scientific fact.

"... story-telling of the highest order... perpetual surprise ... breathless suspense." — NEW YORK SUNDAY TIMES

"... a taut mystery-suspense story." — PUBLISHERS WEEKLY

Arthur C. Clarke's first novel since 2001: A SPACE ODYSSEY.

$1.75

▼ Available at your local bookstore or mail the coupon below ▼

ⒷⒷ BALLANTINE CASH SALES
P.O. Box 505, Westminster, Maryland 21157.

Please send me the following book bargains:

QUANTITY	NO.	TITLE	AMOUNT
	24175	Rendezvous with Rama $1.75	

Allow three weeks for delivery.   Mailing and handling   .50
Please enclose check or money order.
We are not responsible for orders containing cash.   .TOTAL _____

(PLEASE PRINT CLEARLY)

NAME..

ADDRESS...

CITY.....................STATE...................ZIP..........

BB 14/75